It's not the load that

breaks you down,

it's the way you carry it.

Lena Horne

Road Rage

*The Grand Strand's Newest Predator
Doesn't Swim in the Ocean*

T. Allen Winn

Pp
PROSEPRESS
www.prosepress.biz

ACKNOWLEDGEMENTS

Nothing is ever possible without the support and encouragement of family and friends.

I especially owe my beloved wife, Judy, for her many hours of assistance in preparation for my first novel's release.

Finding success is when those same family and friends still support and encourage you after they have read your first one.

Thank you Bob O'Brien, artist, author, publisher and friend. Destiny has a plan for all of us. One must believe and trust in omens. You gave the procrastinator that needed push. Things do happen for a reason.

I toast the caregivers, the unsung heroes.

No man can think clearly
when his fists are clenched.

George Jean Nathan.

Highway 501
The gateway to Myrtle Beach, South Carolina

"Hey, what the hell are you doing?" yelled the ticked off driver, having just barely avoided T-boning the other vehicle.

His thoughts were running rampant. *What were you thinking, running that stop sign? It means STOP for a reason. Out of state tags, I should have known! Guess you don't use stop signs where you come from. I'm so tired of you stinking tourists thinking you own these roads!*

"That's right, act like you didn't do anything wrong! You're messing with the wrong person now," screamed the irritated driver.

Those voices in one's head speak loudly and clearly. *Hey buddy, in case you're interested, my boss just let me go from my job and you want to drive like a jerk and finish me off! I'm really not in the mood for this right now.*

And you, you're all high and mighty living the life, driving your big SUV, you and your kind; I hate every damn one of you! Fools driving crazy like you caused the death of two innocent people that I loved. I can't do this anymore and just let you people get away with this stupid crap! That's it, time to teach you Drivers Ed 101.

"Roll down your window, smartass. Yeah, I'm talking to you! Roll down your window! Don't act like you don't hear me," yelled the enraged driver.

Now you're speeding up! You pull this crap in front of me and now you're speeding up. Sorry, you don't get off that easy! I'm having a bad day and yours just got worse! Okay, good, pull into that hotel parking lot. Can you believe this? Less than a block away from your hotel when you pulled this stunt!

"What's your problem, buddy?" asked the driver of the other vehicle. "This is private property. I'd advise you to get back in your car before I call hotel security or the police," warned the driver, feeling safe now that he was just a stones throw from the hotel office.

"My problem is you ran that friggin stop sign back there and almost caused me to T-bone you. You could have got us both killed! You couldn't even wait until I passed by could you? There wasn't a car within a hundred yards behind me! What's your damn hurry?"

"Just let it go, mister. How about it? You're not hurt and I'm really late. Shit happens."

"You got that right and it's fixing to happen to you!"

"Hold on a minute, back off, you ..."

Conway Medical Center
Room 212

"Doctor, is it okay if I ask him a few questions?" inquired Deputy Woody Anderson.

Standing at only five feet eight inches, Woody was by far the shortest deputy on the force. His hundred and seventy five pound bulldog frame accented by a bushy head of jet black hair, matching thick mustache and side burns gave him the appearance of a much larger and more formidable adversary.

"Five minutes if he's up to it, officer, and no more," answered the young intern. "He's in very bad shape. Someone really did a number on him. He's broken up pretty badly but he'll live."

"Sir, are you up to speaking with me? Your wife is in the waiting room. Neither she nor the hotel clerk said they had witnessed what happened to you. I haven't found anyone at the hotel who saw this incident. I'm Deputy Anderson with Horry County Law Enforcement and I'm in charge of the investigation."

Peeping through the only eye he could slightly open, he nodded to the deputy standing at the foot of his bed.

"You are Walter Ozolins from Youngstown, Ohio. Is that correct, sir?"

Walter nodded again to confirm. He tried to move his head to focus on the deputy but the neck pain prevented him from turning. His jaw ached something terrible too. As a matter of fact, every part of his face and head hurt like hell.

"Age, fifty-seven, two hundred ten pounds, is that correct, sir?"

"You're reading it and looking at me so why ask me such stupid questions? Can't you figure it out on your own?" Frustrated, Walter spoke not much louder than a whisper.

"Well sir, not to sound crude but it's hard for me to match this photo your wife gave me with the gentleman laying in front of me. To be blunt, you're really messed up, sir, and lucky to be speaking at all. I'm not sure anyone could ID you from this photo," responded Woody, not known for being overly tactful.

Opening his one eye slightly wider, Ozolins came back at the young deputy. "You have some nerve. They must not raise any of you down here with proper manners. Can't you see I'm hurting here, damn it?"

"Sorry sir, just trying to do my job, and for the record, the Palmetto State isn't a place overrun with rednecks and hicks like you Yan...northerners like to stereotype us, sir. Give me a couple of minutes and I'll let you get some rest. Can you tell me what the perpetrators looked like?"

"Perpetrators? There was only that one guy. He was huge, mean and pissed."

"So you're telling me that only one person did this to you," asked Woody with a smirk on his face.

"That's exactly what I'm telling you, officer. He sucker punched me or this fight may have had a different outcome."

"Apparently you weren't targeted for robbery. Your money and credit cards are still in your wallet. From what your wife has shared with me, only your driver's license seems to be missing. It seems very peculiar, sir. Why would this feller have lifted your driver's license?"

"Why don't you do your job, find him and ask him. Now, can you just get on with it?" asked Walter, realizing that he hurt from head to toe.

"Bear with me, sir. I've just got to finish the preliminary questioning. Sir, can you describe his appearance? And can you tell me just why this person was so angry with you? You received quite a beating! You must have provoked the attack in some way."

"I didn't start anything! He approached me in the parking lot, started ranting about who knows what and then simply attacked me. I didn't start this! I was minding my own business. If I knew more I'd tell you."

"So I guess you don't have a clue why this person attacked you."

"Are you deaf or just stupid? Either way, it doesn't really matter because I've told you I'm not looking to press any charges. We're driving home tomorrow and I'd just prefer putting this behind me. Like you said, I have my wallet and credit cards, and I really don't have time for all this crap. One thing is for sure. This will be the last time I vacation here on your sunny Grand Strand."

"Sir, you better let the doctor decide when you're up to heading home. Plus, you best wait until you lay eyes on your SUV. I believe it's in worse shape than you if that's really possible. We had it hauled in to dust for prints. It looks like the damage was caused by something like a tire iron. I don't really expect to find any."

"What sort of damage are you talking about, officer?"

"All the windows were smashed. The tires are flat; even the spare. I'm not a mechanic but it looks like the engine could be in need of significant repairs. He popped the hood latch and whaled away at it. Oh yeah, he took your license plate. Maybe he was in the process of stealing it when you showed up. On second thought, that doesn't seem right. You said he approached you and you didn't surprise him at your car, is that correct?"

"I don't know what I said. It could have happened like you described. How many ways do I have to tell you that I have no clue why he attacked me? He could have already been there, I guess. Hold on a minute. You're describing my brand new Lexus as if it has been in an automobile accident," stated Walter, still attempting to construct his lie.

"Could pass for it, but, nope, it appears to have happened while it was parked in that lot. It sure seems this person really had it in for you. This whole attack just isn't falling into place for me, sir. Take a deep breath and think about it. Why do you really think he assaulted you? What happened just before the confrontation? Do you think you would recognize this guy if you saw him again?"

"I told you that it happened so quickly and it wasn't up for discussion. He just did it. Maybe he had just removed the tag. Maybe I startled him. Who the hell knows? It really doesn't matter, officer. I'm not pressing any charges so this interrogation of yours is over," mumbled Walter, struggling to hold his story together.

"That's enough, officer. You're not helping my patient with this kind of talk," interrupted the intern. "Mister Ozolins, you'll be with us a few more days yet and unfortunately won't be driving any time soon. Officer, please come back tomorrow."

"You can forget that notion. I'm due back at work Monday. I have a business to run. I can't stay here over night! By the way, where is here?"

"You're in the Conway Medical Center. Hotel maintenance found you and called 911. And what do you do for a living, Mister Ozolins?"

"I own and operate a machine shop. What the hell does that have to do with anything? This is over! I'm getting out of here," shouted Walter as he attempted to sit up but could not.

"Please stay put, Mister Ozolins. You're in no shape to do any traveling," cautioned the doctor.

"You better listen to your doctor, sir. I'll check back in on you in the morning after you've had a chance to shake out the cobwebs and calm down. Maybe you'll remember more about what happened. I'll send in your wife. Rest well, sir," stated Woody as he exited the room.

"Damn hick town police; I bet he carries one bullet in his front pocket. Okay doctor, what's my prognosis?"

"Officer Anderson is just trying to do his job, Mister Ozolins. With all the commotion I don't believe we've been formally introduced. My name is Doctor Daniel Weatherford but let's drop all the formalities. You can call me Dan."

"Enough already, Danny-boy; what's wrong with me and when can I get the hell out of here? And if you don't mind, spill it to me in layman terms. Spare me the medical garble."

"You're not much on rhetoric, are you Mister Ozolins?"

"Straight shooter, been that way all my life. How about cutting to the chase?"

"Okay, here goes. I'll just start from the bottom and work my way up. Your left leg is fractured in three places and most of the bones in your right foot are shattered. You have a bruised right kidney and three broken ribs. You have a dislocated right shoulder and three broken fingers on your left hand. You have a broken nose, four chipped front teeth, a slight jaw fracture, a crushed left eye socket and badly cut and bruised right eye. You suffer from a mild concussion. Other than that you are the picture of health. I agree with Officer Anderson. This person certainly didn't like you very much. If I were you, I'd cooperate with our local law enforcement. I'll send the nurse in with some pain medication to help you rest. You're going to need it."

Walter said nothing. He just remembered what this jerk had said when he slammed him to the ground. *Best you head back north where you belong and never come back here again. I'm tired of people like you ruining my life. Next time I won't be so nice. Learn to drive, dickhead, before you kill some innocent person. Oh yeah, and keep the police out of this. They can't protect you from me.*

He'd never forget that face or voice as long as he lived, but he intended to live, so that meant keeping his mouth shut and heading home as soon as they would release him. Next year, he'd take his wife on a cruise to the Bahamas and leave the driving to the captain.

Horry County Police Department

"Well, Woody, how'd that tourist assault investigation pan out?"

Sheriff Singleton had been in law enforcement for thirty five years and held his current position for three consecutive terms. At fifty-nine, he pondered whether he'd try for another term. After losing his wife of more than forty years to pancreatic cancer, he just no longer felt the passion to serve the community. The job had gotten rather ho-hum with long grueling hours and an unappreciative public.

"It didn't, Sheriff. I don't think he's going to give us anything. Looks like he pissed somebody off in the parking lot of The Sea Witch and the perpetrator ended up kicking his and his car's asses until he got tired of the cheap entertainment. My gut tells me this guy doesn't want to admit he probably instigated the whole thing. I'll drop by the hospital in the morning and give it one last shot. I don't think he's going anywhere for a few days."

"I wouldn't waste much more time on it after that. We don't have the resources to run down these tussles between tourists and our local hotheads," added Hank as he rubbed his slick bald head and sipped on a glass of ice cold sweet tea.

"Got it chief, but this feller almost became a homicide statistic. This whole thing smells real fishy to me. I think there's more to it," responded Woody with a mock salute.

"Do what you need to do if you think you can really help but don't spend a lot of time on it if it something doesn't turn up real soon. By the way, we've had another rash of burglaries down in Blackmoor. How about going down there and let them know we care. These damn transients pass through the area every year. They hit and run then move on to the next community. We don't have a chance in hell of catching them, but we certainly can't let the taxpayers know that," smiled Hank, rattling the ice in his empty glass.

"I know the drill and I'll take care of it. I hear we've got a newbie reporting in tomorrow. What's the scoop on him?" asked Woody, as he fondled his holstered weapon.

"Not a him, she's a her and she'll be your new best buddy for a while until a patrol car comes available. You get to teach her our style of southern hospitality." Hank chuckled as he stood up from behind his desk, dwarfing Woody with his six foot four inch, two hundred eighty pound girth.

"Come on, Hank, why me? You know I'm like the Lone Ranger out there. Can't you put her with Wilson? Besides, you know how my wife has that jealous streak."

"Sorry, Tonto will be riding with you, Masked Man. You're the best I have out there and you're going to just love this. She's from Columbus, Ohio. She's not exactly a greenhorn," added Hank, remembering that Janice, Woody's little bride, had been born in Ohio, too.

Janice was quite the looker, even after spitting out five little rug rats. Hank knew she really didn't give a shit about Woody except for his guaranteed paycheck, but that was their business, not his. Word had it she spread the love all over town to anyone who had a hefty bankroll. Again, it wasn't his way to meddle in his officers personal affairs.

"That guy that got the crap kicked out of him was from Ohio, too. They don't raise them real smart up there."

"Must not. Janice married you didn't she?" chuckled Hank.

"I rest my case," added Woody, smiling like a possum. "She fell for my southern charm."

"She fell for your southern horse shit."

"Same difference," said Woody, not allowing Hank to have the last say.

"Well, for the record, your new riding buddy has quite an impressive little resume. She graduated top in her rookie class and has crime scene investigation experience. She's been in law enforcement for about six years. She's relocating down here due to family issues. She has an ailing mama somewhere up in the Little River area. We'll both meet her at 1500 tomorrow. Her name is Trudy Wagner," added Hank, eyeing his deputy for a reaction.

"Chief, you know you owe me one for this," said Woody, mimicking aiming a gun at Hank with his right finger and pulling the trigger, then pretending to blow off the barrel.

"You'll owe me a lot more if you don't take this assignment seriously. You're going to teach her the ropes on how we do things here in Horry County. And you'll have plenty of time before the spring tourist season heats up in about four months. Now go do your dog and pony show for the neighborhood owner's association. Try to look sincere when you discuss those burglaries."

"Yes sir," responded Woody mockingly. "Before I head out, have you heard anything from that trial next door? I was just wondering what the outcome was for Bradshaw's case."

"Last I heard the jury was still out. I've known old Ed for almost thirty years. It sure was a shame how that reckless driving of his was responsible for five deaths last summer. It just plain ruined his life to boot. I suspect the jury will do the right thing and put him away for a few years, even though I believe he's suffered a plenty already."

"Call me on the radio if you hear anything. I'd like to know how it washes out," said Woody as he exited the sheriff's office.

Horry County Courthouse
The State vs Edward Bradshaw

"Lance Rocker, Live at Five, reporting from the Horry County Courthouse where we await the return of the jury to determine Ed Bradshaw's fate. If you remember, Mister Bradshaw, owner and operator of Big Ed's Bar and Grill, allegedly caused the automobile accident that took the lives of five people and sent three others to the hospital, two in serious condition. Mourners placed a wreath at that deadly intersection of highway 501 and Carolina Forest Boulevard."

"We're cutting away to file footage from the actual accident," signaled the television producer in Lance's earpiece.

Lance, taking a deep breath, said, "How do I look? My nose feels a little shiny, like Rudolph. Make-up, fix this."

Lance Rocker, aka Sir Lancelot, had been with this local television station for just over three years as the weekend anchor and head field reporter. He had aspirations of moving to the *big* show, the national News, and took advantage of every opportunity to showcase his marketability.

Twenty-eight years old with a chiseled and tanned surfer's body, he oozed charisma. His wavy blonde hair and killer blue eyes owned the camera. He didn't share the spotlight with anyone.

Single, the ultimate bachelor, he had earned his reputation as being the perfect womanizer, burning through women like cordwood in the middle of a winter snow storm. His pearly whites and smooth delivery suckered them in before they knew what had hit them. Only after he had grown tired of his conquests would they realize how foolish they had been, but most of his lovers agreed, the ride had been worth the price of admission.

"Back live in 5, 4, 3, 2, 1 ..." signaled the camera woman.

"Lance Rocker, Channel 12 News, back live at the Horry County Courthouse. This community has healed some of the deeply inflicted wounds from that incredible multi-vehicle pile up. It is still difficult to fathom that the chain of events erupted when Mister Bradshaw apparently, recklessly changed lanes on this major four lane venue to the Grand Strand, prompting the first driver to slam on the brakes when he cut off the driver, and thus the domino effect ensued. Ironically, Mister Bradshaw escaped unscathed. Luckily, eye witnesses recognized the bar and grill logo on his truck and reported him for failing to stop for the incident."

"When the dust had cleared, nine vehicles had been involved, resulting in five deaths. My sources report that two of the injured remained in the hospital for almost three months afterwards. They've since been released and are presently undergoing rehab in an attempt to restore their lives to some sense of normalcy. Neither would agree to go on camera for this report. Mister Bradshaw had to close his establishment to liquidate cash for the many pending lawsuits. Last summer's tragedy will surely be remembered as one of the worst in this small coastal community."

"Sir Lancelot, Live at Five, and waiting for the verdict along with the many of you who have followed this story. We hope to have an update by the six o'clock edition. If not, please check back with us at eleven for further developments. Remember, please drive safely out there. Yours and your fellow drivers' lives depend on it."

"Okay, that's a wrap, Lance...fine job," remarked the producer.

"Certainly; have I ever disappointed you, sweetheart? What's our chance of having a verdict by six? I hate to have to hang around here until midnight. I have a couple of little

Hooter honeys stopping by Rocker-world between now and the eleven o'clock segment," boasted Lance, enjoying pushing the producer's button.

The producer just shrugged as she barked orders in her headset microphone. "Damn arrogant jerk," she whispered as she joined the camera person.

The camera woman heard the comment and signaled thumbs up. She didn't care for Lance either, especially because he had nailed her after last year's Christmas party. Mesmerized like every other female, she had paid homage to Rocker-World. After their little all-nighter Lance had asked if he could keep her panties. She had reluctantly complied, thinking it was sort of kinky.

She had stumbled into his little secret when she prepared to leave the next morning, mistaking the walk-in closet door for the bathroom. All sorts of undergarments were displayed on a wall with photographs of their owners.   She confronted him after realizing he planned to deposit her Victoria Secrets on this little wall of conquest, along with the others she had seen. Kinky transformed into disgust.

He referred to his secluded closet as his trophy room, and explained he only honored those worthy of rocking his world. He told her she should feel proud to have rated a place there. She wasn't proud of her lifestyle, but this had to be a new low even for her. She didn't buy it and asked for hers back.

Rocker refused and threatened to ruin her career if she even considered exposing his little perversion or pressing sexual harassment charges. Too embarrassed to admit what she had done and how he had exploited her, she remained silent, thinking selfishly she'd have a few repeat performances. That never happened.

She had to constantly remind herself that she had done it for the sex and it had been explosive. Plus, she had also seen her producer's crotch-less panties and photo hanging there and figured she had nothing to gain by bringing it to light.

"Hold on Lance, the jury is back in," shouted the producer. "We'll be going back live."

"Must be my lucky day," he muttered. "How do I look?"

"Like a snake charmer," she replied.

"You would know. Keep talking trash and I might just allow you a rare return pass to Rocker-World," he whispered in her ear.

"Make-up," she yelled. "Mister Rocker has a big old booger hanging from his nostril. Never mind, we go live in 5, 4, 3, 2 ..."

Following her producer's cue, she immediately rolled the camera, relishing the look on Sir Lancelot's face. There were other ways to skin a cat, and Mister Alive at Five certainly looked skinned right now.

Lance, obviously rattled, pinched his nose then checked his fingers as the camera rolled, capturing one for the blooper reel. He momentarily looked like a deer caught in the headlights. "Uh, are we rolling? Sorry, folks; we had a minor technical glitch. We have late breaking news in the story we've been following. I'm Lance Rocker with Channel 12 and we're back live here at the Conway Courthouse. It appears the jury has reached a verdict. This came back very quickly. I suspect that spells bad news for our local resident, one Mister Edward Bradshaw, accused of involuntary manslaughter."

Cameras rolling, the jury entered the courtroom. The bailiff collected the decision, handed it to the judge, who motioned it be given back to the foreman of the jury to be read.

"Your Honor, we find Edward Bradshaw innocent of all charges."

"Edward Bradshaw, you have heard the jury. You are a free man." *God have mercy on your soul* thought the judge.

"Unprecedented! The jury has set this man free! Stick with, me folks. I'm going to try to get a word from our exonerated Mister Bradshaw," said Lance, recomposed and in his element.

"Edward, Edward Bradshaw, Lance Rocker with News 12. We have been following your saga. Could you share your thoughts with our viewing audience?"

Tears rolling down his cheeks, Ed looked straight in the camera and said, "I never meant to hurt anybody. It was all just a stupid accident. I've paid dearly for my mistake. I wish I could undo it but I can't."

"And what do you mean by 'paid dearly'?" asked Lance, smelling a twist in the story.

"Well, I lost my business, for one thing. This town turned on me without just cause and I'll never forget that. I sunk everything I had in that bar and grill. Now what am I supposed to do? My life isn't worth nothing now. These past few months have been the worst for me. You and the rest of your news buddies ate it up. You can all now kiss my big old fat ass!"

"Well, there you heard it, right from a very disgruntled but free man. Now back to the newsroom."

"Pack it in. We're done here," ordered the producer.

"Man! Is he pissed or what! That reaction was priceless. I'll work on a follow-up for the eleven o'clock. This has the *Edward R. Murrow* Award written all over it!"

Throwing the remote at the television, "I can't believe this crap. He's walking. He's getting off free as a bird. Nope, that's not going to happen on my watch. Those deaths will not go un-avenged. You just thought this town treated you like crap. You haven't seen anything yet! Your license has been revoked."

Bradshaw Residence
609 Driftwood Drive
9:00 AM

Ed is having breakfast on his modest patio. The bloody Mary soothes his parched throat after a night of binge drinking and a morning of puking out his guts. That jury actually found him innocent of all charges yesterday. Shame this couldn't have happened before he lost his bar and proper place in this fine community.

Pondering his future, he had no plan. Hell, he had no future. It was too late in the game to start over from scratch. He had to come up with a way to turn all this publicity to his favor. Maybe he could do a book. He had a pretty good story to tell. It might just sell.

Who was he fooling? He wasn't a writer. Maybe he could hire somebody to ghost write it. Hell, he didn't have any money and didn't know any authors. He bottomed out his bloody Mary and made a second one to help him think. It wasn't working. His head was throbbing, pounding like a drum. No, it wasn't just his head. Someone was knocking at the damn front door.

Entering through the kitchen and down the hallway towards the front door he wondered just maybe if it was another reporter. He might be able to milk this a little longer if he played his cards right and acted victimized. Maybe the reporter would pay him for a first-hand account of this. This might just work out after all. Opening the door, he didn't see a reporter standing on the stoop.

"What the hell do you want? Get to the back of the line if you're here to threaten me with another lawsuit," barked Ed as he recognized Tim Ford.

Tim and his family had just moved to the area a year before the accident while he pursued construction work opportunities. Built solid as a rock, he stood five eleven, two hundred forty pounds with flaming red hair and mustache. He had two massive tattooed arms, a result of having carried and handled cinder blocks all his life.

Grabbing Ed by the shirt collar, Tim jerked him from the doorway, throwing him down the two steps to the sidewalk. Ed tried to right himself but Tim met him with a right cross, sending him rolling on the lawn.

"No remorse...I watched you in that courtroom showing no remorse whatsoever. Do you actually think this is all about you? My wife and daughter are dead," yelled Tim.

"I said it was an accident. I've said that all along and the jury just saw the light and agreed. Why can't you people get that through your thick skulls?" shouted Ed, as he again tried to get to his feet.

Tim caught him square under the chin with his left foot like he was kicking the winning field goal. "You asshole, what the hell did you lose? You lost a stinking bar and maybe your elite status in this neighborhood. My wife and daughter are dead because of you and your reckless driving. You even left the scene of the crime. You are a pile of dog crap!"

"I'm sorry for your wife and daughter, but it was an accident. It's not like I set out to kill those people."

"They're dead all the same and you're responsible," shouted Tim, grabbing Ed by the shirt almost lifting him off the ground.

A siren sounded in the background as the cruiser came to a screeching halt. Deputy Woody Anderson emerged from the patrol car, pistol drawn. "Mister Ford, please let Mister Bradshaw go. This isn't doing anybody any good. Mister Ford, I mean it. Now, turn him loose!"

Tim pushed Ed to the ground where he collapsed on the stoop's top step shaking his head back and forth. "This isn't right. He killed my wife and daughter. This just isn't right. He deserves to die! How could they set him free? They could have at least stuck him in jail for the rest of his sorry life but no, they did nothing; some justice system we have."

"Mister Ford, you know I'm going to have to take you in. It's for your own good."

"Justice served! I go to jail instead of that bastard! That makes no damn sense."

"Lock his ass up, Deputy, and not a minute too soon if you ask me," added Ed, propping up on an elbow.

Tim landed one last kick to the right side of Ed's head, sending him down for the count this time. Woody tackled and handcuffed the irate Tim, then called the ambulance for Ed, now lying face down on the turf. Tim smiled, gazing down on the unconscious maniac. Justice served indeed.

Horry County Police Department
Sheriff Hank Singleton's Office
10:00 AM

"Mister Ford, just what the hell were you thinking pulling a stunt like that? The man was found innocent. Let it go," lectured Hank.

Hands in his lap and head down Tim mumbled, "But he killed my wife and little girl and they called him an innocent man. That's just not right."

"Listen Mister Ford, I'm willing to cut you a break here if you promise to stay clear of Mister Bradshaw. I'll bring you before the magistrate and only charge you with simple assault with no intent but you'll be spending the night here to mull over what you did. You can pay your fine in the morning but I will be asking the judge to issue a restraining order as a little insurance," explained Hank as he stood and pressed both hands on his desk. "Are we clear on this, son?"

Tim never looked up but sort of nodded.

"Officer Jenkins, book him. Off the record Mister Ford, I do agree. That was a tragic day and senseless loss of lives but we can't bring them back. It's best to move on and put some distance between you and that unfortunate scar in your life. Son, don't let me see you in here again. Take him away, Jenkins."

Tim Ford, never speaking another word accompanied the officer for his prints and mug shots. His only thought, he should have killed the bastard while he had the opportunity. This man had taken everything from him and had not been punished for his sins.

Tim had been the second car in the chain reaction caused by Ed Bradshaw. He had braked and swerved into the right lane to avoid rear ending the van he trailed. He never saw the Ford 150 pick-up along side the driver's passenger door.

The truck clipped him sending his Honda Accord into a spin. The concrete truck caught him broadside on the passenger side killing his wife and daughter instantly. Tim had remained in a coma for almost two months afterwards and had barely escaped death.

Physically he had completed his rehab and had returned to nearly 100%. He had briefly attended counseling to overcome his grief and depression but had finally bowed out when he could no longer stand to relive the incident in therapy. That had been a grave mistake because now his sanity teetered on the edge of the abyss.

He now suffered from blackouts and seldom remembered what happened during those episodes. He did remember kicking Bradshaw's ass and just wished he would have finished the job. He felt no vindication yet. That troubled him and scared him to death. A once peaceful and law abiding citizen had now become a raving lunatic obsessed by revenge.

Conway Medical Center
Emergency Room
11:45 AM

"I understand you're treating a Mister Edward Bradshaw right now. Hi, I'm Lance Rocker with Channel 12 News. I've been covering Mister Bradshaw's story and would like a word with him if he's willing and able to speak," smiled Sir Lancelot, turning on the charm with the duty nurse.

"Well normally we can't give out that information. Am I going to be on TV?"

"Why certainly you will. Roll the camera while I take a statement from...your name, honey?" asked Lance, dripping with testosterone.

"Nurse Jackson, but you can call me Margie."

"Margie, can you tell our viewing audience what happened to Mister Bradshaw?" asked Lance, holding the microphone in front of Nurse Jackson's face.

"I can't really say except that the officer that accompanied the ambulance said he had been attacked at his home. I can't divulge any details of his medical treatment," smiled Margie, patting her hair and hamming it up for Lance and the camera.

"Why Margie, you certainly have such a fantastic smile. I bet you just wow the patients with your upbeat and positive attitude. Do you think it would be possible for me to have a few words with him?"

"The doctor would have to grant you permission and the patient would have to agree to it too. Give me a second and I'll ask," she responded, totally captivated by Lance's charm.

"We'll cut that footage when we edit for the 5 o'clock, sugar," directed Lance, as he gave his camera woman a little flirtatious wink.

She smiled then gave him the finger when he turned his attention to Margie, parting the curtain and motioning him her way. "Mister Bradshaw said to send you right in. He says he would love to talk to you again."

"You're such a little sweetheart Margie," replied the snake oil peddler.

"When will this be aired?"

"Real soon honey, you just stay tuned," he answered, quickly heading down the hallway to Bradshaw's room. "You take care," he shouted back to her.

That was so damn easy thought Rocker to get that heifer eating out of his hand. Would Bradshaw cooperate this time? He'd need luck on his side because his charm didn't work so well on men.

"Well Mister Bradshaw, may I call you Ed?"

"Mister Bradshaw will do just fine," Ed responded harshly. "And let's get one thing straight before you fire up that camera. We're not buddies so cut your crap! You'll pay me for this or it's over before it starts."

"I think I can swing a little cash for an excusive," figuring there was more than one way to skin a cat.

"Cash up front then we talk."

"Here, this is all I have on me but I assure you there will be more if this pans out for our viewing audience," grinned Lance, handing Ed four one hundred dollar bills he had stashed in his wallet. Julie, the camera woman just rolled her eyes in disgust.

"Okay, now you can call me Ed for the camera," he said as he snatched up the money. "This will do for starters. Alright, roll that camera but I'm warning you fancy pants; this is my show, not yours. You got that?"

"Just make this good and we'll see," answered an unfazed Rocker, motioning for Julie to start filming.

"Ed, you were just exonerated yesterday by a jury of your peers on all charges in last summer's fatal accident that took the lives of five people. What brings you to the emergency room? Have you had some sort of unfortunate accident?"

"I was home minding my own business when that Ford feller knocked on my door..."

"Ford, do you mean Tim Ford, the gentleman that lost his wife and child in the accident?" asked Lance smelling gold here.

"Same one... seems he was pissed off about the verdict and came to my house and attacked me. I believe he would have killed me if the police hadn't stopped him. My nosey neighbor across the street saw what was happening and called 911. The old bitty probably saved my life. I suppose I should thank her and I will next time I see her."

"So our Mister Ford turned vigilante and tried to take the law into his own hands. Is that correct?" Lance milked this for all it was worth.

"Guess you could say that. He sure acted like one hell of a crazy man. He needs to learn to leave innocent folks like me alone. That's why I'm going to sue him for the trauma and pain he has put me through, plus he can pay for this medical treatment. About time I had a chance to sue somebody. The damn vultures sure have been after me long enough. All of them wanting to sue me like that and I was innocent all along. Court of my peers proved it."

"And where is Mister Ford now?"

"The deputy hauled his sorry ass off so he's down at the jail I reckon, locked up so he can't finish what he started."

"Thank you for your time, Ed. We certainly wish you the best in your recovery and with your law suit. We will follow up on this story as it develops. Cut...let's head to the county jail, honey. Thank you Ed. I will certainly keep in touch."

"Remember it will cost you more than this chicken feed next time."

Lance smiled and nodded. "Let's go sugar britches," said Rocker, patting her on the butt.

"Bite me," whispered the camera woman. "Never mind, you did that already didn't you, scum bag?"

Horry County Police Station
1:00 PM

Trudy Wagner parked her 1997 four year old Jeep Cherokee in front of the police station. She had arrived a couple hours early for her three o'clock appointment to complete the preliminary paperwork before meeting with Sheriff Singleton.

Trudy had spent the night with her mom after arriving from Columbus late yesterday afternoon. Everything she owned had been transported in her jeep and the small U-haul trailer she had rented. She would probably have never left Ohio if not for her ailing mother and her being an only child, sort of. Well technically she wasn't an only child. She had a sister in Atlanta but she couldn't be counted on to help. She sure felt like an only child. You didn't have to do the math to figure out who'd be responsible for her mom's care in the event of a major illness; not sis.

Amy, her mother, in early stages of Alzheimer's, had begun her struggles in taking care of herself. Her mom's brother, Uncle Freddy had contacted Trudy and insisted she be there for his sister. So, here she was, re-establishing herself in the law enforcement food chain while learning the art of being a caregiver.

The decision to move here hadn't really been that difficult. While she had gotten her foot in the door on the department's CSI unit, they didn't openly embrace her and her woman's intuition and theories. A fresh start in a laid back community could be just what she needed, especially with the care and attention her mom would probably require.

She left behind no baggage such as a relationship. Matter of fact she had not even dated in over a year. She'd seen no reason to include a man in her life. She had her way of living, a most satisfying existence without one.

A blonde haired, blue eyed Amazon at six feet one inch, she turned every head each time she entered the scene. Proud of her hard body and long flowing mane, she thoroughly enjoyed the attention but rarely capitalized on her popularity. She had experienced but one brief relationship and it had ended in disaster. That had been before she had embarked on her career. Now, police work was her life.

At age twenty seven, she had no aspirations of being a wife or mother. Perfectly content with her lifestyle, she did what she wanted to do, when she wanted to do it and didn't have to answer to anyone. She didn't yet fully comprehend the ramifications of her mom's illness and how it would dramatically alter her preferred life choices.

Completing the paperwork, she strolled toward the sheriff's office a little ahead of schedule. She had only talked to him over the phone and had sketched in her mind what he must look like based on his deep gruff voice. The mountain of a man sitting behind the desk had not been who she had pictured.

"You must be Detective Wagner." He stood and offered her a grizzly bear sized paw. "Please have a seat. When did you arrive?"

"Yesterday, sir...I spent the night at my mother's."

"Ah yes, you told me over the phone that she had been ill. I hope she is doing better." He smiled as he oozed southern charm.

"For the moment she's doing just fine. Thank you for asking sir. I do love this area of yours. There's nothing like an assignment that comes with its own ocean and beach." She jested as she tried to relax.

"It would surprise you how seldom we locals actually go to the beach. Guess we have a tendency to take it for granted. I can't recall the last time I had these big old tootsies of mine in the ocean. Well, hope you are ready to roll up your sleeves and make the Grand Strand a safer place."

"My middle name is ready, sir."

"Good to hear but I'm sure it'll take a little time to adjust from detective to deputy; not to worry, much of the same duties apply here. Did you enjoy working crime scene investigation?"

"Loved it sir but I'll be just as satisfied in any roll you have in mind for me here."

"I hope our little coastal community doesn't disappoint you. Don't get me wrong, we do have our fair share of murders and robberies here especially during peak tourist season when the transients pursue easy prey."

"We didn't quite have that problem back in Columbus. The tourist weren't exactly beating down our doors but we did have an extremely high crime rate."

"Horry County's permanent population averages about 240,000. It probably swells to close to a half million on average during tourist season and even more than that when we have our bike weeks. With our limited resources we end up stretched pretty thin during peak season and work long hours."

"Not a problem sir. By the way, where should I put my gear and where will I find my patrol car?"

Rubbing the side of his face and then rubbing his massive hand over his bald head he answered, "Well, we have just a little problem with a cruiser right now. We're one short in our budget. I'm temporarily teaming you with one of my veteran officers. That will give you a chance to get the lay of the land until we round you up one. I hope that won't be a problem."

"No sir. I adapt well."

"Oh, here comes your new partner now. He can show you where to store your belongings." He motioned as Deputy Anderson approached his office. She couldn't help but notice that the officer appeared to be removing mail from his post office. He tugged and scratched at his skivvies apparently lodged in the crack of his butt.

Sometimes she cursed herself for being so observant. This is not the picture of her new partner she wanted burned in her mind. Lucky for her, his probing was being done with his left hand.

"Woody, meet your temporary partner, Detective, I mean Deputy Trudy Wagner," introduced Hank as he stood up.

"Glad to meet you ma'am," stated Woody, extending his right hand. "I'm Deputy Woodrow P. Anderson but every body just calls me Woody."

"Woody, please show our new deputy to the locker room and get her acquainted with the station. I believe you two will be pulling the next twelve hour shift."

"Will do and we are."

"By the way, Woody, how's Ed Bradshaw?"

"He'll live. He was still pretty woozy when I interrogated him but he did ID Tim Ford. They're keeping him overnight at the hospital as a precaution. He took a good lick to the noggin. That Ford character meant business. I tell you what. Bradshaw is one arrogant piece of work. I'm afraid Ford may have bitten off more than he can chew. That old boy has been pushed around just a little too much the past year and something tells me he smells an opportunity to cash in on it."

"Speaking of Ford, I'm keeping him in lock up until the morning. We ought to keep an open mind about those two. I'm not sure they're finished tangling either. I gave Ford a good talking to so I hope it's over. I'm having a restraining order issued just in case."

"Who are these two...Ford and Bradshaw, if you don't mind me asking, sir?"

"Long story, Wagner...Woody will fill you in. Again, welcome to the force."

Horry County Lock-up
4:15 AM

Tim Ford sat on his bunk in his jail cell rubbing his bruised and scraped knuckles. He stared across at the wino jerking spasmodically on the other bed. He reeked of Mad Dog 20-20, the beverage of choice for the derelicts and homeless roaming the city's streets.

He still had no regrets for his actions. He expected to pay a fine come morning and be released to this miserable life he now lived. Jobless, having been fired for his frequent no shows at work; something he had never been prone to do before the accident and his family's murders.

Bouts of depression along with his addiction to pain killers had contributed to his demise. He had gone from a beer drinker to guzzling hard liquor. He wasn't sure what he might try next to help make him forget that awful day when his world came to a screeching halt. Anger had long ago replaced the tears. Now fueled by the anguish of Ed Bradshaw's complete exoneration, insanity seemed to inch ever so much closer.

Lying on his back, the wino grunted, mumbled something and then puked all over his shirt and down the side of the bed. Enraged by the stench burning his nostrils, Tim walked over, plucked him up by the collar and drug him over to their little community toilet.

He shoved his head deep inside the nasty cavity and gave him a couple of courtesy flushes. The wino never flinched when the cold water swirled around his face. Tim let him drop to the floor then returned to his bunk to plan his next visit to Mister Free as a Bird, Edward Bradshaw.

He owed it to his family to make him pay for his sins, something the courts failed in doing.

A restraining order meant nothing to a man hell bent on breaking the law. He would get one more shot before they arrested him. Tim felt his face burning with rage then he blacked out collapsing onto his little single wide bed, a relieved escape from reality. Doctors didn't know why he continued to suffer these bouts of passing out.

He awoke to commotion in the cell. Paramedics were hovering over the old wino. Seconds later they covered him with a sheet, dead. They said something about him having had some sort of convulsive attack. He had probably fell on the toilet receiving quite a blow to his blooded face then died of asphyxiation from his own bile.

Tim had slept through the entire episode and couldn't offer any testimony to what might have occurred. He told them the old drunk had been alive the last time he had noticed.

He wondered could he have killed him. He had no memory of it if he had and didn't really care one way or the other. They pronounced him dead at 8:35 AM. Tim had slept for four hours but he didn't feel rested; only strange and confused. He hoped to get out of this hell and back to his own.

Horry County Police Department
9:00 AM

"Well Deputy Wagner, I suspect it was certainly a boring first night on the job for you. Bet it was a change of pace from Ohio.

"Not at all, Woody, I saw the beautiful Myrtle Beach coastline so what do I have to complain about? I appreciate you giving me the nickel tour and keeping it real."

"What you say we go grab a bite of breakfast after we sign out? I know this great little local spot that has killer pancakes and corn beef hash."

"Thanks Woody but I really need to get home and check on my mom. I haven't really gotten settled in at her place yet and into her routine."

"Rain check then and we'll have plenty of opportunities."

"What's your gut tell you about that Ford and Bradshaw? Both should be released this morning shouldn't they?"

"Yeah, they just kept Bradshaw for observation and hopefully a night in jail has cooled down Ford. I'd just about bet we haven't heard the last from those two. It's really sad for both of them. Ed saw his livelihood go away after that unfortunate accident, lost his business and the respect from the community. It's going to take him a while to rebuild both."

"That's still a far cry from where it left the Ford guy wouldn't you say; losing his wife and child? You can't replace lives. I'm not so sure how I would have handled losing my entire family like that. That had to be devastating."

"Yeah, if I lost my Janice and that little litter of mine I could probably go off the deep end too."

"That's a fact. See you back here around eleven tonight. Maybe we'll have a chance to play cops and robbers." She turned and headed toward the bathroom to make a quick stop before driving back to Little River, about twenty five minutes away.

Woody peeked in Hank's office and saw he was on the phone. Hank tilted the phone's mouth piece away, took a sip of ice tea and motioned him inside. Woody poured a cup of coffee while he waited for the sheriff to finish his conversation.

Hanging up the phone, Hank asked, "So how'd it go last night?"

"She seems to be a smart gal. I'm not sure we're going to live up to her expectations though. You know we hardly ever have anything big happen around here but once in a blue moon. Even then, we tend to get rooted out of the investigation by the state boys or Feds."

"She'll do fine. By the way, Woodrow, I just got through talking to the hospital. Bradshaw should be released within the hour. That news guy, Rocker, was there last night talking to him. He'll probably stir the pot and get what mileage he can out of it. He's a damn showboat if you ask me."

"What about Ford?"

"I expect he'll be set loose before noon if he can make bail. Poor guy, he can't catch a break. A wino died in his cell last night. You remember Skitter Sampson don't you? He's a regular. He apparently slipped and hit his head on the commode and died in his own puke. Ford was asleep just feet away and never knew it happened."

"I'm surprised Skitter lasted this long. Alright, I'm going to stop by Eggs Up and grab a bite before crashing for the day.

Conway Medical Center
Room 201
9:15 AM

"Hello," says Ed as he picks up the phone dropping his second shoe to the floor.

"Bradshaw, this is Rocker. How are you feeling this morning?"

"Fine, I was just getting dressed when you called. I'm heading home directly. Do you have the rest of the money you promised me?"

"I have it and I have an agreement for you to sign giving me exclusive rights to your story just like we discussed."

"You still think you can write a book about me and make us rich?"

"Let's take it one step at a time. I'll drop by your home at, let's say, 7 PM. I have a couple of local bits to cover for the five o'clock segment then I should be free for the evening. Mind if I bring a recorder?"

"I couldn't care a rat's ass what you bring with you as long as you have my cash," snapped Ed, as he hung up the hospital room's phone and finished dressing.

Lance registered the click on his cell phone and turned to face the bedroom's floor to ceiling mirror admiring his naked tanned body. He removed the towel from his waist and gazed on his privates. "You are quite the stallion I must say Rocker. You rode her hard and often. I do believe you plugged every orifice of interest." He gathered up little Scarlet Harper's red thong from the floor pressing it firmly to his nose inhaling its sweet nectar.

He glanced back at the bed where the petite candy striper still snored. The hospital had cultivated a bumper crop this year. "Ecstasy is such a wonderful little aphrodisiac isn't it sugar. You little uncooperative bitches never see it coming. By the time I feed you full of false memories you're always too embarrassed to divulge what you've experienced here in Rocker-World. The staged photos make for excellent insurance." Snapping another digital photo he smiled at his art work then walked over and slapped her on her bare bottom.

She mumbled something but would be out for awhile longer. It would leave just enough time for Rocker to have a little more fun with his guest. Too bad she wouldn't be awake to enjoy it too. Oh well, those were the breaks he thought pressing the record button on the camera strategically located on a tripod then reaching for the Vaseline and a fresh condom.

Amy Wagner Residence
10:35 AM

Trudy knocked then used her key to open her mom's back door entering the laundry room just off the kitchen. She heard the television blasting from the den even before she opened the adjoining kitchen door.

Her mother sat at the kitchen bar staring toward the stove where a large pot boiled over and sizzled on the eye. Its smoldering ingredients, unrecognizable, burned her eyes as she entered the kitchen. Her mom never turned to acknowledge her arrival. Trudy immediately grabbed a pot holder and removed the pot, turning the knob on the eye to the off position.

"Mom, are you trying to burn down the house?" Trudy had never seen her mom in this state before now.

Amy looked at her with an expressionless stone face. "Hello dear, I bet you're hungry. Let me fix you something," she said in a matter of fact tone. "Your sister and you must have breakfast before the school bus arrives."

Trudy shuttered at this response. Her uncle had been insistent that she come and now she understood why. How long had she been like this before anyone realized it?

"Mom, you sit here. I'm going to switch off the television then how about I prepare you breakfast?"

"You don't have time dear. It's a school day. Your father just left for work. Is that sister of yours still lolly-gagging as always? Allison, please go upstairs and make sure Trudy is not late for school."

"Mama, I'm Trudy. Allison lives in Atlanta. Daddy has been gone for over twenty years. You don't even have an upstairs in this house."

Confused, Amy replied, "Nonsense. Such foolish jabber from such a smart little girl... you just go fetch your sister while I finish breakfast."

Taking a deep breath, Trudy had no clue how to handle her mom in this confused state. Obviously trying to correct her was getting her nowhere. She just placed her arms around the woman that looked like her mom and the tears flowed down her cheeks. Amy never changed expression but did hug her back.

Once the burned odor subsided, it was replaced with an even stronger, more pungent smell. Her mother had apparently soiled her underwear so she accompanied her to the bathroom to assist in the clean up. There she realized her mother wore no underwear, was even braless, something her mother would never have done. She removed her dress and bathed her clean.

"Mom, stay here while I get you some clean clothes."

Amy never responded. She slipped into the bedroom and had found only one clean dress and no clean under garments. Dirty clothing was piled in the closet, nothing remained on hangers. Wadded filthy underwear and socks were in the dresser drawers. Her mom had apparently lived with this secret far too long.

She grabbed a pair of her own panties, the bikini briefs, a little tight and not something her mom would normally wear but they were better than nothing. She led her back to the kitchen where she scrambled up the only two eggs in a rather empty refrigerator.

She shook her head as she watched her mom consume the eggs. Amy had seemed perfectly fine when she had arrived less than two days ago. What had happened to her? Had she had some sort of stroke? She'd call the doctor's number her uncle had given her to determine her mother's illness and what could be done to snap her out of it.

In the meantime, she settled her mom in front of the television then started a load in the washing machine. She longed for a cup of strong black coffee but found the canister empty. Very few edible grocery items were stored in the pantry. She'd have to make a list and go for groceries next. Placing her hands over her eyes she just sat on the floor and cried.

Channel 12 News Anchor
Lance Rocker Investigating

Quarter to seven, Lance Rocker pulled up outside Ed Bradshaw's modest home. January darkness had arrived over an hour and a half ago. Strange, he could see no lights in any of the windows.

He checked around back and saw what he perceived to be Ed's pick-up parked in a detached shed. He noticed the truck had no license plate and figured poor Ed hadn't been able to make his automobile insurance payment so they must have confiscated his tag.

He walked up on the front porch stoop and knocked on the door. He waited. Hearing no one approach the door, he knocked again, harder. Finding the front door locked, he stepped off the stoop attempting to peer through the bay window but shades were pulled and he could see nothing.

Lance walked around the house and down the short

drive leading to the shed. The house had a small patio in back, more or less just a concrete slab with old, dilapidated, rusty lawn furniture. Still he could make out no lights inside. He knocked then tried the door. It was unlocked.

He eased it open and shouted, "Ed, are you in there?" He received no answer so he reached in with his left hand and located a wall switch, flipped it on. The entrance opened into the kitchen. He passed through this room and called out again for Bradshaw, receiving no answer. A doorway led to a small room with a nineteen inch television and what looked like an outdated turntable and stereo.

The only other furniture in the room, a Lazy Boy recliner draped with an Elvis throw, a five pronged floor lamp and a metal folding food tray with a half eaten burger, fries and a beer still sitting on it. A rerun of *Mash* played on the television.

A chill ran down Lance's spine. Something didn't feel right here. One door led to a hallway and the other to what looked like a living room on the front part of the house.

He eased into the hallway flicking on the light as he entered. He saw three doors, one to his immediate left, a second near the opposite right end of the ten foot long hall way, and a third on the left side directly across from the one on the right. All were closed.

He decided to try the nearest door first. It made an awful creaking sound, straight out of a horror movie. Lance sighed relief that no closed shower curtain greeted him. He'd not have to venture any further inside the tiny bathroom. It was empty.

Two doors remained. He pulled out his cell phone and keyed in the digits 91 keeping his finger on the 1 key as he approached the door on the right first. The recording device in his front shirt pocket was voice activated so whatever happened he'd capture it for either the police or ambulance. *What I do to advance my career is beyond stupid sometimes* thought Lance.

He changed tactics. This time he turned the knob, kicked open the door as he simultaneously reached for what he hoped to be a wall switch. All went as planned except the switch clicked to a pitch dark room. Startled he fell backwards against the opposite door. It jarred open and he sprawled on his ass into the second dark abyss.

"This is 911. What is your emergency?" The voice blared from beyond. His finger had pressed the second 1 as he fell and his phone was engaged in speaker mode. The dispatcher sounded a second time, "911, what is your name and location?"

Lance now sitting up answered, "I'm Lance Rocker, honey, with Channel 12 News. I was researching a piece for emergency response and I do apologize I accidentally pressed the speed dial on my cell phone. There is no emergency."

"Mister Rocker you must be more careful," spoke the female voice.

"Since I have you on the line and for the relevance of research, just how long would it have taken for a police cruiser to have arrived if this had been a real emergency?"

"Mister Rocker you do understand this call is being recorded."

Lance poured on the Sir Lancelot charm. "Yes and this would be a great lead in for my segment if you'd be so kind."

"Sir, if this isn't an emergency I have no choice but to terminate the call. Please refrain from calling 911 unless you have a valid emergency. Mister Rocker, my superiors will most likely contact your television station and report this unfortunate indiscretion."

"And you have a wonderful night too sugar." Rocker had the final say then got to his feet embarrassed by what he had just done. That's all he needed, bad PR from this stupid dispatcher.

He felt along the door facing until he found the switch. This time the bedroom overhead light did illuminate the room. Taking a deep breath, Lance slowly turned to survey the room. He heard a frantic girlie scream that deafened him until he stopped emitting it.

He recognized the *#2 Miller Lite Rusty Wallace* tee shirt on an otherwise indistinguishable battered and bloodied body lying face up on the bed. The face was not the face of the man he had just interviewed at the hospital less than 24 hours ago. This face had been pulverized into hamburger meat.

He took a deep breath then spun 360 hoping not to see the killer in the room. Pressing redial on his cell phone, the same lady answered, "This is 911. What is your emergency?"

"This is Lance, Lance Rocker. I need the police here immediately!"

"Not you again Mister Rocker... I believe I just warned you that this number is for actual emergencies and not to be used at your whim for a news segment. You are treading on some seriously thin ice with your antics."

"This is an emergency!"

"Sir, please get off this line."

"I'm standing in the bedroom of Ed Bradshaw. He's been murdered! Please send officers now. The killer could still be in the house somewhere!"

"Is this legit Mister Rocker?"

"The man is deader than hell. He's not going anywhere nor am I. Please send the police right here, right now," shouted Lance losing his cool and charm.

"Can you tell me the address?"

"Look it up in the phone book lady. Right now I hear someone else moving around in the other room. I'm afraid I'm not here alone. Hurry damn it!"

"Please stay on the phone Mister Rocker and curb your profanity. I'll dispatch help." She located the nearest cruiser and gave them the address.

Lance cowered in the far corner of Ed Bradshaw's bedroom, his back to the wall listening to the movement across the hall while keeping his eyes fixed on the bedroom door. The sounds were definitely coming from the darkened room across the hallway, he was sure of that.

His own heavy breathing made it difficult for him to focus on the sounds but his mind raced wildly. *Eleven O'clock Edition, Lance Rocker, famed journalist and anchor was found dead in the bedroom of another murdered resident.* He blinked to clear his head because he really didn't like the sound of being on that end of the news.

A figure in the other room contemplated a scenario too. *The bastard got what he had coming. Justice served by Joe the concerned citizen. It was so pathetic how Bradshaw begged for mercy. Big man when the cameras are rolling but such a coward when reality stares him down. Guess what, you'll make the news again tonight. Enjoy your fame and welcome to primetime, Mister Ed Bradshaw!*

Home of one Edward Bradshaw
8:15 PM

"I'll go around back, you stake out the front," said Woody taking the lead.

Trudy asked, "Shouldn't we call for backup?"

"Couple of wrecks on 501 and a burglary reported south on 17 have the department stretched thin. I figure we're it for right now, Wagner."

"Well so much for a boring job. Go, I've got the front covered. Be careful."

"You watch your back partner." He eased around the side of the house.

Finding the back door ajar, Woody entered, pistol drawn. The kitchen light was on so he didn't need his flash light. Den was empty. Cautiously Woody entered the hallway. He peeked in the first doorway and found an unoccupied bathroom.

Two doors remained at the opposite end of the hallway. A light shown from one but the other was dark. He flicked on his flash light deciding to check the dark one first.

Trudy checked the front door knob. It was locked. She slinked around the opposite side of the house and peered around the corner. Something moved in the overgrown shrubbery. The leather of her holster squeaked when she unclipped the strap. Her heart raced. Her breathing became labored.

Suddenly a rabbit scurried from underneath the low growing juniper. She exhaled and focused her attention on the light from a side window. She reached the window and peered through a slight opening in the drapery. She could see part of a person's torso lying on the bed. Even from this vantage point she could see blood, lots of it.

The floor creaked as Woody reached the door to the darkened room. He heard something clicking on the other side of the closed door. Carefully opening it and staying clear of the entrance way, he scanned the room quickly with the flash light and spotted the culprit near the only window.

Trudy saw a shadow. Someone other than the bloody mess on the bed had moved from their concealed position. It could be Woody. He may have reached the room. She strained to see through the narrow slit but couldn't ID the owner of the still moving shadow but her gut told her this wasn't her partner.

She reacted on instinct and broke the window pane, pushed the curtains aside as she screamed, "Freeze, this is the police!"

Woody burst into the room tackling the figure standing with his back to him. Trudy stood at the window, both hands clutching her pistol taking aim at the melee unfolding in front of her. Woody had Lance in a combination headlock-choke hold wrestling him to the floor.

With his windpipe almost closed, Lance struggled to spit out the words, "Turn... me... loose... you... damn fool. I called 911. You're choking me!"

With that, Woody realized who he held in his death grip. "Rocker, what the hell are you doing here?" He broke the hold and sat back on his butt, winded he stared at the newsman.

"What's going on in there?" Do you know this man, Woody?"

"Oh yeah, I know him. Deputy Wagner, meet Lance Rocker, Channel 12 News."

"What the hell is he doing in there?"

"Why don't you ask him?" Lance still gagging from the choke hold said, "And while you're at it, you better check that other room. I think your killer might be in there if you haven't already allowed him to escape. I heard somebody moving around before you arrived and jumped me."

Woody stood up and walked out of the room, his weapon drawn and ready to fire. A half minute later he returned. "You mean this killer? I've already got him in lock up," laughed Woody holding a hamster cage. "The little feller does like running on that wheel! Not to worry Mister Super Sleuth, he won't be able to get you unless I open this little door."

"Real funny officer Anderson but you better save your investigative skills for what I assume is Bradshaw over there on the bed."

"How can you tell that mess is Ed Bradshaw?"

"Super sleuth that I am, I recognized the tee. It's the same one he wore when I interviewed him at the hospital after the first attack."

Trudy had made her way to the back entrance and now entered the kitchen. An eye for detail, she examined the scene as she passed through heading to the bedroom. Nothing had been disturbed; no evidence of any skirmish.

She got her first real look at the victim seconds later. This had been an extremely hostile and brutal murder. "Mister Rocker, please step outside. This is a crime scene and we need to keep it in tact until forensics and the coroner get here. You did call them didn't you, Deputy Anderson?"

"I was just about to take him outside for questioning and make that call Deputy Wagner," snapped Woody not appreciating his partner belittling him in the presence of the dickhead newsman.

After her partner removed Rocker from the crime scene, Trudy had kicked into crime scene investigation mode. She now operated on auto pilot perusing the situation at hand looking for any sign and every detail. She had snapped on a pair of rubber gloves without even thinking. Definitely in her comfort zone, she looked for any clue of the perpetrator.

"Okay now humor me, Rocker. Just what the hell were you really doing here?"

"I had an appointment with Bradshaw at 7 PM to discuss in detail the latest attack by Ford and to expand on the hardships he has endured because of the accident, trial and so forth. I thought it had the potential for a great follow-up story. I guess my hunch paid off but this is more than I bargained for."

"When did you arrive?"

"Maybe about a quarter of, give or take a minute." Lance knew the drill and answered only what the officer asked him.

"Did you notice anything peculiar when you arrived?"

"Yeah, there were no visible lights on in the house until I got to that bedroom. That seemed strange because I knew he was expecting me. I saw his truck in the shed so figured he must be at home."

"What did you do next?" Woody jotted down notes on his pad.

"Next, well... after I had knocked on his front door and he didn't answer and it was locked, I came around to the back."

"Then...?"

"The back door was open so I entered the premises." "You didn't knock at the back door before just entering the man's house."

"Yeah, I knocked then I gave a shout for him but he didn't answer."

"Go on..."

"I flipped on the kitchen light then gave Bradshaw another shout. After he didn't reply, I entered his den, found it empty, and then I eased down the hallway. Something didn't feel right I can tell you. I peeked in the bathroom then headed toward the remaining two doors."

"So you're touching everything as you go... nice work Rocker. You certainly screwed up the crime scene."

"Hey, cut me a break. I didn't know the man was dead and I certainly didn't know I was in the middle of a murder mystery."

"But you didn't mind roaming through a man's house uninvited did you?"

"I had an appointment, like I said."

"Okay, what did you do next?"

"First I checked the room where you found that rat but the light switch didn't work so I investigated the second room. That's where I found Bradshaw. Then I calmly called 911."

"So you stayed in here with Bradshaw until we arrived?"

"Yes, I stayed put. I thought I heard movement and speculated the killer might still be in the house. I hid here waiting to pounce on him if he returned to the scene of the crime. Then you came at me like a linebacker. You can pick it up from here."

"So that is it."

"You got it all. You know what I know Mister One Adam Twelve."

"You stay put right here while I go back inside and don't touch anything else!"

"Yes sir." Lance waited for him to leave then called his television station requesting a crew to the Bradshaw house immediately.

Conway Medical Center
Room 212
9:30 PM

Walter picks up the ringing phone beside his bed, "Walter Ozolins... what can I do you for?"

"You do remember our little agreement don't you." inquires a raspy voice.

"It's you. What do you want? How did you know I was here?" asked Walter in a panicked tone.

"I'll always know your whereabouts, Walter. I thought I made that perfectly clear. I am becoming a tad impatient with your talking to the police. I don't do impatient very well as you should know. It would behoove you to break off contact with our local law enforcement or face breach of original contract."

"What are you talking about? We have no contract." Walter was sweating profusely.

"Do you not honor a gentleman's agreement in Youngstown, Walter? I warned you to keep the police out of this matter. Is it so difficult to stick to the script?"

"Just leave me the hell alone. You've done enough. I get the point!"

"Why Walter, that sounded like you were issuing me a warning. I do not tolerate that tone from anyone, especially someone as expendable as you, you road hogging bastard."

"Wait a minute, I was not threatening or warning you. Please just leave me and my family alone. I'll keep my mouth shut." The line had gone dead before Walter had even started his plea.

He's crazy. I've got to tell the police. They can arrest him. But he knows my name and where I live. What if they release him from jail? They couldn't keep him locked up forever. I just don't trust that deranged asshole. I've got to get out of here. I need a gun. God, what have I gotten myself into?

Home of one Edward Bradshaw
10:05 PM

"You're the crime scene expert, what have you found that will help us crack this case?"

"Well, I have the weapon, Woody. She pointed to the Louisville Slugger splattered with blood, propped up by the dresser. "It says Myrtle Beach Pelicans on the handle and appears to have been autographed by several players. I can't really make out the signatures."

"It probably belonged to Bradshaw. He used to own and operate a Bar and Grill, sort of a sports bar. I bet that's some of the left over memorabilia." Woody pointed to a rack on the wall holding two other bats and one empty spot. "The Pelicans are our local minor league franchise, part of the Atlanta Braves."

"He didn't fight his attacker. There are no blows to his hands or forearms that I can detect. He has a nasty whack to the back of the head then the rest were struck full frontal. The blows made mince meat out of his face. I suspect that back of the head strike was the first. The coroner should be able to tell. Where is the coroner?"

As if on cue, the coroner walked in the door. "Got quite a mess here I see. This is as brutal assault as I've ever seen."

"Didn't hear you come in the back Pat," said Woody.

"Oh, I came through the front door. It was standing wide open and I just figured you left it open for me," answered the coroner.

Trudy's mouth dropped open. She had tried the front door and it had been locked. Her stomach flip flopped. Crap, the killer had been in the house when they arrived.

She had not stayed at her posted assignment and had allowed the murderer to make a clean escape right out the front door.

"Deputy Wagner, I'd like you to meet our coroner, Pat Simpson. Pat, she's from Ohio...CSI expert," said Woody sarcastically as he made the introduction.

"Are you alright, deputy? You look a little blue gilled...all this blood is not getting to you is it?"

"No, everything is fine," she lied. "Where's forensics?" This was the worse she had ever seen too.

"I talked with Hank. It appears we're it. He said for you to give it a shot, Wagner. You're the hot shot expert after all. I'll start dusting the place after I grab the camera from the car and photograph the crime scene. Hank just had Ford picked up for questioning so I wouldn't waste too much time here. We probably already have our man."

"What happened to innocent until proven guilty, Woody?"

"That's just for the innocent."

Pat Simpson interrupted, "Heads up, I saw the News 12 crew outside. Local officers were detaining them and roping off the area."

"Rocker, you can't trust that bastard," snapped Woody.

Standing just outside at the street's edge, "Lance Rocker, live at the scene of a most grizzly and brutal murder. Channel 12 can not give out the identity of the victim until next of kin has been notified. I first found the body and diligently contacted 911. Folks, this one will knock your socks off!" Lance off and rolling again caught whiff of the game breaker. "And I can't say enough about our 911 responders here at Myrtle Beach. They are true professionals."

That should get that dispatcher off my back. And modern technology I owe you one. My exclusive which includes crime scene photos, compliments of my handy dandy cell phone. Oh Lance, the others won't know what hit them!

Horry County Police Department
Interrogation Room
9:55 AM Next Morning

"One more time Mister Ford," stated Lieutenant Grady Wilson.

"I keep telling you, I have been home ever since you released me and no, I have no witnesses to support my alibi."

"And you say you just fell asleep and don't remember a thing until we knocked on your door."

"I remember nothing. I've been suffering from these weird blackouts since the accident. Doctors don't know why but think it's just in my head...brought on by stress."

Trudy, Woody and Hank observed the drilling from the mirrored viewing window. Occasionally Tim glanced at the mirror as if trying to guess who was on the other side.

"Well, he'll break sooner or later. Old Grady will see to that," boasted Woody. "He's about the best we got for getting confessions."

"Yeah, if anyone can weasel out a confession, Grady is our man." Hank cracked his knuckles then stepped away from the window.

"Sheriff, you two appear mighty confident that Ford is our man."

"Duh," mocked Woody. "Wagner, let me recap for you. His wife and kid were killed by Bradshaw. Bradshaw gets off without so much as a hand slap. Ford loses his cookies and goes to Bradshaw's house and beats the crap out of him. Bradshaw and Ford are both released from the hospital and jail just hours apart. Bradshaw turns up dead. Don't you catch the theme here? It's pretty simple. Ford returns and finishes the job he started not more than 24 hours earlier. There you have it in a nutshell."

Before she had an opportunity to counter, her cell phone rang. "Yes this is she. You've got to be kidding me. Thank you for calling. I'll be right there."

"Problems?" asked Hank.

"It was the sitter. I've got to go if that's alright. I'll finish up my preliminary report and have it on your desk in the morning after Deputy Anderson has a chance to review it."

"Go, you've been working this thing over fifteen straight. Hope your mom is alright."

"Thank you sir. Woody, I'll meet you back here at 1800."

Woody just nodded resenting that Hank had given her full rein on only her second day on the force. "Open and shut case the way I see it, Hank. Process the paperwork and throw away the key. I'm going to drop by the hospital on the way home and check in on that Ohio Yankee feller."

"Then you get your ass home, Woody, and catch some shut eye. Tell Janice and the kids hey for me."

"Got it chief...let me know when he confesses."

Amy Wagner Home
Little River
3:10 PM

Trudy pulls into her mom's driveway and for the first time succumbs to the pressures of mental fatigue and physical exhaustion. She places her hands on the steering wheel and rests her head there just for a minute before going inside to face her next challenge.

A tapping on the window startles her. "Are you alright in there?"

Moistening her parched lips, she turns and tries to focus on the face staring at her from outside the driver's side window. "Are you okay lady?"

She recognizes the uniform of a postal worker. The mailman stands there waiting for her response. "Yes sir, I'm fine. Just had a long night and needed to rest my eyes for a few seconds." Satisfied she is alright, the postman heads down the street.

She yawns and glances at her watch. "Damn!" She opens the door and rushes into the house. She has been out for almost an hour. How is that possible?

"Lordy, I've been fretting something terrible waiting for you to get here, Miss Trudy. Your mama, she's been showing out something terrible. It's not like her to cuss me like she's been doing," whined Lullabelle Tolbert. Lullabelle was a black woman in her mid sixties, family friend and only a couple of years younger than Amy Wagner's sixty seven years.

"It's took every breath I got to talk her into staying. She said she's got to go to Daddy Bill's house. Who's Daddy Bill and where's his house?"

Trudy let out a long sigh. "Sorry Miss Tolbert. It has been a long day. I got here as soon as I could," she lied. "Daddy Bill was mom's father and he's been dead for probably forty or more years. He was killed in a train accident when mom was a teenager. I never met my grandfather. Where is she now?"

"Pacing a hole in the den carpet and I'm afraid her poor old heart is going to explode. She's been at it for hours."

Trudy stood at the den door for a couple of seconds and watched her mom pace back and forth the full length of the room, rubbing her hands like she was trying to start a fire. Alzheimer's was certainly a cruel fate. She mustered up the courage, positioned herself and stood in her mom's walking line.

Her mom simply adjusted for Trudy's presence, stopped short, turned and continued walking. She never acknowledged Trudy standing in her path. New tactics, "Mom, it's Trudy; you need to stop this pacing."

She did and gazed long and hard into Trudy's blood shot baby blues. "Trudy, where have you been?"

Trudy broke down and let the tears flow. Her mom just patted her on the back telling her everything would be alright. Everything wouldn't be alright thought Trudy.

Her mom's long term prognosis was bleak. She was in the middle of her first big case with her new department and she needed to focus on it. She could sure use someone to lean on but had nobody and up until now had never wished she had.

Trudy remembered what she had read in an article on line at the police station earlier. The article had indicated that one in seven Americans age 71 and older, about 3.4 million, has dementia, according to the National Institutes of Health. In this age-group, 2.4 million people have Alzheimer's disease, research has shown. Alzheimer's disease is the most common cause of dementia.

Amy is only sixty seven. She wondered what the stats were for those younger.

"Lullabelle, you will come back tonight won't you?"

"I'll be back. Don't you fret honey child. We will get your mama through this. You can count on me."

"Thank you. You don't know how much this means to both of us."

"Honey, are you going to be able to get you any sleep before you go back to work?"

"Hey, I'm a cop, I'm used to it." Trudy lied. She was really about to go down for the count. She was beyond mere exhaustion.

Conway Medical Center
Room 212

The knock on the door almost sent Walter Ozolins diving under the bed even in his battered state. When Woody entered the room Walter looked even more terrified. "How are you feeling?"

"I told you I was done. Why are you here? Please leave!"

"Calm down. I was just on my way home and thought I'd check on you. I'm off duty. I'm not here to grill you. You made it perfectly clear you were not going to help us find your attacker."

Walter buzzed the nurse. As she entered Walter shouted, "Please escort this officer out of here now. He shouldn't be here."

"No need nurse, I'm leaving. Take care Mister Ozolins. I hope you get back to Ohio real soon."

What a jerk? I almost feel like kicking his ass.

Woody stopped by Sam's Corner on the way home and grabbed hotdogs for the whole family. The kids loved Sam's hotdogs; the best dogs on the beach.

"Where in the hell have you been Woodrow?" snapped Janice. "Your shift ended almost eight hours ago!"

"I've been in the middle of one hell of a big murder case and it's going to blow your drawers off when you hear who committed it," bragged Woody, ignoring Janice's typical bitchy attitude.

"Surprise is on you Deputy Dog. Sir Lancelot has already broken the news on channel 12 and he had photos of the bloody murder. That gorgeous hunk can do it all," she said, fanning herself with a magazine.

"Impossible... we haven't released it to the press yet! Where did he get photographs? Shit, his cell phone!" Woody was furious.

"I'm sorry to have to break it to you but he called it an exclusive. He even said he discovered the body and says that Ford man was the prime suspect." Janice so enjoyed pushing her Woody's button.

"Damn that Rocker! He just had to scoop the competition. It's all about him! I've got to call the sheriff."

"You're too late on that one too deputy. He called about half hour ago to ask if you'd seen the news yet and old Hank sounded fit to be tied."

"Hotdogs are in the bag. How about you feed the kids before they get cold? I better return that call."

"Yes sir mister policeman, Sir. We'll snap to!" She snapped back as she saluted him then gave him the finger.

Janice hated her miserable life. Right out of high school she and Woody had gotten married. Pregnant, she really didn't have a choice. She had squeezed out four more chaps since and felt shackled to this pathetic existence. She had remarkably maintained a killer body and used it to her advantage having had countless affairs.

Woody had allowed his career to consume him, spending more time away than at home. That suited her just fine. She gave him the occasional slam-bam-thank-you-ma'am and an occasional knob job. It kept him happy and would hold her over until her next liaison.

Her real happiness came from her many flings making each man's fantasy come true by being what they wanted her to be. She made it a habit not to go out with the same guy more than once. No strings attached ensured she never got caught with her panties down so to speak.

"One more thing sweetie pie before you make that call. Hank said they would have to release that Ford guy in the morning if you and your partner don't give him something to hang his hat on."

Woody placed the phone back on the table and didn't say a word and shoved a Sam's foot long down his throat.

Horry County Police Department
7:00 PM

"I've read through your report three times and we have absolutely nothing," said a frustrated Woody.

"Don't blame me. It looks like the only clean prints you got other than Bradshaw's were Rocker's. His were everywhere. He fouled up the whole scene."

"Do we have anything from the coroner yet?"

"No more than what we already knew. The bat was the weapon and he died from severe head trauma. Like we figured, one to the back of his head immobilized him then the killer laid him in the bed and pulverized him. Wagner... you do realize that Ford is going to be cut free in the morning if we don't come up with something concrete so Hank can hold him."

Trudy continued to relive her big error. The murderer had been in the den and slipped right out the front door she was supposed to have been watching. She had failed to follow one of the initial responses of Crime Scene Investigation: *Remain alert and attentive. Assume the crime is ongoing until determined to be otherwise.*

"Woody, let's go back over there and check the place out one more time. Maybe we're missing something from one of the other rooms."

"What makes you think that?"

"Call it a hunch, woman's intuition or just sheer desperation." She was getting way too good at this lying.

Channel 12 News Room
Eleven O'clock News

"Our lead story continues to be the murder of Edward Bradshaw. We join Lance Rocker reporting from the Conway County Jail," stated the late night news anchor.

"Thank you Neil. We are indeed live just outside the jail where Tim Ford remains in custody. As most will recall, Mister Ford recently attacked Ed Bradshaw at his home after Mister Bradshaw had been cleared of any wrong doing in the deaths of Ford's wife and daughter. Tim Ford is now the prime suspect in his death after the second attack on the deceased. I discussed the altercation with Ed just hours before he was killed. Please roll that interview."

"Cutting to file footage from the interview," spoke the producer into Lance's ear piece. "Lance, we'll cut back to you next then run the footage on the crime scene.

"How do I look?"

The producer gave him the okay sign. They finished running the segment and Lance decided to call it a night. He had an entertainer from one of the local theaters lined up to join him for a nightcap at Rocker-World.

He walked to the parking lot and schemed how he could milk this story for all it was worth and decided he'd try to secure an interview with Tim Ford just to stir the pot. He had gotten whiff from his sources that the case against Ford was extremely weak and falling apart.

That Deputy Wagner intrigued him too. He most definitely would be scheduling a private meeting with her. His mind raced with all the possibilities. He had room for her on his trophy wall.

While a tumble with her sounded wonderful, his mind drifted back to the case. He pondered the scenario. If Ford didn't kill Bradshaw, which he believed he did, then who could the killer be and why would another person attack Bradshaw? For now, he decided to play the Ford angle. He really had no reason to suspect another killer either and couldn't understand why the cops were botching it up so badly.

Bradshaw Residence
12:00 AM

"How much longer are we going to be at this, Wagner? There's nothing here."

"Damn it Woody, there has to be. There's always something else at a crime scene if you look hard enough. Let's go over the check list again and do one more room to room search."

"You realize that Hank is going to have no choice but to release Ford don't you? The big man is going to be fit to be tied."

"I'm fully aware of that fact but what if he's not the killer? Have you given that any consideration?"

"Why would I? It's a no brainer like I've explained to you until I'm blue in the face."

"I'm just saying we need to keep all options open."

"What's the matter deputy? Are you afraid you're going to flop on your first big case here on the Grand Strand?"

"Just what the hell is that supposed to mean, *DEPUTY*?"

"Look, you've been here all of three days. Nobody is expecting you to bring your Yankee know-how down here and solve all our crimes." He smiled, "Nobody but you and maybe the sheriff."

"Kiss my royal ass deputy. Oh, by the way, for the record, I lived and worked in Ohio for seven years but I was born and raised right here in the Palmetto state, Mister Redneck, sir."

Woody's jaw came unhinged and he had no rebuttal for the newly identified southern belle's revelation except, "Let's go over your check list one more time and then get the hell out of here. I'm hungry."

"Me too, we'll cover this as quickly as possible. Alright, we arrived at Bradshaw's after the 911 call. We have all that information so we're good here."

"Check."

"Did we cover all the bases? We didn't see any people or vehicles leaving the crime scene, right."

"I certainly didn't, did you, partner?"

"No I didn't. The only vehicles in the drive were the Z28 convertible you identified as owned by Rocker and Bradshaw's pick-up in the shed in the back."

"We didn't run any plate checks and we should have before we entered. That was a bad assumption on my part."

"Yeah that was a blunder on our part. Luckily we did ID both of the vehicles after the fact."

"Bradshaw's registration was in the truck's dash box."

"There were no strange smells or things out of place that would have prevented us from entering the house."

"Affirmative, there were no odors that I can recall."

"We obviously treated it like a crime scene because we had the 911 confirmation. We covered all the safety procedures."

"I saw us take no unnecessary risks."

"We covered protocol for emergency care."

"Well we certainly didn't need an ambulance or any medical assistance. Bradshaw was obviously deader than hell. Rocker came close to requiring medical attention."

"You should have kicked that bastard's ass," laughed Trudy.

"I regret my failure to act properly," grinned Woody.

"I feel we secured the crime scene and got Rocker out of there."

"Yeah I got him out of there and questioned him but unfortunately he had already contaminated the scene before we arrived."

"Woody, one more time, did we do our job and secure the crime scene?"

"I believe we did don't you?"

"Yeah, we did it by the book." She lied remembering how she had allowed the murderer to escape through the front door but only she knew this fact.

"We contained the scene and kept any unauthorized personnel from entering."

"We did it by the book Wagner, so enough already. I've read the CSI Guide for Law Enforcement issued by the U.S. Department of Justice and we did everything by the book so lighten up."

"I just want to make sure we didn't botch anything up. The Sheriff is counting on us."

"Look, I even questioned the nosey neighbor that witnessed the first attack by Ford and called 911. She saw nothing this time. Ford... I mean the killer covered his tracks."

"Okay, let's go to that joint you were telling me about. I'm famished."

"River City... now you're talking...burgers that will make you slap your mama. I'm sorry, I shouldn't have said that. How is your mama?"

She's fine lied Trudy, "Let's go get a burger."

Horry County Police Department
8 AM

"Alright you two, do you have anything for me?" asked Hank.

"No sir. We have no physical evidence linking Tim Ford to the crime scene and Ed Bradshaw's murder. We found nothing to point us to any other suspects either," responded Trudy.

"I guess he didn't confess either," asked Woody.

"Not even close," responded a frustrated Sheriff Hank Singleton.

"Looks like we're screwed then Boss," added Woody.

"I reckon the media will have a field day with this one."

"Rocker and the Channel 12 News van are already parked outside and he's licking at the chops to talk to Ford. I hate that asshole," said Woody.

"Sad thing, we can't stop him. He's within his right," admitted Hank, pausing to take a sip of sweet tea.

"Sheriff, let me try talking to this Mister Rocker and see if I can get him to cut us a little slack on the case. I'll woo him with my natural charm." She wasn't sure why she volunteered. She had the looks but had never possessed the ability to charm any man. What made her think she charm Lance Rocker?

"Anything is worth a shot but Wagner, be very careful with Rocker. He is one hell of a player and can raise the stakes, suck you right in before you even know the hand is a lost cause. We call fellers like him...never mind, you'll figure it out." Whore hounds thought Hank...

"There's no offense taken, sir. I've neutered much worse than our Dan Rather wantabe." *Where did that come from? I am not a charming person and certainly have no experience with gigolos.*

"I doubt that," added Woody. "This old boy has a reputation and can kick it up a notch, if you catch my drift." *This is going to be good thought Woody.*

"Guess I better go cut our Mister Ford loose. There's not much more we can do without hard evidence to keep him here," said Hank. "This is a sad day for Horry County law enforcement."

"Sorry we came up empty sir," replied Trudy as she headed to her encounter with Lance Rocker.

"Here comes our new Deputy Wagner. Roll the camera. Let's capture us a little footage for the noon segment," advised Lance. "Let's see if I can rattle her cage."

Trudy was up close and personal before Lance had a chance to prepare his TV face. "Well Mister Rocker, here to scoop the other channels again? You certainly have no professional ethics, reporting on the death of Edward Bradshaw and showing the bloody crime scene before the gentleman's next of kin had been contacted. I certainly hope this will not prompt a law suit against you and the television channel from his bereaving family members."

She had him on his heels and back peddling right out of the chute. "Uh, excuse me. We owe it to the fine people of our community to report such brutal incidences." He responded and was relieved that this wasn't live and he'd have an opportunity to edit it.

"At the expense of his love ones...now that was very classy Mister Rocker. This is certainly all about you and your career isn't it? You do realize that you're on the short list of potential suspects?"

"Me, how preposterous..." Rocker had lost complete control of the interview.

"Should I recap for you Mister Rocker? You were found hiding in Ed Bradshaw's bedroom with the murder weapon propped against the dresser less than five feet away while he lay dead on the bed. Your fingerprints were discovered on the back door entrance way, the light switches and all relevant door knobs within the house."

"Hold on here..." Lance tried to interrupt.

"There were no other fingerprints found in the house other than those belonging to Bradshaw except yours."

"But..." Lance tried to regain control.

"Your confession on camera stating you were the last person to see him alive in the hospital and then admitting you followed him home and there you were in his bedroom. Please don't leave town."

"You can't possibly be serious with these accusations. I called 911 remember."

"And thank you for reminding me. The 911 responder reported that you called her twice from Bradshaw's residence. The first call you made you claimed it was a mistake and you made up some cockamamie story about accidently speed dialing 911 because you wanted to interview her on response time for 911 calls. Were you trying to make sure you had adequate time to stage the crime scene?"

"This is unbelievable."

"I agree. Anything for a story I suppose. You then called back to report the murder. That certainly appears very suspicious. First it's an accident and then there's a murder," she said, looking dead into the camera.

"You can't be serious. I'm no murderer."

Bingo, he had lost it. "We have the recorded transcripts from both calls Mister Rocker. Stick close to the station here if you don't mind. I do believe Sheriff Singleton might have some additional questions for you." She smiled as she dropped the big one on him.

"You can't really be considering me as a suspect?"

Grinning she added, "I'm afraid so Mister Rocker. There are certainly a lot of gaps in your story. You better consult a lawyer before the Sheriff asks you to step inside." She had lied rather convincingly.

"That's a rap. Let's get the hell out of here. We can edit this later." Pissed, he eyeballed his producer.

"Edit what?" she asked. "If we take out her dialogue about you as a suspect, we have nothing left. I've never seen you with both feet shoved down your throat like that before. It appeared to me that she was doing the interviewing. I must admit. That was most entertaining but very poor journalism. I think I'll start my own wall of shame."

"I'll make several copies," added the camera woman feeling somewhat vindicated too.

"Screw both of you and as I remember, I already have!" Lance was on unfamiliar ground at the expense this new adversary. He didn't like it one bit! "This is far from over," he whispered.

Trudy buzzed Hank on her cell and got his voice mail. "You can release Ford now. Rocker decided to can his interview. He's following up on a new lead. I'm calling it a day too and heading home to check on mom."

Conway Medical Center
Room 212
10:00 AM

Walter Ozolins listens to the phone ringing by his bedside. On the forth ring he finally musters the courage to answer it. "Hello."

"My, my, Walter, you really are one hard headed Yankee boy aren't you? You just don't know when to quit and my warnings were for your own good. This is my final reminder. I said no damn police."

"But you don't understand. I didn't call the police. He wasn't here questioning me about you," pleaded Walter, but he heard the click before he finished making his case.

Conveniently an orderly walked into the room carrying a tray and wearing a surgical mask. Walter wiped the sweat from his brow and smiled, relieved to have company after the disturbing phone conversation.

"Please call the police. Ask for an officer Anderson. His card is on the nightstand there. The maniac that is responsible for my condition just called and threatened me. I'm in grave danger!"

"Indeed you are Walter. It's time to tidy up a few loose ends." The orderly removed his mask to display a most sinister smile.

Amy Wagner Residence
12:00 PM

Trudy had found it necessary to hire a second part time sitter for when she was off duty so that she could catch some shut eye between shifts. Thankfully Amy was having a good day today and she had spent a couple of very rewarding hours with her mom.

Amy had even remembered who she was and had carried on very normal conversations. An outsider would have had difficulty recognizing that she suffered from Alzheimer's today. Her mom had actually prepared breakfast for her. She had scrambled eggs and salmon, her specialty and Trudy's favorite.

"Mom, I'm so glad to see you feeling better today," said Trudy as she kissed Amy on the cheek.

"Feeling better? Why honey, I haven't been sick. I've never felt better in my life. You know me. It takes a lot to pull me down. I'm healthy as a horse! Tell that sister of yours to be home from her friend's before dark. She has school tomorrow. You too young lady and don't forget to do your homework. I expect all A's on that report card and so does your father."

A tear ran down Trudy's cheek watching her mom go about her business, washing the already clean dishes. She sighed, "The Pavilion has nothing on our little Wagner roller coaster ride. Spills and thrills and never a dull moment for us I can assure you."

"Did I hear you mention The Pavilion, dear? You know I can't take you to the Myrtle Beach Pavilion on a school night and I forbid you and your sister riding that dangerous roller coaster. I heard one of the cars left its tracks and injured a whole passel of youngsters at that park up north. Nope, roller coasters and helicopters, those are two things I refuse to allow my children to ride. Your father would let you if I didn't keep an eye on him but not me. He'd probably ride it with you. He's just a big kid you know."

"We'll go another time Mom and I'll make sure sis comes in before dark." She went along with the charade. She had learned not to correct her.

She heard her cell phone beep in the bedroom indicating she had missed a call. She retrieved the message. "Wagner, it's Woody. Sheriff released Ford just before 9 AM. They slipped him out the back; no reporters. Ford opted not to let them take him home and set out on foot saying he needed to clear his head. I just figured you'd want to know. See you at 1900. I heard about how you slammed Rocker. Damn good job that was. Hope your mom is doing alright."

Woody had received a message of his own but sleeping soundly he had not yet retrieved it. "Woody, Hank. I'm just calling to tell you your tourist, Walter Ozolins, was found dead in his hospital bed during routine rounds. Doctors suspect complications from his numerous injuries. His wife didn't want an autopsy. His body will be transported back to Youngstown tomorrow. We now officially have a homicide with our only witness dead and soon to be buried. I expect this one to go cold case if we don't stumble into any new leads. Besides, it appears the wife has no intentions of pushing for an investigation for whatever reason so I wouldn't waste much time on it for now. Have a good one, buddy."

Surfside Beach
Three Days Later
7 AM

"So how did you find the body, Mrs. Fletcher?" asked the young policeman.

"Well it was actually my dog, Napoleon, that found it," answered the elderly lady.

"And you say you had noticed this golf cart parked in that same spot for how long?"

"It's been there for almost a week."

"And you didn't think that was strange?"

"Regardless of what you think, I'm not a nosey busy body like you young people have the elderly pegged. I just didn't think it was any of my business. Young man, how come the police haven't noticed it and done something about it? They drive by here all the time. It seems you coppers should have done something before now. That's no way to protect us now is it sonny?"

"You got me there. Please remain here while I call this in ma'am. I have more questions for you."

"I'm not going anywhere officer. This is the most exciting thing that has happened to me in more than thirty years. I hope you find out what happened to Mister Cochran and please take care of his golf cart. He was so fond of the cart. He even took me for a ride in it a couple of times. I really didn't like being alone with him. I think he was the typical dirty old man."

"Why didn't you tell me you recognized the victim and his cart ma'am?"

"Why young man, you're the professional here. I figured you must have known him too since you didn't ask. You must be one of those rookies."

"Is there anything else you wish to share with me?"

"What did you have in mind?"

"Forget it for now, Mrs. Fletcher."

"I wish you'd make up your mind. Aren't you going to frisk me or pat me down and then take me downtown and lock me in the slammer?"

"Now why would I do that ma'am?"

"Well, how do you know I'm not Mister Cochran's murderer?"

"What makes you think he was murdered?"

"You are new at this aren't you? Why would his driver's license be crammed in his mouth? I don't think that's where Mister Cochran would keep it do you?"

"Damn," he exclaimed.

"Damn is right young man. Now do you want to cuff and run me in? Don't forget to read me my rights."

Heading up highway 17 Business, they heard the incoming call. "Well partner, what you say we check this out? I know it's about quitting time but..." said Woody as Trudy cut him off.

"We're just a few blocks away from Ocean Drive so let's go."

Horry County Police Department
11:45 AM

"Sheriff, we filed the report and are heading home."

"Woodrow do you have a gut read on this one?"

"The body was badly decomposed but the old lady at the scene identified him as Raymond Cochran. His driver's license confirmed his identity. It's required when operating one of those carts on the street and apparently someone didn't like his driving. The officer on the scene found it lodged between his lips.

"That's a sick thing for somebody to do to an old man." Hank attempted to visualize what it must have looked like.

"Stranger still, sir, his wallet was back in his pocket. Credit cards and cash undisturbed," added Trudy.

"So much for robbery as a motive," said Hank.

"Yep, money was still in it. Why wouldn't the perp have taken the money? They removed the license and had obviously seen the cash. Sheriff, the old guy's dentures were in the cart's storage compartment. Either he wasn't wearing them at the time or the perp removed them and replaced them with the license."

"Woodrow, this one is a tough one to follow. Maybe I should just wait and read your report. Do you have any suspects?"

"None yet but we're still questioning the elderly lady who called in the discovery," said Trudy with a little snicker. "Mrs. Fletcher wanted the officer to take her in."

"Do you think she's a suspect?"

"No way. She was just enjoying the attention, sir."

"Guess we could wait and catch the Channel 12 News to hear what the expert has to say."

"Woodrow don't tell me Rocker showed up there too. Does he know this is a possible homicide?"

"Negative, boss. We kept our witness away from him but as usual he was in rare form."

"You get your butt home, Woodrow. You look like hell. I'll let you know if I hear anything."

"Sheriff, sorry we haven't gotten anywhere with the Ford case."

"You can't get blood out of turnip, Wagner. Go home and check on that mama of yours and get you some shuteye too. We're not even into tourist season yet and the whackos are already out in full force."

Channel 12 News Room
Live at Five

"The body of Raymond Cochran had been lying in the drainage ditch for numerous days. Mrs. Sarah Fletcher and her dog, Napoleon, discovered the body. She remarked that local police had passed the spot for days and never checked on Mister Cochran's golf cart parked precariously alongside the road. So much for serving and protecting I suppose. I'm not sure if foul play is suspected. We'll know more after the coroner completes the autopsy. This is Lance Rocker, Channel 12 News."

"I hate doing these types of reports. The old fart strayed away from his golf cart, stumbled into the ditch and drowned. He should have been wearing one of those alert buttons around his neck then he could have yelled *'I've fallen and I can't get up.'* I didn't have a chance to interview the old lady thoroughly, but I'll get over it."

"Lance, what all of a sudden makes you think you're too good to take the assignments I dish out. And it really pisses me off when you show no remorse for the dead," scolded the producer.

"Q-tips, there are millions of them retired here. Have you ever been following a couple of them poking along in their vehicle? Their white haired heads on those frail little bodies resemble Q-tips in a box. They get old and they die. That's what they do. I'm heading home and tomorrow's my day off. I'll call you if I need you."

Viewing the news segment then yelling at the television, "I cannot believe you have this all wrong you stupid prick. That old fool driving the cart was hogging the damn road.

He was just snailing along and backing up the traffic. He thought he owned the damn highway. I honked. Hell, everybody honked and he just flipped us the bird. The nerve of him! Nobody gives me the finger! He had that stupid sticker on his cart, *Invite someone to heaven.* That's an RSVP to you old man. And Rocker, where's good investigative journalism when you need it? You didn't even mention my calling card, his driver's license!"

Still enraged and thinking, *that's okay, he won't be hogging any more highways. I've decided I don't have to put up with this crap any more! Long as I have my pain medicine and an abundant supply of meth, I'm on top of the world. Until one of you highway maniacs attempts to take me out with a cut-off or running the red light or weaving while you have your cell phone stuck up your butt, or just backing up the traffic like old Raymond. Don't even get me started on mopeds.*

Raymond S. Cochran, I remember him so well...born in Detroit, Michigan, April 22, 1923, one hundred seventy pounds, blah, blah, blah. Eat that damn license Raymond old pal! And Sir Lancelot, you've lost your edge. You used to be quite the entertainer and a damn good sleuth. What has happened to you lately?

"So what have we learned here people? That's right. Drive like you got some sense and quit ruining my life. The highways belong to me now; not you. I'm putting you all on notice! Drive responsively or die! It's really so very simple! The highways can be your dieways! Make the right choice or I'll do it for you."

I guess my old pal Walter has now returned home to Youngstown and has started feeding the worms. You just wouldn't heed my warnings would you Walter? Oh well, you're responsible for your fate. Sometimes it pays to listen. Take your wife. She got the message loud and clear...mums the word right lady...no autopsy. Thank you.

Murrell's Inlet, Hot Fish Club
Trudy Wagner's Day Off
5:45 PM

Trudy's sister, Allison had called and then had taken their mother to Atlanta for a couple of weeks to give Trudy a break from the grind of being a caregiver. Allison and her husband really wanted to assess first hand their mother's mental deterioration. Lately Amy had been having more bad days than good.

Good old sis and that money hungry brother-in-law must think there's a hefty inheritance involved. Let them think so thought Trudy even though this ruined Trudy's self proclaimed only child status.

As a child, she had always told strangers she was either an only child, an orphan or adopted because it was much easier than claiming she had a sister like Allison. Deep down she knew she shouldn't feel this way but sister dearest had always given her just cause. Oh well, freedom for awhile.

Amy Wagner now suffered from the dreaded sundowner's syndrome. This caused her to hallucinate when the night approached with her convinced she occupied someone else's house and that they would return and catch her there. The only solution, take her for a ride and pretend to be driving her to her own house. She'd be fine when they returned. Sis, enjoy!

Trudy, having three days off, decided she would treat herself and enjoy some of the local cuisine. Right now she sipped on her third Vodka and cranberry juice, alone and at the Gazebo Bar enjoying the sights and sounds of the waterway and marsh in Murrell's Inlet while a live band played shag music.

She would need at least a couple more drinks to dull her senses and prevent her from thinking about her mom, her job and her loneliness. She toasted her sis, "Here's to you and my two week leave of absence."

She then pondered the Bradshaw case while Tim Ford roamed free. It frustrated her that almost a month later they had been unable to make any headway. She felt the evidence dangled out there somewhere but she just couldn't grab the carrot. She ordered another drink.

The Surfside homicide haunted her too. The coroner had confirmed that Raymond Cochran had indeed drowned but only after receiving a blow to the back of his head that most likely rendered him unconscious. Why had the murderer not taken his wallet or cart or something? What a senseless killing. That old guy didn't deserve such an ugly fate.

And that driver's license affixed inside his mouth. That was just plain sick and seemed just too screwy for around here. An investigation team had returned to the site and found plenty of footprints trampled along the ditch and surrounding area because the area was used frequently as a path to the inland marsh. No witnesses had come forward.

She had not performed too well in her CSI debut opportunities. She wasn't sure how many more chances the sheriff would give her. No patrol car had come available but she and Woody were getting along better now. He seemed to ease up on her once she went off on him and confessed being a southerner.

Her mom's mental health continued to decline. Two sitters had quit, unable to deal with the wild and wooly situation. She had an interview scheduled with a third. Lullabelle had remained faithful and stayed around the clock when needed.

The sun had finally disappeared on this unseasonably warm late January weekend at the beach. Trudy sipped on her drink and did a double take when the clown entered the bar. Dressed in a gaudy pink, black and green argyle vest and matching knee socks, a pair of funny flared Capri looking pants and one of those Van Gogh flat painter's hats he stepped up to the bar like he owned it. The circus had indeed come to town she thought.

She waved the waitress down to bring her another drink and asked, "Has the Ringling Brothers Barnum and Bailey Circus just arrived? Who's the Bozo over at the bar?"

The waitress snickered, "No, afraid not. That's Brady Pierce, a local, and let me tell you honey, he's single and loaded."

"What's with the outfit?"

"He's a golfer and on top of that, he owns his own golf apparel business."

"So that's a golf outfit?"

"Yeah, you don't remember that famous golfer that used to dress like that all the time?"

"Was he one of the Little Rascals, *Spanky* maybe?" She laughed out loud when she said it. Brady turned and made eye contact with her.

"No, Payne Stewart...he was killed in that airplane crash."

"I'm glad I'm not a golfer. I wouldn't be caught dead in an outfit like that! Hey, maybe that's what happened to that Pain guy." She laughed even louder at her own humor.

"Another Vodka and cranberry?" asked the waitress.

"Why not? I'm a liberated woman tonight, and while you're at it how about sending something over there to match circus boy's outfit. Make it something fruity with a big old umbrella.

"Should I tell him it's from you?"

"Let's just see if he's smart enough to figure it out and don't forget about mine."

Trudy shifted her focus to the flat screen plasma TV in the corner where she realized Lance Rocker was doing a live report on the seven PM segment. The television was set on Closed Caption. She almost had to close one eye to focus on the words being displayed.

Rocker was live at some sort of accident. She laughed, "Got him on traffic detail, serves him right." Then she read the words homicide and road rage. Some woman had been forced off highway 22 near the highway 31 exit ramp.

Rocker was pointing to a child's restraint in the back seat of her automobile. The child, a little boy, had been found unharmed strapped in the seat. "Thank goodness the kid wasn't harmed."

Rocker continued. She couldn't believe what she was reading on the Closed Caption. The mother had been found thirty yards away, dead. Cause of death had not been released but sources said she had not been thrown from the vehicle and appeared to have been attacked and beaten.

"Excuse me. I believe I owe you a thank you."

She flinched and turned, startled to see circus boy standing at her table. He had gorgeous white teeth, a mouth full of them. They were surrounded by a neatly trimmed reddish brown beard. He had just a hint of grey on the sides. He had killer brown eyes to match.

An eye for detail she measured him head to toe, standing at least six feet two or three inches and evenly proportioned to boot. "Owe me for what?" she asked, slightly slurring the words.

"That little specialty beverage with the umbrella you sent over. It had an interesting taste to it. What was it?"

"I have no idea but I'm glad you liked it," she replied as she noticed a slight bulge in his Capri pants. "How did you know I sent it over?"

"Waitress is a friend. She ratted you out." Extending his hand he said, "Names Brady Pierce and yours would be?"

"Dep...Huh, Trudy Wagner. It's a pleasure to meet you, Mister Pierce."

"Likewise, are you new in the area or just here on vacation?"

"New. I live in Little River with my mom." She couldn't believe she had just said that! "Uh, she's been sick and I've been staying with her until she gets better then I plan to find my own place."

"You have quite a drive back to Little River from here so best pace yourself. The law enforcement around here takes DUI pretty serious. Are you okay to drive?"

"I'm absolutely able to operate any vehicle," She slurred. "My sister has actually taken my mom to Atlanta with her and her family for a couple of weeks. I'm staying in a friend's ocean front condo over at Garden City taking in the beach for the next week." *Good scramble girl but that was way too much information to give a stranger. What the hell was I thinking?*

"I love the ocean too. I own a beach house down in Litchfield." Brady was wooing her with his gorgeous smile and dark brown eyes.

"What's up with that outfit? Waitress told me you like to dress up like some famous golfer."

"I just finished a round of golf at the True Blue golf resort. Wearing this outfit is my style of cheap marketing strategy and you've proven once again that it works."

"Marketing..."

"You spotted me dressed in the funny looking clothes and an inquiring mind had to know the rest of the story. That's the perfect opening for me to hawk my goods," he explained as she once again made eye contact with his goods increasing her desire to get inside that pair of funny looking pants. *What am I thinking? This is beyond stupid...got enough on my plate right now.*

"I don't get it. Why would you really want to wear that getup?"

"I sell these, among other golfing apparel. The pants are golf knickers. Some people call them par fours."

"And those socks, long and loud aren't they." *What am I saying? That didn't even make sense.*

"I specialize in these. We actually have a Golf Knickers Chapter here at the beach, three hundred strong and growing. I've lobbied to make them the official golf wardrobe for the state but there's no such category right now."

"So do you have a store or something?"

"Have three actually, two in South Carolina and just opened a new one up in Wilmington, North Carolina. They're called The Missing Links. Our creed is *Look Good, Feel Good and Play Good.* Plus I have a strong internet following where people can order directly from my website."

"Catchy name..."

"See how well this is going, marketing strategy at its best."

She nodded, "Hooked me right in didn't you?"

"And we customize them to match the color schemes of your favorite sport teams, NFL, major league baseball, college, or NASCAR."

"So who are your favorites?" She motioned to the waitress for another round.

"Carolina Panthers, Atlanta Braves, Coastal Carolina Chants and Rusty Wallace, and make mine a Jack on the rocks. And what do you do for a living?"

I knew he was bound to ask sooner or later. Here comes the show stopper, the reason my social calendar stays open. "I'm in law enforcement."

"What type?"

"I'm a Deputy with Horry County."

"Interesting, do you enjoy it?"

"Immensely, I can picture myself doing nothing else. I specialized in Crime Scene Investigation before I left Ohio." *CSI sounds better than deputy doesn't it?*

"Tell me more about the life of a law enforcement officer and crime scene investigation."

"Is this more of your marketing strategy?

Brady sat down beside her. "Not hardly. It sounds quite intriguing."

He seemed really sincere but she'd rather be putting him in hand cuffs about now. *Has it been that long, girl? Yes it has.*

The drinks arrived and she slurped hers down very un-lady like. He did the same and ordered another round. She forgot about mom and the cases, deciding to live for the moment for a change, something she never did.

The band began playing Shag music, a Swinging Medallions tune, and all of sudden she got a case of happy feet. "You want to dance?"

"So you're telling me they Shag in Ohio."

"Hey, I'm an original southern belle so you just try to keep up." She took him by the hand and led him to the dance floor.

"You're just full of surprises aren't you?"

"I have my moments." *Screw it, this is my night!*

"Guess I better stick to you like glue. It wouldn't do for one of Horry County's finest to get busted for DUI, now would it?"

"Stick it where ever you want," she laughed as she stumbled into his arms. *I know I didn't just blurt that out.*

Elsewhere, while Deputy Wagner became lost in her moment, he had been watching Lance's earlier news segment. *Well done, Lance, you're looking more like your old self. Of course...I would never harm a child. He can't drive yet and ruin my life, but give him a few more years and he'll be out there terrorizing the roadways. But that mother of his was one reckless little bitch. I so hate lane switchers, especially those that don't give signals or pay attention that the lane is already occupied.*

Worse still, she kept her ear glued to that damn cell phone of hers the whole time. Wonder if they can hear her now with it shoved deeply up that tight ass of hers? And her son, he was so precious and innocent, and now motherless because of her senseless carelessness. Too many people make it all about them!

Such a lovely name, Anna Marie Costello, so young at twenty three with her whole life ahead of her and I for one don't believe you lied on your license. One hundred twenty pounds looked about right to me. Fit perfectly in that luscious mouth of yours didn't it? I should have left it there but seemed like too much of a dead give away. I must keep them guessing.

"You had to talk on that damn cell and disregard everyone else's safety! You changed friggin lanes without even verifying that you were about to occupy my space! Hell, if I hadn't laid down on the damn horn and swerved into the median, you'd have forced me into oncoming traffic."

"If the vehicle ahead of me that you almost ran off the road too, had found a turn around spot sooner you'd probably still be alive. I hate having witnesses but I was gone before he returned! As it stands bitch, you won't be pulling this stunt again on either one of us will you?

You made me ruin my new pair of leather gloves with that cutesy little face of yours, Anna Marie. You screwed up a perfectly good paint job to boot. I'll have to fix that myself. I can't report it to my insurance. You certainly were a long way from Branson weren't you? I do like that Missouri tag by the way but didn't care much for you.

"Now they suspect road rage! Those bastards sure are slow learners. Of course it was road rage! I'd never harm a responsible law abiding driver. I only remove the assholes from the roadways! Don't mess with me and you'll be just fine! It's your choice!

And Anna Marie, just like the others, you certainly made a bad decision didn't you? You won't have an opportunity to kill innocent people like that Bradshaw did.

Garden City
Unit 1005 Beach Front
2:00 AM

"I must say officer you are just a little shagging machine aren't you? Nice view here." Brady stood on the balcony breathing in the ocean and Trudy.

"It all came back to me thanks to you. Yeah, that's what I like about this place. It came with its own ocean and beach. I could settle into this life style if..."

"If your mother didn't need you right now," he finished for her.

"Well, you have to play the hand you're dealt but I really don't want to think about that right now. I have two weeks of freedom. That didn't come out so good did it?"

"Keeping it real, there's nothing wrong with that. You're doing the best you can." Brady pulled her close.

"Circus boy what do you have in mind? Is this part of your marketing strategy too?"

"I told you. It works every time." He pulled her even closer.

"Tell you what circus boy. Let's just see how fast you can lose your advertising attire and if you're lucky, you may just score a hole in one. How's that for marketing strategy?"

"Impressive and effective," he replied as he removed his vest, shirt and knickers in record time.

"Keep those argyle knee highs on. I think they're sexy and it makes you look sort of slutty, another excellent marketing tool I must say."

To the sounds of the crashing waves, they tested the balcony and Brady did score that hole in one followed by an eagle then a birdie putt.

Trudy woke to the smell of fresh coffee. Glancing at the clock that displayed nine fifteen, she turned over to see Brady sitting on the edge of the bed, naked and sipping a cup of brew.

"Yours is there on the night stand."

She reached over and grabbed the mug then slid out from under the covers and sat naked Indian style facing him. She was surprised by her boldness with him.

"Nice socks," he said as he pointed to his argyles on her legs. "You're right, they do scream slutty when worn by themselves don't they?" He placed his hand on her thigh.

She placed her mug back on the night stand. "Well I'm not one to waste a marketing moment." She removed one of the socks and handed it to him. "You slip this one on and we'll see if it has the same impact as it did last night."

He became aroused. "Yep, it must be the socks all right."

"Next time I'll bring my cuffs. We'll see if they have the same impact as these funky socks."

"And your uniform I hope! I'm a repeat offender, book me Dan-o."

They finished the round under par. She had learned a valuable lesson tonight. Knickers do make excellent marketing strategy. She didn't want this moment to end. And for the next three days, it wouldn't.

While she played and distanced herself from work and her tormented home life, Road Rage continued to wreak havoc. This time he struck one county over. The connection would not be made quickly. Justice would be served on his terms, circumventing due process; judge, jury and executioner in one swift delivery. Evil never sleeps.

Horry County Police Station
Three Days Later
7:00 AM

"Well partner, did you enjoy your little stay over at the beach in my cousin's condo?"

"I did. Thank you for doing that, Woody. I hadn't realized just how overdue I was for a little down time."

"Did you do anything interesting?"

"Not really. I just had a lazy streak and curled up in bed with a good read. I spent way to much time doing the same old thing over and over. Guess I'm a creature of habit." She figured fibbing might be best for now.

"What about you? What'd you do on your days off, Woody?"

"I ended up just taking one day. Janice was in one of her moods and got pissed having me under foot so I came back to work. I'll use it as comp time later." He had so much vacation time built up he'd be able to retire a year ahead of schedule if he wanted to, if that time ever came.

He was much happier working. Janice was even happier with him working so she could do her own thing. He had offered to take the kids to the Aquarium but she had thwarted that effort saying she had just taken them. She hadn't but he didn't know it. Next she instigated an argument to frustrate him.

Daylight hours didn't offer the necessary cover for her to prowl effectively and Woody cramped her space when he was off duty. Ah but when he worked the night shift all bets were off. Queen of the nightlife, she became the perfect predator and had just the right bait to lure her prey. Poor

Woody, he never suspected a thing and that's the way she intended to keep it.

Janice was proud of how she could so easily manipulate her husband and even prouder of her killer hot body and young school girl looks. She'd wait until he returned to the night shift in a couple of weeks then she'd satisfy her hunger. This required the cloak of darkness to hide her sinful ways.

Woodrow was so predictable. She had picked a fight with him and he quickly returned to work. Dealing with the kids was a breeze and something she really didn't mind. She didn't fare so well with Woodrow. After having her run of the candy store for so many years, settling for milk duds had gotten less appealing.

She constantly reminded herself that he was a good father and excellent provider. She had convinced herself two out of three wasn't bad. That third thing was a biggie though and a void Woodrow could no longer fill.

She was finding it more difficult to fulfill her marital obligations. It didn't seem to matter to him because he loved his job more than he apparently loved her. Two more weeks and she would again be the lioness on the hunt.

"So what else is new?" asked Trudy trying to appear focused and interested.

"Sure does seem like we're having quite a rash of homicides lately. Henderson and Price investigated what they thought was a hit and run a few days ago up near the off ramp at 31 and 22. It turns out to be a murder. They think it's a case of road rage."

"How so?" she asked, now vaguely remembering seeing Rocker reporting on this before Brady swept her away.

"Well for one thing, her cell phone had been shoved up her pie hole. That happened after the attacker strangled her to death. A witness saw some sort of sideswipe collision in his rear view mirror that sent her car off the road, but he had to ride almost to business 17 before he could find a turnaround and drive back."

"Could he ID the other vehicle?"

"I'm afraid not. The other vehicle had been behind him and her, and it happened well after dark. He did report that she almost veered into him while she jabbered away on the phone. He hurried and got past her to avoid her erratic driving and said she kept weaving out of her lane more interested in her phone conversation than the roadway," added Woody as he removed his hat and ran his hand through his hair.

"So that's it?"

"Not by a long shot. Henderson and Price found a kid strapped into a child's restraint in the back seat unharmed." He looked up to the heavens, "Miracle, wouldn't you agree?"

"That's one lucky child except for the loss of his mother."

"You want to hear something really weird? She had driven all the way from Branson, Missouri with no tag on her car. No driver's license was found but records indicate she had a valid one. The car was registered to her husband. According to her parents they were separated. She had her social security card in her purse along with a wad of cash, almost twelve hundred bucks."

"Where's the husband?"

"So far they have not been able to locate him. He's on the *person of interest* list. Missouri police records indicated a long history of domestic abuse. She may have been fleeing from him."

"Sounds like a good possibility he caught up with her."

"Problem with that theory, phone records indicated she was talking to someone at their Branson residence at the time of the incident. If it was her husband it clears him."

Trudy struggled to stay focused on this case or any police work right now. Her thoughts drifted back to the past three days spent with Brady Peirce. She planned to meet him after her shift.

Something almost struck her as relevant to this case and the others but she just couldn't embrace detective work right now. For the first time in her life, and unlike her partner Woody, the job just didn't rank as the number one priority right now.

With Amy still at her baby sister's, she planned to seize the opportunity and enjoy the next week and a half of freedom, and do something just for her. She felt young and alive and missed Brady. Work was just a necessary evil. She wished she had vacation time but unfortunately she didn't. Shift's end crept like a tortoise.

Georgetown Police Department
10:00 AM

Detective Daniel Newton reviewed his report from last night's crime scene. The brutality of the incident, still vivid in his memory, haunted his thoughts.

Report prepared by Detective Daniel Newton, Georgetown Police

Badge #1291

Case # 1764

Location: Highway 17 and Rice Bluff Road, Georgetown County

Date: February 11th, 2001

Time: 2:25 A.M.

Crime: Apparent homicide

Victim: Hispanic, Male

Coroner: Dr. James Hanna

Autopsy Surgeon: Dr. Patricia Robinson

Pronounced dead: 10:12 a.m.

Discovery
The body was discovered at approximately 1 a.m. by one Aniston Childers, a local delivery truck driver. Childers stated that he noticed the automobile twenty yards off the highway near Rice Bluff Road when he stopped, pulled down the road to relieve himself. He walked over and found a body in the back seat, bloody and battered.

Childers stated he opened the driver's side back door and checked the victim for a pulse and found none. He returned to his truck and called 911.

Witnesses
Aniston Childers (See Discovery) No other witnesses have come forward.

Scene
This section of highway 17 is remote and has very little traffic this hour of the night. There is thick undergrowth making it difficult for those passing to ID a vehicle. McCurry stopping enabled him to see it.

Victim
The body was discovered lying on its back, head on passenger side back seat and feet on driver's side.

The perpetrator(s) apparently forced the driver off the road then pulled the victim from the automobile where he was attacked and killed then the body was placed in the backseat. There are no obvious signs of a sexual assault.

Evidence recovered at the scene

An Assortment of tools (saw, power drill, screw drivers, claw hammer, tape measure, level) in the backseat floor board presumably belonging to the victim

Wallet: containing one hundred twenty seven dollars, no identification information. Wallet was empty except for the money.

1995 white Toyota Camry, four door - there was no license plate on the vehicle.

Blood samples: on the ground near driver's side door, on the back door and window and in the interior, second claw hammer found on the ground

Fingerprints: Driver's door handle, passenger door handle, second claw hammer found on the ground

Victim Identification: Can not make a positive identification at this time (no license, registration or license plate)

Mumbling out loud Detective Newton said, "Maybe the serial number on the auto will turn up something. My gut tells me we have an illegal alien here which will make things much tougher. I won't get any help on this one."

Back in Horry County, *Hector Jorge Gonzales, Hispanic male, five feet, three and a half inches tall, blah, blah, blah.*

"Hey Mi Amigo, this looks too much like a phony damn license to me! Taco Bell, what's with pulling out in the highway in front of me like that? I nearly ran off the road trying to dodge your sorry ass. Lucky for you 17 is four lanes. Is that the way you little bastards drive down there in Mexico? Hey boy, this is America. Learn how to drive here and live longer! Oops, too late for you. Sorry. You made me late getting home because I had to turn around and run you down to teach your illegal ass some manners. I hate being late! Thanks for letting me borrow that versatile hammer of yours. It did the trick. Too bad they hadn't finished that border fence yet. It could have saved your butt! Oh well, there's one less of you taking American jobs!"

"I'm the angry American making the roadways safe ways for God and my country. I hate inconsiderate and rude drivers! I got all of you in my cross hairs so best you stay in your lanes, off those miserable phones and pay attention to the red lights and stop signs! Use your damn turn signal when you change lanes. You'll live longer!"

Sea Captain's House
Ocean Blvd, Myrtle Beach
8:23 PM

"This is very nice Brady," said Trudy, holding his hands across the table.

"One of my favorites and right here on the ocean," he responded as he squeezed her hands.

"Did you protect us from the riff-raff out there today?"

"Just another day in the neighborhood I suppose. It seems that this beach paradise sure has its fair share of homicides."

"The criminals need their fun in the sun too. They just add their own demented little twist to it."

"Well, how about you? Did your marketing strategy land you any hot little beach honeys today?"

"Nah, it seems to just work on deputies in heat."

"You excluded horny, hot bodied and depraved," she said as she pinched his fingers.

"I was saving those for later."

"Wine me and dine me first and if you're lucky you might just have a slim chance but I'm not easy."

"Who needs easy? Did you bring your cuffs?"

"Did you bring your knickers?"

They still couldn't believe they had found one another. Neither had been married or had really even come close to walking down the aisle. Trudy always had her career and a very ambitious appetite. Brady had spent his years building his little empire. Trudy ended up on the short end of relationships compared to Brady but both had been content in their lives until now. Four days ago the game had changed.

Her cell phone rang. "Hello...what's wrong? Oh...Are they Okay? I'm sorry. She's getting worse for sure. No it won't be a problem...really! No, I fully understand and agree. You will stay the weekend won't you? Okay, see you then and I'm sorry about what the kids had to go through."

"You look stressed. Can I help?"

"That was my sister, Allison, in Atlanta. They're bringing my mom home this weekend instead of the next. She's been terrorizing my niece and nephew." Trudy felt her life being sucked from her body...

"How so?"

"Well, maybe terrorizing is a little too harsh but she has frightened them. She became disoriented and tried several nights to climb in bed with them. A neighbor also found her on their front porch early one morning ringing the doorbell. Sis couldn't handle it. I should have stayed an orphan."

"Can you handle it?"

"I have too."

"Let me help."

"NO," she almost shouted out too loudly.

"And why not?"

"Because...she is my responsibility and not yours and besides, I need you, she doesn't. I'm selfish with you."

"But," he started to say but she interrupted.

"We have a few more nights. Let's not waste them. I'm easy after all so take advantage of me. Please take me to your place. My appetite hungers for only you right now."

"I'm in, let's go," he replied as he motioned over the waitress and gave her a fifty.

Not accustomed to juggling priorities, Trudy felt her life coming unraveled. She had always had just one focus, her career and nothing else. Now she had her career, her mom and Brady. Ranking them had become complicated. For the next few days Brady would rank number one. She'd reassess the pecking order when her mom returned.

"Where'd you go just now? What were you thinking," asked Brady, placing his hand on her cheek.

"Thinking only of you my dear and I can't wait to show you how much."

"I love how you think."

She kissed him passionately and tugged him toward the exit. Tonight would belong to them. Tomorrow, she would deal with tomorrow.

Intersection of 501 and Church Street
Conway
10:45 PM

The traffic light turned yellow then red and the car rushed through heading eastward on 501 just missing the front bumper of the driver entering 501 from South Church Street. The driver laid down on his horn and the traffic offender flipped him the finger. Two passengers, each pointing, turned, laughed and mouthed F-bombs.

"Mister Driver, did you just shoot me a bird? I hate getting the finger! Ask the Q-tip. You ran the damn red light, not me, so why are you the one acting like such a smartass? And you sure can pick your friends! Jump off the damn cliff and the others must follow. They gave me the finger too. "I'm driving along and minding my own business...and now this...you brought it on yourselves."

I see by your license plate that you boys are from North Carolina. This is no way to treat your neighbor state! You just couldn't let me go home peacefully could you? Nice night to drive to the beach I guess. Lead on boys! Here comes the welcome wagon!

Horry County Police Department
6:45 AM

"Partner, you look like you're dragging ass this morning," commented Woody. "Rough night?"

"On the contrary, the night was quite wonderful. I actually hated to see it end."

"Guess you're still seeing that guy, huh."

"Guess you could say so. Allison is bringing mom home Friday so I have to enjoy it while I can."

"I thought she was keeping your mom for at least another week."

"Long story, it didn't work out. Is there anything on the radar screen for us this morning?"

"Nope, I guess we could act like cops and go for donuts. By the way, I heard Hank say you may have you a cruiser by the weekend. It's going to feel sort of strange being on my own again."

"What's the matter Lone Ranger, you going to miss your buddy Tonto?"

"Actually it's going to be nice to have my own space again."

"Anderson, Wagner, get your butts in here," yelled Sheriff Hank Singleton, blocking out the doorway of his office with his massive girth. "I've got a hot one for you."

"What's stewing boss?"

"Well Woodrow, there's a possible triple homicide over at the Admiral's Quarters, Ocean Boulevard between 8th and 9th avenues. Local police have the crime scene contained. I called and told them you'd be arriving to lead the investigation. Snap to it and be thorough. This could be bad for our hospitality market."

"Got it," said Woody as he exited the sheriff's office.

"Wagner, hold up a minute," Hank motioned for Trudy.

"Yes sir."

"I really need your experience on this one and would appreciate it if you personally take the lead in the investigation. It sounds damn bad. Three young men from Greensboro were found dead by their cousin this morning and the scene has been described as a blood bath. We want to keep the news media at bay until we know more."

"I know the drill sir."

"And Wagner, how's you mom?"

"She's fine sir," she lied as she joined Woody who stood patiently outside.

Woody was waiting down the hallway. "What was all that about?"

"He just doesn't want the crime scene to turn into a three ring circus so I'm going to need your help to make sure that doesn't happen." She didn't want to degrade Woody with the chief's request for her to take the lead.

"You're thinking Rocker aren't you?"

"He's your problem this time, Woody, so make sure he doesn't get inside that hotel."

"Trust me. That lowlife won't set foot on the property," he boasted, underestimating Lance Rocker's tenacity.

Rocker had already arrived at the hotel after hearing the chatter on the police radio frequency that he had conveniently monitored. Using his charm and the promise of fifteen seconds of fame on the news, he had begun his questioning of the hotel staff. He already knew more than the newly appointed crime scene investigator.

Admiral's Quarters
Ocean Blvd, Myrtle Beach
7:25 AM

"This is Lance Rocker reporting live from the Admiral's Quarters in Myrtle Beach. I'm at the scene of a suspected triple homicide. Details are sketchy. What we do know from sources here at the hotel is that the three young men were Coastal Carolina Alumni. They had returned to the Grand Strand for a few days of golf but events turned tragic for them unfortunately. My source tells me that a golf club may have been the murder weapon. Please stay tuned for the developing story. This is Lance Rocker, Channel 12 News."

"Lance, you do realize you're pushing the limit on this one," warned the producer. "We do have the scoop on the other networks so I'm warning you. Don't screw this up."

"How's my hair?"

"A category three hurricane couldn't move a hair on that head."

"Look, we got to keep the heat on this storyline. I smell something big and Sir Lancelot is never wrong. Perfect timing...there's that hot deputy and her little sidekick, the Woodpecker. I owe her one so start that camera rolling on my cue."

"Lance..." pleaded the producer to no avail.

"Work with me on this," he said, giving her *the look*, reminding her of their little dirty secret.

"Asshole," she whispered. "You screw this up by making it personal and I'll have you doing remotes from the mall."

"Just have them roll the camera," demanded lance. "This is Lance Rocker, Channel 12 News, with a late breaking report at the Admiral's Quarters, scene of three grisly murders. I see a couple of Horry County's finest. Let's see if I can catch a word with Deputy Wagner."

"You see who I see?" asked Woody.

"Why should that not surprise us?"

"You said you wanted me to handle him."

"I hoped we would have beaten him here. He is resourceful I must admit. I tell you what. Let me head off our newsman, Woody. You secure the crime scene."

"Deputy Wagner, what can you share with us about the three bodies discovered in unit 317? Is it true that they were plummeted with their own golf clubs? I'm sure this has shaken our fine community. My source tells me they were graduates of CCU."

Rattled by Rocker's information, Trudy grabbed the lens of the camera and pushed it toward the ground. "I must ask you to vacate the crime scene."

"Deputy Wagner, is it true a cousin to one of the deceased discovered their bodies?"

She pushed the camera aside then grabbed Rocker by the collar. "These people have families. You're worse than a damn tick in a blood bank! "

"Deputy, I resent those remarks," whispered Lance.

Woody stepped between the two of them. "No news crews on the premises...clear the area...now!"

"You heard Deputy Anderson."

"Cut the feed," ordered the producer and the camera woman complied with her request. "This is getting out of hand."

Lowering his microphone, Lance crept closer to Woody. "The runt of the litter sure jumps to the alpha female's orders. I guess you really look up to the Amazon don't you, Shorty? It appears to me that she's rooted you off the Sheriff's main tit."

Woody cocked a right hook but Trudy grabbed his arm. "Don't let him push your buttons, Deputy Anderson. He's baiting you for the camera."

"Mind your mama," mocked Lance.

"Enough Jimmy Olson...now get out of my sight before I run you in for destroying yet another crime scene."

"Did you hear what she just said? She can't roust us away just like that." Lance eyed his producer and camera woman for support.

"It looks to me that she was just doing her job. I could certainly take pointers," stated the producer. "Let's pack it up, Jimmy."

"Can't say I heard anything unusual," added the camera woman. "Then again, Sir Lancelot spending the night in jail with a couple of bubbas might be worth the price of admission.

Trudy smiled and sensed something more than just dislike for Rocker from the others. They both acted like women scorned. Whatever, she didn't have time to deal with it. She stepped on the elevator and rode it to the third floor.

Entering unit 317, she paused to take a deep breath after catching a glance of the carnage. An officer pointed to the cousin sitting on the balcony. She began her interrogation.

She had to admit Rocker was good. The cousin had found the bodies when they didn't show for their 8:18 tee time at Arrowhead golf course. They were alumni of Coastal Carolina having graduated three years prior. The alleged weapon had been a Big Bertha Driver.

Two of the young men had been identified by their driver's licenses but the third had been identified by his cousin as one David Thompson. His driver's license had not been located. Ages ranged from 24 to 27.

Prints and photographs had been taken and the coroner wrapped up his preliminary assessment. No motive had been determined. She met Woody near the elevator.

"What'd you find, partner?"

"Other than three badly beaten bodies, not much but maybe the prints or blood samples will turn up something. It was a forced entry by the looks of the door jam. The killer did do something sort of strange. He severed the middle finger of each of the three victims. Their pants were pulled down to their ankles and the fingers were positioned in their anal cavities like candles."

"Damn, stuck in their butts? That's perverted and sick and too weird even for here. That took some time to do."

"I agree. This sure isn't the quiet tourist community I was expecting. Whoever did this came prepared...definitely premeditated."

"I can't remember ever having so many homicides in such a short stretch. Oh yeah, we found their automobile in the parking garage but it took a while. We had to get the make and model from the front desk before we matched it. It must be some sort of new fad around here to lift license plates."

"No plates...," she said to confirm what she had just heard.

"Mean something?"

"Might. Let's get back to the station. We need to pull a few files."

"You're on to something aren't you? I can see it in your eyes."

She nodded. "I hope I'm wrong but I think the facts might just support my suspicions."

"Can you at least give your partner a hint?"

"Only if you keep it between you and me until we have the evidence to support it."

"You've got my word. Now what's up? Spill the beans."

Lowering her voice to just above a whisper she said what she really dreaded saying, "I believe we may have ourselves some sort of serial killer here on the Grand Strand."

"Holly crap, a serial killer," exclaimed Woody.

"Holly crap indeed," whispered Lance Rocker, standing at the door of the stairwell.

Equally concealed from view, an interested spectator heard both comments. His mind processed the events.

So my good buddy Lance Rocker got the scoop on the law. Seems we may have a little rivalry developing here. It's a shame you folks just don't get it. I'm saving innocent lives by taking care of the threat on America's roadways but you're just too damn stupid to realize it. That's alright. I'm not in it for the fame. It's my civil duty to clean up the streets.

Damn it. I'm out of meth. Looks like a road trip to me! At least the highways are safer right now. Mister Eric Southard, I bet you and your little yuppie buddies from Greensboro wish you had a mulligan about now. Interesting, just twenty four years old, college smart and you're such a shitty little driver with a smartass attitude, but no more. Your pals are not better. Never ever give me the finger.

Gulf Stream Cafe
Garden City
9 PM

Trudy had returned to the station and had run a query to single out any cases with similarities to the triple homicide at the Admiral's Quarters. She had gathered those files but had not had an opportunity to review them in detail. That alone had her a little antsy.

She now sipped on a glass of Chardonnay as she waited for Brady to arrive. She had contemplated returning to her car and retrieving the files but decided against it. She didn't want to ruin one of her last three evenings with Brady before her mom returned. She owed that to him and herself.

Still she reviewed the cases mentally. The missing plates and driver's licenses in the triple homicide with the symbolic severed fingers, the old guy on the golf cart with the driver's license staged in his mouth, the Missouri lady with the phone inserted in her butt with her tag and license missing, an Hispanic victim in Georgetown county yet to be identified, his license and tag also missing and the clincher...the Bradshaw murder. That one dragged Tim Ford back into the picture, although no evidence linked him to that murder yet or to the others. She was thinking too much like Woody now; guilty as charged.

The murder methods all differed slightly. The three young men had been brutally beaten in their sleep with one of their golf clubs. The old guy had been struck from behind in the head with an undetermined weapon and had then been drowned. The lady had been strangled then sexually assaulted with her cell phone. The suspected illegal alien had been killed with his own claw hammer. Bradshaw had been beaten severely with his own baseball bat. They were somehow linked. She had to make the connection and make it stick before she dared share it with anyone.

She ordered another glass of wine. Where was Brady? It wasn't like him to be late. Now what did she really know about his promptness. She hadn't known him for a week yet but she perceived him as being a person that would always be punctual. He certainly shouldn't waste a precious second of their time. After all, the clock was ticking. Mom would return Friday and all would change.

The waitress refilled her glass. What did all those people have in common? This part of the puzzle didn't fit. They had nothing in common. Three young men, an elderly gentleman, the Missouri lady with a child, the unidentified Mexican and Bradshaw, she just couldn't draw a correlation. She didn't know about Walter Ozolins yet because his case had not shown up on the radar. It had been ruled natural causes in the hospital but had been a result of the brutal beating. Coincidence, his tag had been removed.

Her serial killer theory wasn't falling into place very neatly if indeed there was really a serial killer. She still had not openly introduced it to the sheriff and wouldn't until she had something she could hang her hat on and right now those chances seem slim to none. She had no motive, no link, and most of all, no suspect but Tim Ford and other than Bradshaw, why would he kill all those other people?

Maybe by killing them, he was trying to throw them off the original trail. No, even he wouldn't kill all those innocent people just to hide one murder. She just couldn't make that work out in her head.

"Hey pretty lady. Can I wipe those frown marks off your face before they become etched on there permanently?"

"I don't know, circus boy, can you? Where are those funny pants?"

"I'm off duty just like you and it's too rainy for golf today, even for the beach."

"Yep, it's a nasty day for sure."

"Looks like it could possibly match your mood," he said as he motioned for the waitress. "Would you like to talk about it?"

"I'm off duty too," she replied as she bottomed out the second glass of wine.

"Are you sure about that? I don't think your mind has punched out yet."

"Okay, so you twisted my arm but you must keep this confidential or I will have to shoot you then arrest you and possibly hang you," she replied as she pointed to her empty glass.

"I love it when you role play with me, Deputy," he said, pretending to take a position for frisking.

"Who said I'm kidding? I don't know if you caught the news today or heard about that triple homicide at Myrtle Beach. It was very brutal and I'm trying to tie it in with a few more homicides in the area."

"So if I'm hearing you right, you think you have a Charles Manson or Ted Bundy type terrorizing our fine tourist community."

"Possibly but I can't make all the puzzle pieces fit," she replied, reaching for his hand.

"Feel free to abuse me as your personal sounding board. I'm quite the amateur sleuth. Just ask McCloud or Colombo or even McMillan and wife."

Snickering, Trudy said, "Now you're really dating yourself. Those shows haven't been on TV in forever. They didn't even know how to spell DNA back then."

"Haven't you heard of reruns? It's nice to hear that laugh by the way."

"Is that how you solved them, by watching them more than once?"

"I can't hide anything from you."

"Nope, circus boy, I know all your little dirty knickered secrets," she whispered as she stroked his fingers.

"So what do you have that makes you think Charles Manson is wreaking havoc among us?"

"Well, I have six homicides and in each of the four incidences, the *perp* may have taken the victim's license plate and/or driver's license or did something with the license to make a point. Other than that, I have no other similarities or motives or common ground for any of the victims. How's that for building a case for a serial killer?"

"So what then makes you conclude these were all done by the same person?"

"Mostly gut right now but I can't overlook the missing items because this has to be more than just coincidence, don't you think?"

"Yeah, the murders do have a connection it seems," he said as he downed his Jack and Coke. "What do you feel like having?"

Her look said it all. "Waitress, forget the menu. Here, this should cover our drinks. We have an emergency and will be leaving." He winked as he grabbed Trudy around the waist and headed for the door.

Pink Cadillac Bar and Grill
Myrtle Beach
10:27 PM

Lance ordered another cocktail while he warmed himself by the cozy fireplace. He sank in the plush leather sofa while eyeing this one particular hard bodied cutie sipping her drink in front of the Plasma television. She had to be all of nineteen and prime for his picking. He'd send over a drink once he confirmed she waited for no male companion. Then he'd rock her world if all went as planned.

In the meantime he pondered Deputy Wagner's haunting revelation, serial killer indeed. He had to determine why she had made that comment and what other cases were linked to those three murders at the Admiral's Quarters. This could certainly make the national news and pave his way if he did his homework and called in a few favors in the police department.

He couldn't just throw out the serial killer scenario on the news without the facts to support it, or could he? Would she take the bait if he let it slip? This would require more thought, and another drink and for sure that coed now standing by the bar. Priorities first, nail the sweet young thing then he could think more clearly.

Horry County Police Department
7:00 AM

"Well, how's your theory going, Wagner?"

"Woody, it blows chunks right now so please keep it close to the vest. There's no need in either one of us looking foolish if it doesn't pan out."

"Not a word from these lips," Woody replied, locking them with an imaginary key then unlocking them as he said, "Looks like you may have your own car in the morning. Hank told me it was supposed to arrive today. It's been repaired from a high speed pursuit a couple of months ago."

"Well partner, guess we better enjoy the last day sharing a ride."

"Guess so and is your mama still coming home Friday?"

"As far as I know...it'll be good to have her home." Was she? She wasn't sure how she would manage that new juggling act...her mom, Brady and her job, specifically this case.

"How's it going with Payne Stewart?" Woody asked while demonstrating his disjointed golf swing.

She smiled and nodded to confirm all was going well. "What you say we pay your buddy Ford a little visit? I'd like to ask his whereabouts for the Admiral's Quarters' homicides to see if he squirms."

"You think he could be your alleged serial killer?"

"Don't say that too loudly. I wouldn't go that far yet but we at least know he had motive for Bradshaw's murder and had previously attacked him. You reported Bradshaw's license plate missing from his truck in the shed didn't you?"

"But his driver's license was in his wallet," Woody pointed out. "So maybe it's not related."

"Woody, I excluded something from our final report, something I shouldn't have and I'm ashamed for doing it. When I deserted my position at the front door, I cleared the way for our murderer to escape."

"How can you be so sure?"

"I tried the door right after you went around back. It was locked but the coroner entered by that very same door. He said it was standing wide open. I'm so damn stupid," she shook her head in disgust.

Woody discharged a winded blow of air, "Damn, we had him didn't we?"

She nodded, "Someone was in that living room when we entered the house, hiding and unable to escape until I cleared the path."

"Does Hank know?"

"Nope, only you and I know now."

"Then it stays right here, partner. No good would come out of telling him about this now. He'd shit a brick." He placed a reassuring hand on her shoulder.

"Thank you, partner...just telling someone has helped me tremendously," she said as she placed her hand on his arm.

Woody blushed, "Let's go talk to Tim Ford. Maybe we can make him crack."

Rocker World
7:30 AM

Rocker had made good on his promise about nailing the cutie he had scoped out at the Pink Cadillac Bar and grill. Now strutting like a rooster he admired his handy work.

A mighty tasty morsel you were my dear but now it's time to see you on your way. I don't suppose you'll make it to my wall of fame seeing that you were wearing no underwear. I'll make sure you receive an honorable mention. Now what the hell was your name again? Oh well, guess it really doesn't matter does it?

Rocker noticed his answering machine light blinking and pressed the play button.

"Rocker, its Bert, I did what you asked and you owe me big time. If I ever get caught, it will be mine and your ass on the line. Horry County has had ten homicides in the past six months but one of these was a domestic squabble gone badly, another, the result of a break-in and two were gang related. That leaves six of the ten presently unsolved. I've made copies and placed them in the usual location. Remember, I deal in cash only so I will look forward to your contribution. Don't forget to bury this message."

Bert Bell, a dispatcher at Horry County Police Station, had come through for him once again. Bert greedily accepted bribes to support his gambling addiction.

"So there are only two others. One has to be Ed Bradshaw and the other would have to be that little Branson mommy. How can a serial killer case be made from those two and the three visiting golfers? I'm missing something here," Lance spoke out loud.

"What did you say baby," slurred the little hot redhead just awakening from her drugged stupor.

"I said it's time you got your sweet little ass out of here because I have work to do," he responded, pulling the covers from her perky tanned body. "On second thought, I believe I have a few minutes to spare. Say *'yes Rocker I'll have another'*."

Tim Ford Residence
North Myrtle Beach
8:55 AM

"Knock on the door one more time, Woody," urged Trudy. "His car is in the drive so I suspect our Mister Ford is just trying to avoid the long arm of the law."

The door eased open and Tim Ford peeked through, his right eye being all that was visible. "Well if it isn't my two favorite law enforcement officers. To what do I owe this visit? Are you still pissed because I wouldn't confess to that bastard Bradshaw's untimely demise? Sad, someone went long ball with that bat on him didn't they? What a waste of a good autographed Pelican's bat."

"You seem to be mighty familiar with the details of the case now don't you Mister Ford."

"Come now Deputy Wagner, it is pretty common knowledge isn't it? It has been on the news and in the papers so what are you holding back? My bet, nothing or you would have booked your man by now."

"My we have a smart mouth to go along with a somewhat cocky attitude this morning don't we."

"Do you mind if we come in?" asked Woody.

"And if I do?" asked Tim, now exposing the right side of a wide grin through the narrow opening.

"We have no warrant if that's what you mean," stated Trudy.

"But we can certainly acquire one," added Woody.

"On what grounds officer?"

"On the grounds we have new evidence that prompts us to search your premises more thoroughly than the previous time. Hope we don't break any valuables this time!"

"What say I join you out there?"

"Something to hide?" asked Woody.

"No more than you have cause for entry but out there in the open keeps you from whacking me around doesn't' it?"

"Alright, outside it is. We'll do this on your terms, *this time*," she emphasized in her not so forgiving voice.

Tim eased out the door, closing it behind, him facing his two interrogators. He stood only a couple of inches shorter than Trudy at 5'11" but drew comfort in looking down on Woody some three inches shorter.

"Who's first, you or the half pint? Let's get his over with because I'm a busy man."

"Just give me a reason to kick your ass," said Woody, taking a step towards Tim Ford.

"Police harassment or brutality; let me tally up the score."

"Enough, both of you," interrupted Trudy. "What have you been doing with your time lately?"

"As in lately, I assume you are referring to after that bastard met his maker."

"In lately, I meant lately," she replied. "But since you brought up the Bradshaw homicide first, carry on."

"Can you wait here while I go grab my diary?"

"You're certainly confident aren't you Ford," stated Woody, as he tugged on his gun holster.

"Got nothing to hide, just like how much I hated Bradshaw for killing my family. You have the records. I kicked his ass and would have probably finished what the court wouldn't do if that nosey neighbor of his hadn't called 911. Nobody wanted him dead more than me. Are you satisfied? I said it. Toss some confetti."

"Too bad that same neighbor didn't call 911 the second time," added Trudy.

"Yep, it might have saved his miserable life," snapped Tim sarcastically. "There is a God."

"So tell me, Mister Ford, did it make you nervous hiding in that living room until you had an opening to exit the premises," Trudy asked, trying to rattle Ford's cage.

"What in the hell are you talking about Deputy?" asked Tim, as cool as a cucumber. "Living room...what is this really about?"

Ignoring his question Trudy asked, "Do you have an alibi for Tuesday?" She baited him intentionally not being specific with the time hoping he'd fill in the blanks to coincide with the times of death of the three murdered men.

"Tuesday, what time Tuesday...matter of a fact, which Tuesday?" he asked, not falling for it as she had hoped.

"The 11th, let's say between the hours of midnight and eight," she replied, intentionally opening up the hours for a wider spread than the coroner's proposed time of death.

"Doing what most honest law abiding folks do, I was sleeping of course and no, I don't have any witnesses. I don't usually ask anybody to watch me sleeping in case I require an alibi."

"What time did you retire?" asked Woody.

"What is she doing, throwing her voice? Nice trick, it looked very convincing."

Woody edged toward Ford but Trudy blocked the maneuver. "Answer Deputy Anderson's question please."

"Probably around midnight and before you ask, I think I must have awakened at around eight."

"Smartass," lashed out Woody.

"Smarter than you two apparently...is that all officers?"

"One more question," added Trudy. "How would you react if we told you Bradshaw was still alive and in a coma and we were waiting for him to wake up and identify his attacker?"

"After thinking what a crock of crap, I would probably consider pulling his life support systems, hypothetically speaking of course."

"Thank you Mister Ford. We have no more questions," she replied as she motioned Woody to head to the cruiser.

Sitting in the cruiser, Woody commented, "See, he's guilty like I said and so damn smug about it."

"I don't know. If he is, he's one demented killer for sure. I never saw him break a sweat."

"I tell you, he killed Bradshaw! Now I don't know if you can link him to those others or not, but he damn sure killed him. I'll stake my reputation on it."

"Let's don't go that far yet. Let's see if we can talk to the officers that investigated the Costello woman's homicide."

"It'll probably have to wait until Friday. I think they're in seminar in Charleston for the next couple of days."

"Just our luck, Friday it is. What you say we take an early lunch? I have a few personal phone calls to make."

"Your Mama?"

"That's one of them," she hedged.

"And I guess you're pining for that boyfriend of yours."

"That would be the other one," she lied again. She had received a phone call from Lance Rocker just before they had left the station stating he had something urgent to discuss with her, and her alone, pertaining to the Admiral's Quarter's homicides.

"I know just the place, Cracker Barrel. I just love Cracker Barrel. I take Janice and the kids there at least once every couple of weeks. You can order lunch or breakfast anytime. The kids love it too. I'm not sure about Janice though. That woman is getting harder to read all the time," said Woody as he licked his chops.

"Cracker Barrel it is. Call it in would you?"

"Sure thing partner...hey look, Ford's pulling out of his drive. Should we follow him?"

"No, he's just chomping at the bits to scream harassment. He knows we're onto him. That's good enough."

An hour later...

"What's the hurry asshole? Stop that damn honking! I'm going as fast as I can. The hick on the John Deere is holding up traffic, not me."

Why do they even let these Gomer Pyle characters ride on the highways with their farm equipment? And now I got the bitch in the BMW riding my bumper and laying down on her horn like it's my frigging fault! Apparently neither knows they're fueling road rage here!

"Come on farm boy, shit or get off the pot! Pull over and let traffic through! Quit hogging the highway!"

No that would be way too damn easy! It would ruin the future farmers of America's right of passage!

"Woman, get off my ass! And if you blow that damn horn one more time I'll shove it up yours!"

What the hell is wrong with America? Have we forgotten how to be kind to our fellow man? Why is everyone in such a damn hurry? Start earlier if you think you're going to be late! Hell here at the beach you better allow extra time if you're going to the grocery store!

"Okay, so finally Mister Douglas you're pulling into your yard. And a fine Ponderosa you have there I must say! Park the John Deere and drive an automobile next time!

Are you happy in the BMW? We're moving now."

Oh so now you're going to whip around me like it was my entire fault! I see you're a realtor. You wear that advertisement proudly don't you? Were you late for a condo showing? Not to worry, I may be interested! Good gimmick, advertising on your car. I now know your phone number! And don't think I've forgotten about you either sod buster! I know where you park your tractor. I just love living at the beach! It is so relaxing...NOT!

Cracker Barrel Parking Lot
Windy Hill Area, Myrtle Beach
9:59 AM

Trudy made her phone call. "Hello Rocker, what do you have to share with us?"

"This is for your ears only Deputy Wagner. Can we meet after you get off duty? Drinks and dinner are on me. I would prefer not discussing this over the phone and don't bring short stuff." Lance poured on the charm with a twist of sarcasm.

"This better be good, Rocker. I'll meet you for one drink. My shift ends at seven."

"Call me Lance and may I call you Trudy?"

"Rocker is just fine and you may call me Wagner. Deputy actually works even better." She spoke into the phone trying to stress her point.

"Is that a way to treat a friend?"

"I'd never speak to a friend like this."

"I know a cozy little bar and grill in North Myrtle Beach. I can give you directions and I'll meet you there say around eight.

"Too intimate for me I assure you. I'll meet you at eight thirty in Murrell's Inlet at Drunken Jacks. You best get to your point quickly and if you try anything, I will neuter you for the mere hell of it."

She would be meeting Brady there at nine. She had been staying with him at his place and avoiding her mom's Little River residence except to pick up clean cloths and drop off her dirty laundry.

"Trudy, you're such a hard sell but I so like it when you trash talk."

"And Rocker, be there on time and I repeat, be prepared to get to your point or suffer the consequences."

"I'm fascinated by your take charge personality. Does Deputy Anderson feel the same way?" he asked, trying to egg her on.

"Eight thirty, Rocker..."

Just what are you up to Rocker? Instinct tells me nothing good will result from our rendezvous.

"I've got us a table. Did you reach your mama and lover boy?"

She nodded to confirm the lie.

Sun, Sand and Sea Realty
12:00 PM

"Yes sir, it will be my pleasure to show you that unit, Mister Jones. You have remarkable taste. The Penthouse offers a wonderful view of the beach and the seclusion most people desire. How did you acquire my name and number?" asked Rachel Winslow.

"Oh you saw me earlier as I drove by. You'd be surprised how advertising on my own auto has paid off. Yes I can meet you there at one thirty. You won't be disappointed. This is prime property."

"No you don't have to check in with security. Just park at the Check In parking area and take the elevator to the fourteenth. I will meet you at the condo."

Rachel hung up the phone and immediately began to calculate her commission. The Penthouse had been on the market for almost a year. "It's my lucky day to be at the right place at the right time."

Sonny Boggs Residence
6:00 PM

Well, well, well Mister Green Jeans, you sure have a fine little shop here. You possess such expensive tools and gadgets to choose from too. What is a man to do? All I require is your company and a few minutes of your valuable time.

Please don't make me wait out here too long. Your little bride had nothing to do with your rude behavior and it would not be appropriate for her to be so unfortunate as to pay for your sinful road hogging ways.

Ah, I see you now and heading in my direction, simply wonderful. I must rush my decision so not to disappoint you with my choice of gadgets. Ah yes, this will do just fine and battery operated, excellent. Nice overalls! You really do play the part well.

Sadly, you're actually no better than my old pal Raymond in that stinking golf cart. He wouldn't yield to the traffic either. He had his ten seconds of fame in the news so I suppose he got what he deserved. I still see no value in allowing such vehicles on the highways, golf carts and tractors.

Sonny opened the shop door. "Who the hell are you and what are you doing in my shop?" Sonny instinctively reached for a shovel resting by the door.

"I stopped by to inquire if your John Deere might be for sale. It's such a fine looking machine and green is my favorite color."

"What would give you a damn fool idea like that, boy?"

"Pardon me, my bad. I saw you earlier on the roadway and the speed you were driving gave me the impression you may be tired of your little toy. I thought you might wish to opt for something that can maintain the minimum speed limit. I'm sure it would do well in a parade but not on my highway."

"Your highway...you're damn near crazy aren't you boy? Get the hell out of my shop before I call the police!"

"Sure thing, I know the drill and I do apologize."

Sonny leaned the shovel back against the wall turning his back for only a second. "Damn fool," he spouted.

I heard that. "You're the damn fool and one inconsiderate road hogging bastard," he commented, planting the drill against Sonny's back and drilling clean through to his heart. No struggle, he died almost instantly.

"Cordless is definitely the way to go, don't you think? I crack me up sometimes."

Drunken Jacks
Murrell's Inlet
8:27 PM

Entering the bar, Trudy immediately spotted Rocker sitting at a secluded table. He saw her and smiled almost blinding her with his self righteous charm.

"My, I almost didn't recognize you out of uniform. That deputy outfit doesn't do you justice. I like it." Rocker thought the tight fitting jeans and a body hugging sweater was certainly eye candy for a sweet tooth!"

"Stuff it. Cut to the chase. What do you want?"

"Sorry, excuse my manners but I'm a sucker for perfection. What can I have the waiter bring you Trudy? You did tell me I could call you Trudy?"

"Vodka and cranberry with a splash of lime and Deputy works for me."

"So tell me. Have you gotten settled in yet? Are you staying busy enough to prevent boredom from setting in? It is not Columbus, Ohio. I did my homework."

"Cut the crap, Rocker. I'm not here to be wooed and impressed and no chit chat is required. What do you have that might interest me?"

"Now you're talking my language Trudy. You haven't been properly welcomed to the beach yet have you? I have just the thing to interest you and rock that little world of yours. Possibly once you get to know me, we can take our relationship to the next level."

Her drink arrived and she killed half of it with the first swallow. "Time has almost expired on your meter. If you wish to waste your time like this then it's your quarter. When I finish this drink I'm out of here."

"Let's discuss how you're going to capture your serial killer," Rocker answered watching for her reaction.

"Serial killer, I have no clue what you're babbling about. How many drinks did you have before arriving here?"

"But you must be mistaken my little deputy delight," he said and he never broke eye contact with her. "I heard you reveal your theory to short stuff."

"I don't know what you thought you heard but..."

"But nothing," he cut her off. "We can work as a team on this or I can break it on the 11 PM news. It really doesn't matter to me. It's your call."

"I'll have your ass if you start these foolish rumors," she said as she pushed her finger against his chest.

"There you go with that sexy talk of yours again. You and I should spend a little time back in Rocker-World and compare notes." He licked his finger tips then caressed her finger stroking it affectionately.

She jerked her hand away and wiped it on her jeans. "One last warning, don't even think of starting this nonsense."

"Bring me in on this and promise me an exclusive and I'll hold back but only for awhile."

"There's nothing to bring you in on. If you think there's a serial killer out there, convince me with some evidence to support it and we'll talk."

"Should I recap for you?" asked Rocker as he removed a note pad from his pocket. "Let's see, you said to short stuff, *'I believe we may have ourselves a serial killer here on the Grand Strand'*. Short stuff replied, *'No crap, a serial killer.'* Did I leave out anything? What makes you think we have a serial killer, deputy?"

Furious she replied, "It's your word against mine. Don't push it or I'll..."

"What do we have here?" asked Brady as he walked in on the obvious heated discussion.

"We're finished," replied Trudy "Let's go."

"Sir Lancelot, Channel 12...what an honor it is to meet you."

"I know you. You're that Mister Knickers aren't you?"

"Very good, see I told you my marketing strategy works every time dear," smirked Brady as he winked at Trudy. "I've been running those spots on Channel 12 for the past two months."

"Excuse us Mister Lancelot, we have dinner plans," interrupted Trudy.

"And I, too, have plans Deputy. Sorry we couldn't *come* to an understanding," Rocker replied as he caressed her forearm.

"And you remember what I told you," she warned him one last time.

"And you do the same."

"What was that all about?"

"He overheard me telling Woody I had a hunch about a serial killer and now he wants me to bring him in on it or he's going to run it on the news tonight. That's not going to happen."

"So what do you think he'll do next?"

"He's a sleaze but I hope he's not stupid. He's got no more evidence of a serial killer than I have right now."

"Not going so well, huh," he said as he sympathized with her dilemma. "You apparently haven't been able to connect the dots yet."

"It's there. I know it is," she said as she rubbed her eyes. "Let's forget it for now. Time is running out. Mom will be back Friday. Let's not waste valuable time."

"Are you sure you can?"

"I can do anything as long as you're part of it."

"Then let's get out of here and head to my place. I'll cook you an omelet after we have had dessert of course."

"Sounds like a plan to me," she said as she kissed him.

Horry County Police Station
7:30 AM

"Good morning crime investigators," greeted Hank, jiggling the ice in his glass of sweet tea.

"Back at you sheriff," responded Woody.

"Good morning, sir," added Trudy.

"Any progress on the golfer case..."

"Unfortunately we have uncovered no new evidence, no witnesses and have no suspects," Trudy responded as she tried not to make eye contact with her superior.

"Not so, we did visit our friend, Tim Ford and asked him a few questions," blurted out Woody.

Trudy shot Woody a one of those *what the hell are you doing* looks then glanced at the sheriff for his reaction. She didn't need this right now.

"Ford...care to explain where you are going with this," asked Hank as he frowned then sipped his tea.

Trudy, now scrambling, said, "Well sir, we just followed up on one similarity to the Bradshaw case from those at the beach resort."

"And what would that similarity be?" asked Hank, as he slipped his glasses down on the end of his nose.

"Uh, in both incidences, the license plate had been removed from the victim's vehicle and all the victims were beaten to death with sports equipment."

"Interesting angle but why would Ford commit the murders of the three young men from Greensboro? What's his motive?"

"Well, we haven't made that link yet, sir. Possibly he could have been trying to throw us off the Bradshaw murder and convince us there was another murderer out there."

"Not very sound if you ask me, him killing three more to cover up one. Does Ford know he's being investigated for these other murders?"

"Not exactly...,"

"What does not exactly mean, Woodrow?"

"We asked if he had an alibi for the hours between midnight and eight but we didn't tell him why," Trudy jumped back in to clarify.

"So do you not think he may eventually put two and two together and, if he does, don't you think this could be bad news for the department? What the hell were you two thinking?"

"I take full responsibility for our actions," replied Trudy.

"Indeed you will if this turns ugly," Hank said, now looking larger than ever standing behind his desk. "Don't go down this road unless you have concrete evidence."

"Yes sir. We will not question Ford again without just cause," she assured the mountain of a man standing before her.

"One more thing... your car is ready in the lot. You're on your own now. Thank you Woody for assisting Deputy Wagner and showing her around our wonderful beach community,"

Woody nodded, wishing he could launch an escape pod and get the hell out of Hank's office. He didn't like seeing the big man pissed.

"How about you two doing some constructive detective work and at least solve one of these open homicide cases. Take your pick. We have plenty to choose from right now. The local media is ripping us a new butt hole for not doing our job to protect the community. I've got dead people falling out of the sky and we can't seem to arrest anybody for their murders. What's wrong with this picture, deputies?"

"We're doing our best, sir," answered Trudy.

"Best is not good enough. I expect results, so arrest someone please and today wouldn't be too early. But let's make sure we have probable cause first and aren't going off on another silly witch hunt, do you read me?"

"Yes sir," both deputies chimed in.

Exiting Hank's office, Trudy pulled Woody aside. "Where did that come from, telling him that we rousted Ford? I'm the lead here. What were you thinking?"

"You're the lead? Where the hell did that come from?"

Trudy had screwed up with that comment and she knew it. "What I meant to say was that the chief expects me to utilize my investigative experience. That's why he hired me."

Woody wasn't buying it. She could read it in his eyes. "You just pissed me off in there and I tried to get even, that's all."

He changed the subject when he heard radio chatter at the dispatcher's desk. "You hear that?" It seems that we have another homicide in our wonderful retirement community."

The body of Sonny Boggs had been found by his wife in his shop this morning over in Aynor. "You take it Super Sleuth. You have your own car now and a ride out in the countryside might just clear that big ego of yours."

Lance Rocker had heard the call too, monitoring the police radio frequency as always. He was already heading toward Aynor on westward 501. Traffic on 501 this time of morning had him traveling at a snail's pace but still well ahead of Deputy Trudy Wager.

The Anderson Residence
Thursday, 8:25 AM

Janice Anderson, now counting down the days, couldn't wait until Woody returned to his night shift in just over a week. She had already arranged a sitter for the munchkins. Anticipating the potential of a coupling with a stranger had almost gotten her off through sheer thought. She finished the job with a battery operated friend and was now primed and ready for the hunt.

Growing so tired and bored by this marriage of convenience, she always fantasized of a way out. The only fantasies falling in place so far had been those shared with her chosen partners. These never included an escape route from her existing world. They only provided a temporary distraction.

She would be traveling across the border to Shallotte, North Carolina, this time to a little bar she frequented a couple of times a year. She would leave shortly after Woody, forwarding the house phone to her cell just in case Woody tried to reach her which he never did. She believed in covering her bases.

She had enough cash for a room and adult beverages but seldom ever had to pay for either. Her companions took care of this. She would only be about an hour from home and an easy return trip if push came to shove. She always picked the kids up on the way back and easily arrived before Woody finished his shift. She had never come close to being caught. She could con her way out of anything so the prospect never worried her.

Standing naked in front of the full length mirror she

admired her body. Flat footed, Janice stood a good three inches taller than Woody and towered even more over him when in high heels.

Proud of her figure, she liked to flaunt her assets, two very large and naturally firm breasts, nipples still pointing skyward even after five kids. She still had a fine booty, no lard ass like many of her friends. Her belly was flat and firm. She had the full package.

"Now that's one damn fine looking piece of prime merchandise old girl if I do say so myself. Who'd ever imagine five chaps have passed through man's play ground?" She snickered as she turned slightly and slapped her ass with thundering authority. "I am the perfect predator, queen of the ocean sands! Hang in there gentlemen just a little longer!"

Sonny Boggs Farm
Aynor, SC (Rural Horry County)
8:57 AM

Trudy spotted the John Deere shaped mailbox and pulled into the driveway. The first thing that caught her eye was the Channel 12 News van and Rocker holding a microphone, already conducting an interview. "I can't believe this," she spouted as she slammed her fist on the steering wheel.

Wheeling in, she leaped from the cruiser almost before it came to a complete stop and approached Rocker. She stepped directly in front of him, her back to the camera, before she thought clearly about the repercussions of her actions. "What in the hell do you think you're doing," she snapped as she stared him down.

"Deputy Wagner, could you please face our cameras and share with us what you can about this alleged homicide? I'm sure our live audience is very interested in what you may have to say. We seem to have quite a bloody crime spree on our hands don't we?"

Rolling her eyes she couldn't muster up a response, too infuriated. She momentarily considered pulling her revolver and dropping him where he stood.

"I must apologize for our good deputy. She must be under considerable stress as is Horry County's Sheriff, Hank Singleton, trying to capture the serial killer responsible for the ever increasing body count in our small God fearing resort community. He now felt slightly vindicated for the earlier interview where she totally stepped on his profession and reputation, the interview that he had been unable to use until now.

"Let's cut to an earlier clip when Deputy Wagner expressed similar contempt for local media coverage, accusing yours truly of being at the scene of one of the killer's first victims. She accused me of being a suspect. I suppose our local law enforcement agency doesn't appreciate fine citizens of Horry County trying to help them apprehend a ruthless killer among us."

The clip from the court house had been conveniently edited to now portray Trudy as one trying to accuse anyone of the Bradshaw murder and it appeared as if she was badgering and accusing Rocker of the crime. "Perfect," commented Lance.

Once she was sure they were off the air she spoke candidly to the *fine upstanding citizen.* "You despicable low life. You have crossed the line and have opened Pandora's Box. You'll turn this into a media circus and compromise our investigation. What makes you think this homicide had anything to do with the others?"

"I didn't know for sure there were others until you just admitted it. Thank you. I assume Bradshaw and that Missouri lady are on your list. Who else has fallen victim in our little crime spree?"

The Sheriff now exploded over her radio. She tried to compose herself before responding but had obviously lost control of the situation. This was unfamiliar ground because she had always been in control of every situation. She needed a drink. She needed Brady. She needed to be anywhere but here right now.

Also watching the telecast..."Serial Killer, I'm no damn serial killer! What have you done Mister TV Reporter?"

A serial killer chooses his victims and has a twisted, perverted reason for killing his prey! These people have chosen themselves! They came to me! I didn't seek them out, crave to kill somebody! I am a mere extension of the judicial system! I just eliminate the due process of the system and save the tax payers money. I prevent these maniacs from killing innocent people!

"Serial Killer indeed, that's downright insulting even for you Sir Lancelot!"

You want a serial killer? I suppose it is my responsibility to provide you with one. After all, your audience will now demand it. Confession cleanses the mortal soul they say. Game on, let's play who really done it!

133

South Ocean Boulevard
10 AM

Woody had been summoned to a suspicious death on the 14th floor of a well-to-do resort. The body of Rachel Winslow, realtor for Sun, Sea and Sand Reality, had been found dead on the balcony of a unit she had been scheduled to show the previous day.

A competing realtor had discovered her body when he met a client at the same location. Unmarried and living alone, no one had reported her missing. Her employer suspected nothing because Rachel maintained and coordinated her own schedule.

"Officer, you found no driver's license on her person or in her purse," Woody questioned one of the Myrtle Beach policemen on the scene.

"No sir," replied the officer. "Her BMW is parked near the lobby. Desk manager recognized it. Weird, somebody had lifted the plate."

"Bingo, Wagner was right. We have a serious problem here."

"Sir," asked the officer confused by Woody's comment.

"Did you find a murder weapon?"

"Why, do you think someone killed her?" asked the officer. "There are no obvious marks on her body. She just seems to be resting peacefully on that chase lounge. I just assumed natural causes."

"We'll see what the coroner says."

"Sir, do we really have a serial killer on the Grand Strand?"

"Where'd you hear something like that?"

"Channel 12 reported it about an hour ago."

Rocker, what have you done now, boy?

Woody combed the condo. He found water puddled up in front of the john in the master bedroom and a partial foot print smudged on the tile, too large to be the woman's shoe. The killer had gotten sloppy.

The clothing around the victim's neck felt damp as did her hair. Like the officer had reported, he could find no marks on the body but he suspected she had been drowned in that toilet.

One thing for sure, this murder was linked to Bradshaw's, the Costello woman and the old guy and those three young men. The missing driver's license and tag could no longer be considered mere coincidence.

It hit him like a bolt of lightening. The Walter Ozolins attack, his tag had been stolen. *Oh crap...the murderer paid him a visit at the hospital and finished what he had started. That's why he was so nervous about police involvement. His attacker had told him to keep his mouth shut.*

"Damn it, there was no autopsy," Woody now babbled out loud. *But, we have the missing plate to link his attack to these murders and we still have no motive unless Ford has really flipped out. I've got to radio Wagner. She'll want to hear this.*

"Officer," he motioned for the young man, "Tell the coroner to contact me once he has determined a time and the cause of her death. I'm betting she drowned."

"How could she have drowned on a balcony fourteen stories up?" asked the officer. "And you think she's linked to others and that Ford guy is the serial killer?"

Woody didn't respond, too deep in thought to even hear the officer's questions. He had to call Wagner.

Sonny Boggs Farm
12:13 PM

The body had been removed and the crime scene secured. Rocker had been escorted from the premises. Trudy now interviewed Sonny's widow, Catherine. She looked like everyone's grandmother, blue-gray hair in a bun and face as sweet as an angel, wearing an apron over a denim skirt with a plaid blouse.

"Mrs. Boggs, I really appreciate you doing this and especially here in your husband's shop," consoled Trudy.

"I just want his killer caught. Sonny would have never harmed a fly. He was a good man. He loved this farm and that tractor." She pointed to the John Deere.

"You say you didn't find him in the shop until this morning? Strange, don't you think? The coroner suspects he died at least ten or more hours before you discovered his body? Why did you not miss him before now?"

"Not so strange, he often stays out here to the wee hours piddling with something or another. I usually retire about 9:30. I need my beauty sleep."

"But wouldn't you have become suspicious when he didn't come to bed?"

"Heavens no, You see he snores like a wild bear."

"But wouldn't you have noticed him not snoring along side you?"

"I think not, dear. You see we haven't shared a bed in over fifteen years." She blushed as she realized what she had admitted. "I couldn't sleep with that thunderous snoring of his and he couldn't sleep with those sore ribs."

"Sore ribs, you lost me again."

"I elbowed him until he was black and blue but couldn't stop those gosh awful sounds. We decided on separate bedrooms so we both could sleep peacefully and live longer."

Trudy smiled. "And you say you didn't notice anything out of place or missing when you discovered your husband's body."

"Just his drill next to him, everything else looks as neat as a pin like he always kept it," she said as she sobbed openly.

"I know this is difficult but we must cover the bases. Did you notice anything about your husband when you found him?"

"So much blood, there was just so much blood. I didn't know a person could bleed that much." She cried louder.

"Did your husband have any enemies?"

"Certainly not. Everyone liked Sonny. He was the best neighbor and husband anyone could ever wish for and I sure wish I had him back right now," she said with a slight smile, tears still rolling down her cheeks.

"Thank you. That will be all for now. I may have additional questions later if you don't mind."

"I just want to help. Sonny would have expected it out of me."

"We'll find who did it, I assure you." She wasn't at all sure of that. Her track record sucked of late.

"His hat," commented Catherine, wrinkles appearing on her forehead.

"Hat?"

"Yes, his hat, his John Deere hat. He wasn't wearing it when I found him. He always wears that dingy old John Deere ball cap. Only time I can pry it off his head is at meals and bed time. He wasn't wearing it and I don't see it anywhere. Who would want that nasty old hat?"

"Do you remember anything else?"

"No, I'm afraid not, dear. I don't know what I will end up doing with that tractor of his. I certainly can't drive it. He would expect me to keep it though. He kept it polished and shiny like a new penny. He would rather drive that tractor down to the store instead of his old truck, and did most of the time. I told him that tractors are not meant for the highway but he did what he wanted. I always knew when he was almost home."

"How so?"

"I would hear all those horns honking. People didn't appreciate him driving on their road. I told him he was the root of road rage in Aynor. He paid me no mind and just let them honk at him. Personally, I think my Sonny enjoyed all the attention. I suspect the traffic will improve without him clogging up the road. We were supposed to grow old together. I know we're already old but we had a few good years left."

Trudy's imagination was swirling with Catherine's last comments. She may just have provided a motive. She remembered the report for the Costello homicide. The witness mentioned how her driving may have instigated the attack. What about the others?

She still had no positive link with Sonny and the others. No missing tag but of course, the tractor had no tag. No missing driver's license but then again, it did not require one to operate a tractor. What then?

"My heavens, why lookey yonder," she pointed. "The John Deere emblem has broken off Sonny's tractor. After forty three years of marriage to that man, I know him better than anybody. It would have troubled him to no end until he fixed it. He would have never left it like that. He was, now what do they call people like him that have to have everything in its proper place?

"Obsessive Compulsive..."

"Yes that sounds right, dear. Thank you. He was so fanatical about his equipment. He would have told me about it I'm sure."

"Do you have some friends or family you can stay with tonight?"

"My sister is coming over from Florence. I'll have to work myself to death to see after her. She's so needy and has that oxygen tank she drags around with her. I keep telling her she needs to lose some weight but look at me, I'm one to talk."

"You look just great, not one pound too many. Take care and here's my card if you think of anything else."

"Honey, what sort of person would do this to a harmless old man?"

"Pure evil and someone with uncontrollable rage I'm afraid."

"I'll pray for that person's soul. Sonny would have wanted me to forgive."

Trudy returned to her car and radioed Woody. "I think I have something."

"I was just about to call you because I think I have something too."

Hesitating to mention serial killer over the radio she said one word, "motive." Woody repeated it.

Woody now speaking in code and loving it said, "What say I meet you at that open front door?"

"Open front door it is in about twenty."

Channel 12 News Station
1:00 PM

"You really did it for us this time, Lance," screamed the producer. "I have no idea how I allowed you to talk me into letting you play up that serial killer angle and then run that chopped footage!"

"Honey, you're not stupid. You know good stuff when you see it. Hell, you banged me didn't you?"

And I'll regret that for the rest of my life. "Cut the crap, Lance. We have the station execs all over us. They've been blasted by the sheriff, the mayor, sponsors and have been flooded with calls from irate viewers on the verge of going vigilante," she screamed in Lance's face.

"See, I told you this would boost our ratings," he replied as cocky as ever. "I have a nose for it."

"Yeah, I know where that nose of yours is capable of going. Ratings are spiraling in the wrong direction, you stupid prick. They've pulled the plug on us. No more live broadcasts from crime scenes for you or me. We've been reassigned to special interest coverage, puppy dogs and touchy-feely segments with old people and kids, nothing live or remote. The network will view and edit everything we film before it airs. We're damn lucky to still have our jobs," she explained then slapped him hard across his face.

"That wasn't very professional," he shouted as he felt his stinging cheek.

"It wasn't intended to be. That was for that night! It had nothing to do with what happened today. You can return my panties and that photo or I'll share you dirty little secrets with our viewing audience." She stormed from the room giving him the finger.

Still rubbing his face but not really impacted by her comments he said, "They can't do this to Lance Rocker. This story hasn't even started to sizzle yet. It might be time for me to do a little freelancing."

The producer came back into the room and handed Lance a piece of paper. "Drive up to Shallotte Saturday. I'll have your new cameraman meet you at that address at the scheduled time. Mike Stewart will be your traveling buddy. Have fun with that sea turtle story and I'm sure Sir Lancelot will put his own special spin on it," she laughed as she exited a second time. "And remember what I said about returning my belongings."

"Screw all of you," he shouted to an empty studio. "You haven't heard the last of Lance Rocker!"

Edward Bradshaw Residence
1:39 PM

"Here, I picked you up a coffee, loads of sugar and cream just like you like it," Trudy told Woody handing him the cup.

Woody laughed, "And I grabbed you one of those funky lattes you drink."

"Okay, Woody, what you got?"

"You go first. After all, you do have the lead on this investigation," he quipped with a half smile.

"Ouch, and I am truly sorry about that. I just left the scene of that murdered farmer. I'm not sure if his death is related to the others yet but his wife got me to thinking so hear me out."

"You still have the floor."

"I've been focusing on the people and have gotten absolutely nowhere. They're such a sorted group at best, males, females, old, young, tourists, locals, blah, blah, blah, so I couldn't make a serious connection there. What do they have in common though? The cause of death tends to vary, brutal beatings with a bat, a hammer, golf club, strangulation, head trauma and drowning. Again, it's not the MO for the typical serial killer. We can't hang a time sequence on the homicides. They tend to happen with no rhyme or reason. Serial killers often, but not always, go by the clock or lunar events or something. These have been more random don't you think?"

"Yeah I agree. I've been reading up on them ever since you first threw it out. The typical serial killer usually feels a need to kill every so often or coincide with some special alignment of the stars or something like that."

"Catherine Boggs, that's the farmer's wife, got me to thinking. What if all the homicides were a result of something like road rage? What if our Perp is reacting to road rage incidences? Catherine mentioned how her Sonny enjoyed driving his tractor down the road and how it enraged the drivers, backing up traffic. Now he's dead."

Woody nodded to confirm he was following what she said. Not a bad assumption he thought.

"The Costello homicide, she had been seen driving erratically while talking on her cell and eventually a motorist forced her off the road. Look where that cell phone ended up! The child was not harmed. The child was not driving and deemed innocent of any wrong doing."

"Plus, the kid was too young to be a witness. Go on. I'm right there with you so far."

"Raymond Cochran, the elderly gentleman driving the golf cart, now how many times have you cursed one of those carts backing up traffic on the Grand Strand streets?"

Woody smiled. "They do piss me off. Please continue partner."

"The three young men murdered with the golf club, only one driver's license was taken along with the tag from the car owned by that very same driver. The severed birdie fingers planted in their rear ends, I'm betting signified these boys had given our Perp the finger."

"It makes sense. You have been doing your homework."

"The Hispanic death over in Georgetown County probably pissed Mister Road Rage off somehow too. His license and plate were lifted. We still have no ID for him and probably never will but doesn't that sort of fall into place too?"

"That's at least seven victims you've mentioned so far including Bradshaw."

"Yeah, Bradshaw was the first and Sonny Boggs the most recent."

"Not necessarily..."

"I don't follow," she said with a most puzzled look on her face.

"Well...I'm not so sure that Ed Bradshaw was the first. Walter Ozolins, a tourist from Ohio may have been the first victim."

"I seem to remember seeing his name on a record query I ran."

"Ozolins was attacked but not killed, at least not the first time. Severely beaten in a hotel parking lot, he survived but his car was demolished, beaten even worse than him. And guess what?"

"Plates and driver's license were stolen."

"His tag was indeed missing, as was his license. Later he was found dead in his hospital room supposedly of natural causes. His widow would not authorize an autopsy and his body has since been cremated."

"You don't think his death was natural do you?"

"Not any more. He was extremely nervous when I paid him a second visit like he didn't want to be seen with a cop. Then he died."

"I'm with you. The attacker probably contacted him and warned him not to talk to the police."

"Exactly...I showed up and that Mister Road Rage of yours decided to tidy up loose ends. I suspect he also threatened the widow. That's why she had him cremated and no autopsy. After what happened to her hubby she would never admit it I suspect."

"Damn, that's eight!"

"Hold your horses, there's more," he said pulling his notebook from his shirt pocket. "Rachel Winslow, Realtor for Sun, Sand and Sea Realty was discovered dead this morning in a unit she had been showing to a client yesterday."

"And..."

"We're not sure of the official cause of death yet but..."

"Her license and plate were missing."

"Bingo! We have a winner and that makes nine if your farmer turns up being number eight."

"I'm afraid we need more evidence to link Sonny Boggs so we won't count him in just yet, but my gut says he's a victim."

"What are your thoughts on Tim Ford? Do you think he should remain on the top of our list?" asked Woody, staring at Tim's house less than a block away.

"I'm not sure about the top but let's keep him on the short list."

He laughed, "Some list, he's the only name we have. Maybe Ford snapped after his wife and kid was killed and he started taking it out on erratic drivers."

"Good theory if we can prove it. The homicides did start after he finished his rehab. Either way, I don't think these killings are going to stop anytime soon. Look around you. The drivers here drive like maniacs. Mister Road Rage has his pick any given time, any given day."

"He just drives until one crosses his path and pisses him off, and then he delivers their punishment."

"You know what I hate about this...playing into Rocker's hands because he's a real A-1 jerk."

"I can't argue with that. I guess we need to bring Hank in on this ASAP."

"You've got that right. He's one angry sheriff right now. I'm not his favorite deputy. He may allow me to stay in Horry County if we can make this stick."

"One big and pissed off puppy and I've been on the wrong end of that stick before and it's no fun I assure you. To make our case we need a suspect. Doesn't your mama come home tomorrow?"

She nodded. *One more night of freedom and I better make the most of it with Brady.*

Tim Ford Residence
4:30 PM Thursday

Even though his Z28 had no Channel 12 markings, Lance decided to park on an adjacent street and walk over to Ford's house. He watched from the corner until he spotted Tim Ford hoping in his car and leaving. An anonymous tipster had assured him he could find something of interest here if he was willing to toss the dice.

Nonchalantly he strolled down the sidewalk in front of Ford's house until he reached the drive then he quickened his pace, veered down the drive and disappeared in the hedged back yard.

The double garage in back had a side entrance but it was locked. The garage had one window on the opposite side from the door. "Eureka, exclaimed Lance. "It's unlocked and has no screen."

He raised it and scampered inside. Tim had driven off in the only car. Ford's other vehicle had been totaled in the accident and with him as the only surviving driver he had apparently decided he didn't need the second one.

Lance jiggled the entrance door from the garage but found it locked. Just as well, the house probably was equipped with a security system.

He rummaged through a couple of drawers in a work bench but located nothing of interest but he wasn't really sure what he was looking for just yet. An unlocked cabinet offered nothing but paint buckets and various other items you'd find in almost anyone's storage. Had the tipster been wrong?

He checked the door to a closet and found it securely locked. This raised his curiosity. He had learned a little trick or two from interviewing felons, like how to pick a lock so he gave it a shot. After several attempts, the door opened.

He clicked on the light switch and discovered several plastic containers marked Christmas decorations. He opened the first to verify the contents and sure enough, it contained lights and ornaments. He set the first on the floor and checked the next, more of the same. This seemed like too much of a wild goose chase and he hated chasing geese.

Pushed back in a little nook he noticed an old computer cardboard box sealed with duct tape, no outside markings to specify its contents. He dragged it toward him to get a better look and carefully peeled free the silver tape.

Inside he found a collection of old books, Dean Koontz, Ann Rice, and Stephen King. Either Tim or his deceased wife apparently loved reading horror and suspense novels. Something caught his eye tucked behind Ann Rice's *Interview with a Vampire*.

He reached for the cloth and carefully unwrapped the contents and found a tattered John Deere ball cap. Inside the cap he found additional contents wrapped in a section of newspaper. His eyes bulged from his head when he realized what he now held in his hands.

"Shit," he almost shouted out too loudly then he began to shuffle through the cards realizing they were drivers' license. He began reading the owners' names out loud. "Edward Leonard Bradshaw, Walter Allen Ozolins, Anna Marie Costello, Hector Jorge Gonzales, Andrew Davis Thompson, and Rachel Ann Winslow." He recognized some of the names as being murder victims and suspected the others were too.

"I have found the bloody Holy Grail."

Shock number two came when he noticed that the newspaper was a clipping from the Sun News describing the accident that took the lives of those unfortunate people, including Tim Ford's family.

"I've got what I need to blow this thing wide open. Hold onto your asses, Sir Lancelot is going live."

Reality kicked him square in the nuts. He couldn't remove this evidence because then it would be inadmissible in court. Tim Ford would walk. Breaking and entering...the law would just love to have a reason to put him away and toss the key.

Even a bigger mystery remained. Who had tipped him off in the first place? He smelled a rat. *Maybe Ford planted this figuring I would take it and screw up the investigation. Sorry, you can't outwit Lance Rocker.*

First things first...he had to put it back like he had found it. Next he'd make nice with that hot ass deputy and tell her that his reliable sources had tipped him off about incriminating evidence that could be found in Tim Ford's garage. She would agree to allow him to accompany her here of course and he would be guaranteed the exclusive coverage and credit.

He'd break the case. The station would be happy. Conway's finest would be off his back. Tim Ford would be in jail and Sir Lancelot could name his own price with any major network. "Damn, I'm good," he whispered as he closed the closet door just as the first bay garage door began opening. Ford had returned. *Maybe he's been watching and waiting.*

Horry County Police Department
6 PM

Hank Singleton was fit to be tied. "So now you're telling me that Rocker knew what he was talking about with this serial killer business."

"Not exactly, sir...he overheard Woody and me discussing it and he played the hunch. He did approach me before but I refused to deal on his terms and denied the theory. While the murders do have the earmarks of a potential repeat killer, it still doesn't exactly fit the text book description for a serial killer.

"I must say it is an interesting theory Deputy Wagner and could be some mighty fine detective work if, and only if, you can scare up a suspect from the brush pile."

"What about Ford?" Woody reminded Hank.

"What about Ford? You have nothing to tie him to any of these homicides, including Bradshaw's. Stay away from him unless you have something concrete and you two best not do didley squat without my permission."

The dispatcher knocked on the sheriff's door. "Sorry to interrupt but Deputy Wagner you have a call on line three."

"Please take a message and I'll return the call later."

"It sounded mighty urgent!"

"Did the caller leave a name?"

"Sure did, it's that newsman, Lance Rocker." "That's all we need," exclaimed Hank. "He's crapped in my mess kit just one time too many already."

"Excuse me sir, I've been just itching to talk to that ...how can I best describe him?"

"Asshole," said Woody. "Excuse my French but he is the spitting image."

"Stand in line," barked Hank. "I'd like to lock him up and throw away the key but I don't have any charges to hang on him. Take the call here Deputy Wagner. Use my phone," he pushed it across his desk toward her.

She picked up the handset, "Rocker, what lies are you spreading this time?"

"Officer Wagner, I was wrong. I overstepped my boundaries and I apologize." He poured on the charm to hopefully hook and reel her in.

"Sorry, I thought the dispatcher said you were Lance Rocker."

"I can't say I blame you for feeling this way. Again I'm sorry but I have a lead for you. This is the real deal."

"I told you I'm done dealing with you, Rocker. Peddle your threats and lies elsewhere," she raised her voice staring across the desk at Sheriff Singleton.

"And I certainly don't blame you for feeling like this but I do have information from an extremely reliable source. It has to do with your alleged serial killer. Please stifle the laughter deputy. I mean this."

"So now it's alleged since your little stunt on the news backfired. Humor me, Rocker, just what do you have that I'd be so interested in hearing?"

I've got something for you alright and in due time you'll get the experience of your lifetime he thought then responded, "My source says that if you obtain a search warrant for Tim Ford's premises and specifically search a closet inside his garage, you will find all the evidence you'll need to make this an open and shut case."

"Your source certainly has the facts all the way down to the specific closet to search. And just how reliable is this source of yours?"

"I'd trust him like I'd trust my own mother. This is the real thing I assure you."

"Bringing in your family tree doesn't exactly reassure me of anything."

"I've talked to the station and they have granted me live coverage of your search if you agree of course."

"I should have known. It's all about you and your exposure on the news."

"This is bigger than both of us. I'm sure it will exonerate the police department of all previous wrong doings concerning your case. We'll shoot from the street curbing I promise. No tricks, no unauthorized interviews, you run the show." *Just tell her what she wants to hear. We know who runs the big show and it's not Horry County cops.*

"Where's Rocker? Did he get abducted by aliens and you're the new and improved clone delivered by the mother ship?"

"I'm serious as a heart attack deputy. The evidence is there. I've seen ...I mean, my source says he's seen it."

"Breaking and entering is a serious offence."

"Only if you get caught, deputy," and he almost had. He had hidden in the closet until he had heard Ford close the garage door and enter the house then he slipped back out the side window.

"I'm going to place you on hold. I'm in the sheriff's office as we speak and will run this by him. If he buys your little story then we may request the search warrant. I don't suspect we'll be able to get one until tomorrow."

"Thank you Deputy Wagner." *Bite me.*

She recapped Rocker's side of the conversation for Hank and Woody. She eyed her partner and the sheriff waiting for their reaction.

"I don't trust him as far as I can throw him, Deputy Wagner. Do you really think this is legit?"

"Honestly, with Rocker I'm not sure anything is on the up and up. He sounded different this time but do I trust him? Hell no! He's in it for him. We all know that."

Hank deliberated the request wringing his big old hands and then cracking his knuckles. Burn me once shame on you, twice, shame on me he thought. Reluctantly Hank agreed to the request for the warrant and granted the search but only after warning Wagner her ass was on the line. None of them really trusted Lance Rocker.

"I'll finagle the request and hopefully we'll have your warrant tomorrow morning. I'll warn you one more time, Deputy Wagner, and you can pass this on to Rocker. This department will not be made a fool of again and there will be hell to pay if this thing backfires." Hank stood and pounded his bear paws on the desk to make his point.

Trudy almost blurted out for him to forget it but she had gone this far, she may as well finish it for better or worse. Rocker better be right about this.

Woody whispered, "I sure hope you know what the hell you're doing. This could cost us both dearly if Rocker doesn't deliver."

She swallowed what felt like an egg, mouth parched like a desert, and pressed the phone's button. "Hello, Rocker, are you still there?"

"Still here, so what's the verdict from our Sheriff Singleton?"

"We're in but you better be damn sure this evidence exists! You screw this up and we all go down."

Going down, now you're talking. "Trust me Deputy Wagner, you will not be disappointed. I promise."

"I'll contact you when we have the warrant. It most likely won't happen until Friday morning."

"I look forward to your call," he replied hanging up the phone. *Yes, my man. You still have it! Money in the bank this time!*

"See you back here in the morning, Woody."

"Will do, partner. What time does your sister bring your mama home?"

"Probably midday...Lullabelle is scheduled to meet them." She was reminded this would be her last full night with Brady.

Brady Pierce's Beachfront Home
8:25 PM

Sitting on the oceanfront balcony with Brady by her side, sipping on a glass of vintage Chardonnay, listening to the waves crashing on the shore was exactly what Trudy needed. She sorely needed to block out the distractions of the case and her mom's pending return, at least for one more night. She wasn't sure if she could.

"Okay, I recognize that cop's red hot little body sitting next to me but I fear her brain is still in overdrive. Would you like to talk about it, deputy?"

"Was it that obvious? Do you know me that well after such a short time?"

"You're a quick and easy read, even for someone as shallow as me." He reached over and kissed her deeply.

"Sorry, I'm not accustomed to having to deal with romance. My life has always been occupied by my career and now my mom."

"Well, at least I now know where I stand on the priority list, third," he said with that gorgeous smile of his.

"I didn't mean it that way."

"And I really didn't take it that way," he replied with a squeeze of her hand. "Let's get it all out on the table then we can focus on us the remainder of the night."

"I hate to sound like such a dreadful daughter but I'm not looking forward to mom's return tomorrow. Her sickness is going to impact us dramatically. You do realize that don't you?"

"We'll deal with it. She's your mother and thinking that way doesn't make you a terrible person. This caregiver role is new for you and tough I'm sure."

"If I knew her condition was only temporary or even had at least a slight chance of improving, I think I could deal with it but she won't get better and..."

"And we'll deal with it together," he interrupted.

"Brady Pierce, I do believe I am falling in love with you," she blurted before she thought about what she was saying.

"Works for me, I'm still shooting for that number one spot."

She smiled and kissed him.

"So tell me, how's that mass murderer case of yours coming? I saw the Channel 12 News segment and I'm sure the crap must have been flying afterwards."

"Oh you don't know the half of it! My reputation is on the line big time! I've single handedly allowed this investigation to spiral out of control. And I've always prided myself on being a control freak."

"So tell me what you can, you have my shoulder." He playfully nibbled on her ear lobe.

Unfazed, she continued, "I may have overstated this serial killer scenario of mine."

"So now you don't think there's a serial killer?"

"Yes and no...I do believe there is a connection to possibly as many as eight homicides but it just doesn't fit the routine stereotype for serial killers, or at least not yet."

"So there's a *How to Book* on being a serial killer?"

"Not exactly but enough studies have been conducted to at least lead one to water and right now, I'm not sure my killer is at the watering hole like the other case studies."

"Okay, so what makes you think this?" Brady was becoming more intrigued by her lesson.

"I don't want to get into all the technical garble, not tonight anyway, but in a nutshell the killer profile doesn't conform to the MO of a serial killer. They don't seem to be sexual in nature and have not been singled to just one gender, race or age. The murders just don't fit the mold for a single murderer's behavior."

"Maybe you've stumbled onto some new hybrid killer or a cult."

"Could be...I sincerely believe that road rage is the motive. This could explain the randomness of the victims."

"Do you think that Ford guy is still a suspect?"

"Funny you mention him. We're supposed to do a search of his home tomorrow," she said with a long frown on her face.

"You don't look too sure about this."

"Still reading the pages of my book I see," she smiled as she confessed. "Lance Rocker told me that the evidence is there in Tim Ford's garage and that it will break the case wide open."

"And you believe him? Excuse me for saying so but a zebra doesn't suddenly change his stripes."

"Normally I would blow this off but it seems our scoop reporter somehow broke into Ford's garage and saw the evidence first hand. I'll give the bastard that much credit. He left it there and came to us, a very un-Rocker like thing to do."

"So what's in it for the news hound?"

"He just wants the exclusive, filming there live. His butt is on the line just like mine and the departments, as well as the credibility of Channel 12. He seems so confident this time and I believe he smells fame and fortune."

"It's all about him so you're probably right. Why the long face?"

"I guess this case has bitten my butt so many times that I fear the next bite will be the lethal one. Cases like this just don't suddenly fall in place in such a neat and tidy package," she said as she bottomed out her wine glass.

"Let me pour you another," Brady said as he reached for the bottle.

"The only thing I do know for sure is that the killer will continue killing until either he is caught, he dies by our hands, he kills himself or he just grows tired of killing. I'd rather us catch him."

"Me too, but for now let's move on to number three in your pecking order, me," he said as he began unbuttoning her blouse.

"Nice marketing strategy circus boy. Get me drunk, then have me confess my sins, use the ocean setting then seduce me with reckless abandon on the balcony where anyone can see us. I like it!"

"I'm a professional. Don't try this at home."

There would be no sleeping tonight and tomorrow would test her moral fiber. Not to forget, mom would be back again she would assume her role as the primary caregiver. She sucked terribly at this caregiving role. She sucked at everything right now.

Elsewhere...

Awakening at five in the morning, Road Rage cursed Edward Bradshaw. *You're dead but I'm still bearing the brunt of your stupid moronic driving. You have stripped me of my mortal soul. You've subjected me to being demoralized as a serial killer! You haunt me even from your worm infested grave! See you in hell Edward Bradshaw.*

Standing under the hot pelting spray of the shower he declared, "Please drivers...behave just once...I am not the serial killer they've made me out to be."

Tim Ford's Residence
Friday 9:12 AM

Accompanied by four uniformed police officers, Woody and Trudy reviewed procedure and prepared to serve the warrant to Tim Ford. Lance Rocker and his camera man listened in as the final instructions were repeated.

Trudy pulled Rocker to the side and asked him one last time, "You're sure that what you saw is on the up and up?"

"Now Deputy Wagner, I never said I saw anything," he responded with a wink. "My source guarantees you will have Tim Ford in custody by the time you complete your search. Focus on that garage closet first."

"Alright then, you can film whatever you wish from here at the curbside but I warn you, make no comments on camera about what we find inside. Stick to the script and I will make sure you're privy to any media releases first."

"Hey, that's all I can ask of you."

Exhaling like a deflating balloon she gave the command to close in on the house. Woody knocked on the front door as a pair of officers watched the back yard exit. Tim answered the door on the first knock as if he had expected their arrival.

"Officers what can I do for you this time? Do I need to disclose my whereabouts since your last visit and have all my alibis lined up?"

"Tim Ford, I'm Deputy Anderson and we have a warrant authorizing us to search these premises so please step aside and allow us to do our job."

"Hold on there officer." Tim raised his hand like a stop sign. "On what grounds?"

"Reliable sources have indicated to us that you have concealed information relating to recent homicides in our community," answered Trudy.

"That sounded plural."

"Step aside, Mister Ford," Woody insisted, taking the first step through the entrance doorway.

"Hold on," shouted Tim, grabbing Woody by the shirt sleeve.

Woody slipped free in one quick maneuver and had Tim pressed face first against the wall, cuffed and secured. "Behave yourself until we're finished."

"I have my rights!"

"Presently, because of your resistance you have the right to sit quietly in that squad car until we finish our job," warned Woody, then he read him his actual rights.

Trudy stood speechless wishing Anderson had not gotten so physical with Ford. Pandora's Box now open, she had no choice but to go with the flow. Rocker and his camera man unfortunately had captured Woody's little debacle live on camera. The only thing that could now save face would be locating the sure thing evidence in that closet.

Channel 12 News periodically broke to Rocker for updates in the search but before now all he had to shown them was the replay of Ford being cuffed and shots of the house's exterior. The search took over three hours.

Lance Rocker, as did his viewers, watched as Deputy Wagner extracted Tim Ford from the police patrol car, said something to him and allowed him to return to his house. He and his cameraman approached Anderson and Wagner for a statement as they returned to their vehicles, obviously empty handed.

"Deputy Wagner, may I have a word from you for our viewers? Why is Tim Ford being released?"

"I cannot comment on the case at this time," she responded and he could see the rage in her eyes.

"What," Rocker said rattled by her response. "This is Lance Rocker live from the Tim Ford residence where a search has just been completed. We'll return to local programming. Please stay tuned."

Once the camera light went out, Trudy grabbed Lance by the collar and pushed him up against the television van. "You son of a bitch, you did it again!"

"What do you mean? Didn't you find it?"

"We found absolutely nothing. We'll all be lucky if we're not sued over this little stunt of yours."

"You didn't find that box in the back of the closet?"

"There was no little box of goodies in that closet or anywhere else in the house that contained anything that incriminated Ford, unless it's illegal to store Christmas ornaments and old novels. You screwed up this investigation for the last time," she said, finally releasing his collar.

"I have the names written here on my pad. All of their driver's licenses were in that box."

"You have one vivid imagination, asshole," added Woody.

"I'm telling you, they were there in that box. Everything was inside a raggedy John Deere cap."

Trudy made eye contact with Woody. "Damn, the missing link," she exclaimed. "That ties in Sonny Boggs!"

"Sonny Boggs...I didn't see his license."

"Damn it. Ford is playing a game with us and we're being held scoreless," she said as she kicked the tire on the van. "He's played us and the news media like a fiddle and has guaranteed that we'll have to keep our distance now. We've cried wolf one time too many." She slammed her hand on the hood of the cruiser.

"Just got worse," stated Woody. "Hank is on the radio and said we better get our asses back to his office pronto. He said to bring Rocker with us!"

"Crap, we're cooked," she exclaimed. "This is like being told we just won a multi-million dollar lottery and can't find our ticket. We have nothing..."

"We're screwed, that's for sure, partner."

"But I'm telling you, it was there."

"I'm sure it was yesterday. We've been had and now it's time to go take our medicine and this time it is going to be a damn nasty dose," she said as she rubbed her fingers in her eyes.

"Hey Rocker, save the groveling for that super sized sheriff! You're in up to your neck with the rest of us," snapped Woody, pointing a loaded finger and pulling the trigger.

"I'll show him this list. He'll understand. It was there. Everything was there."

"Show him any damn thing you want but without the supporting evidence you may as well wipe your ass with that piece of paper."

Trudy remained silent. She envisioned her once promising career burning off like the morning fog. Her mom would be home in a few short hours and she didn't know how she would work in time for Brady. Moving back south had certainly taken its toll on her life. Maybe she just wasn't cut out for this southern belle stuff.

Woody noticed his partner's demeanor but said nothing. He could no more help her than he could himself. This had to go on record as the worse day of his life. He really didn't cherish facing big Hank Singleton right now and hated Rocker's guts.

Serial Killer indeed; you can kiss my ass and kiss your investigation and reputations goodbye. I got all of you in one clean sweep. Ruin my life and steal my thunder will you. And isn't that just a fine bit of detective work again by Horry County's elite stooges. That's exactly what you get for letting Bradshaw walk in the first place. I think I'll take a well deserved vacation and do a little fishing. You heroes sort out your next career moves.

Amy Wagner's Home
Friday 8:00 PM

Trudy sat in her cruiser in the driveway, fully awake this time as she prepared to meet and greet her mom. Her ass still stung from Hank's thorough and intense chewing some six hours ago. He had taken no prisoners but for now she, along with Woody, still had a job.

Hank threatened to bring Lance Rocker up on breaking and entering charges but thought better of it. The department didn't need more bad publicity. Letting it go would be the best for all but he did warn Lance that if he ever interfered with his department again he'd show no mercy.

Unbeknown to her, Rocker had received a weekend assignment in Shallotte. His face would be absent from the nightly news. One thing she did know for sure, he had personally been dealt an ugly blow to his own career. She had heard him mumble he wasn't sure if the station would renew his contract set to expire in a couple of months.

She figured that Rocker had been outraged knowing Tim Ford was guilty as hell and had outsmarted them. He had taken them all down in one clean sweep. Rocker had the evidence in his hands and tried to play it by the book and look where it had gotten him. Look where it had gotten all of them.

She and Woody would be starting the night shift a week early, tomorrow night. Both had volunteered after two deputies were summoned to testify for a federal case and after Hank insisted it would be in their best interest. That would minimize their contact with the sheriff for the next couple of the weeks which suited them just fine.

It was time to face the music. Trudy opened her car door and made the first step toward an uncertain future. Her mom's return screwed up everything but she knew deep down that she shouldn't blame her. Trudy was in a dark place. Self pity is not pretty.

She entered through a side door and saw her mom sitting on the sofa, Lulabelle sitting next to her. On the television a repeat episode of an old *I Love Lucy Show* played loudly on the TV Land network.

Lulabelle saw her first. "Look who just walked in the door, Miss Amy."

At first her mom didn't turn then she started looking around frantically. Finally she made eye contact. She squinted; her eyes stared intensely at the woman in the police uniform.

"Mom, it's good to have you home. How are you feeling?"

Stone faced, her mom did not respond.

"Mom, what are you watching on television?"

Amy remained expressionless like a marble statue.

"Is she okay?"

"She's been like this since your sister, Allison, dropped her off. She ain't said a word. That sister of yorn, she didn't say much either before she headed back to Atlanta. She did say she'd call you sometime tomorrow. I tried to get your mama to eat something but she only took a little swallow of Orange Crush and one bite of that moon pie over yonder."

"I tell you what Lulabelle, why don't you go home for the night. I don't have to be back at work until Saturday night. You just plan on coming back around 5:30 tomorrow afternoon."

"Are you sure honey child? I don't mind staying."

"No, it'll be alright. I should spend some time with her before I start my next shift."

"Alright then, I'll call my niece to come pick me up."

After Lullabelle left, Trudy grabbed a bottle of water from the fridge and sat down on the couch with her mom.

She grabbed her by the hand and spoke softly, "Mom is there anything I can get you?"

"You can make sure you don't leave me by myself with that darkie again. You know they can't be trusted. Wait until Daddy Bill gets home and finds out you're letting them come in the house like that. He'll whip you good."

"Mom, that was Lulabelle. You've known her for ages."

"I don't care if you want to call her Tinker Bell. You keep that darkie out of my house except if she's here to do some ironing or cleaning. I damn well won't tolerate it. Shit, they'll steal everything we got if you let them! You have to keep them in their damn place and don't ever let them out of your sight."

Trudy had never heard her mom carry on in this tone and had absolutely never heard a curse word roll off her lips. She was crazy about Lulabelle. If her mom wouldn't allow Lulabelle to stay with her, she was screwed! Who else could she round up on such short notice?

Her cell phone rang and she checked seeing the incoming call was from Brady. She decided to let it go to voice mail. She couldn't talk to him right now. She noticed her mom became disturbed by the catchy song now bellowing from her cell so she flipped it to vibrate mode.

Over the next few hours, she played along with her mom and her rants and raves, and dialogue from her past life. Eventually she persuaded her to go to bed about 1 AM. Trudy collapsed on the couch shortly thereafter. It would be a very short night. She just didn't know it yet.

She woke to the smell of something burning. Glancing at her watch, the time was 4:40 AM. Her eyes burned and she smelled an odd scorched odor. She jumped from the sofa seeing black smoke drifting from the kitchen door.

Rushing into the kitchen she found her mom holding a smoking and sizzling frying pan under the kitchen water faucet, a dish towel smoldering on the stove and a Tupperware bowl melted to the large stove eye.

She screamed, "Mom, what are you doing?"

Amy answered in a calm and matter of a fact tone, "Why I'm cooking your father's breakfast before he goes to work, dear. What does it look like I'm doing? That's no tone to use toward me young lady. Best you brush up on your manners."

She grabbed the skillet from her hand noting the slab of bacon, melted in its plastic package, and placed it in the sink. She smothered the smoldering dish cloth and switched off the stove eye registering *high* on the setting. She could do nothing for the melted Tupperware bowl right now.

She thanked the good Lord above that her mom hadn't been burned. Lucky too, the house had not caught fire. She escorted her from the kitchen only after promising her she'd finish cooking her father's breakfast. How much more of this could she endure she thought before she too would be in Looney Tune land.

Once she got her mom away from the swirling smells of the kitchen, she zoomed in on another foul odor. Amy had soiled herself again. She now saw it caked to her inner thighs, smeared down to her ankles.

Tears rolled down Trudy's cheeks as she bathed her mom in the tub. Amy just looked off in the distance and occasionally back at her and smiled but uttered not another word. She got her a fresh change of clothes and called her doctor. She needed medical advice for her mom's condition and for hers.

Woodrow Anderson Residence
Saturday 6:00 AM

Woody's biological clock sounded a wakeup call even though he wasn't due at work for another twelve hours. He snuggled up behind Janice, sleeping with her back to him. Woody reached over and fondled her right breast. The kids were still sound asleep so maybe they could slip in a little morning session. He had a piss hard-on and hated to waste it.

She felt his erection against her buttocks as she lay there with her eyes wide open. She let out a series of snores then squirmed away from him giving the illusion she still slept soundly. She could just have easily given in to his needs but it would have been over in two minutes so why bother.

Woody sighed and turned over on his back, rolling his eyes toward the ceiling. A minute later he sprung to his feet and headed to the bathroom. She heard him take a long piss, the toilet flush and the shower start. Woody was so predictable. She would pleasure herself tonight but not with Woodrow. She needed a real man, someone to take their time with her, not mister slam bam, thank you ma'am.

Still tickled with Woody's news of starting the night shift tonight, she had altered her plans. She would be on the prowl earlier that originally anticipated. Today she'd send him off to the park or movies with the kids while she pampered herself for tonight's potential activities.

When Woody stepped back into the bedroom to check if she had awoken, she snored loudly to dismiss any thoughts he might have. He stood there a second just to make sure then gave up, got dressed and headed to the kitchen. She lay there until she heard him flip on the television in the den to Fox News then returned her thoughts to her next greatest adventure.

After hearing a rattling of dishes, she arose and slipped on a dingy old house robe to discourage any further advances. To ensure her success, she discreetly woke the youngest two children. There would be no hanky-panky in this house this morning but Shallotte was another matter.

Saturday Night
9:00 PM

Miraculously, Amy had greeted Lulabelle with open arms when she arrived this afternoon. She had acted like her old self. Trudy had managed to get the kitchen back in order, all except for the melted Tupperware bowl. That would still take more work. For now it would remain a conversation piece.

Trudy prayed for an uneventful night. She had called and left Brady a brief message but had not actually spoken to him directly. She thankfully had no contact or messages from the sheriff nor had she talked to Woody.

Woody felt just the opposite. He craved for something to happen. He couldn't deal with the boredom. He had bonded with the kids earlier but had seen very little of Janice and he did mean *very* little. She had seemed colder than usual. She could be so bitchy lately.

He hoped tomorrow would be a better day on the home front. He ached with sexual tension. Teenagers called it blue balls. He was married and no teenager. It wasn't supposed to be this way for him. Maybe she would be in a better mood next try. Unfortunately matters didn't improve. The hours flew by and soon Woody had left for duty.

Without a minute to spare, Janice had dropped off the kids and put her plan in action. Taking highway 17, she headed north up the Grand Strand. She could hardly contain herself just thinking about what might happen. Her panties felt moist from anticipating an encounter. She passed through North Myrtle Beach toward Little River. The North Carolina border seemed but a stones away.

Time had passed quickly. Janice now sat in the secluded Shallotte bar and had been there for about forty minutes. So far, she had seen no prospects but the night was young. She nursed a Gin and tonic. Janice would not waste much of her own money on drinks and really wasn't a big drinker. She just used the cocktail as a prop. Sometimes she would do the same with a cigarette but preferred not smelling of smoke. She didn't need to invite any questions from Woody.

Lance had finished his shitty little human interest story and wrapped it up for the weekend. Typically he'd be anchoring the weekend news but the station had even put that on hiatus for awhile. He was an outcast after that last foiled stunt. The station was giving that hot young black girl a shot at it this weekend. He'd like to give her a shot and eventually he would no doubt.

Right now, his throat was parched and he needed a drink and desired female companionship. He had spotted the little out of the way bar earlier and decided to give it a try. Parking the Z28 in back he strolled in like he owned the place, the only way he knew how.

Glancing around, he saw a couple of locals drinking beer and shooting pool. He could pick out the locals from the tourists because locals never wore anything with the touristy logos. One overweight bleached blond sat at the bar eyeing the young barkeep like candy in a store. Good luck he thought because even from his vantage point he could tell the bartender was gay as a daisy.

An old fart sat at a table glued to a basketball game on the big screen. The Tar Heels were playing some no name little college and had a thirty point lead. What a great little place he had picked. He figured he would finish his drink and call it a night.

Then he saw her returning from the lady's room. Bingo! Even in this light he could tell she was a keeper and presently she was alone. It's time to pour on the Rocker charm and work my magic. He boldly approached her table over in the corner.

Janice Anderson had noticed him as she returned from the powder room but didn't let on to him that she had. The game had begun, winner take all and she never lost.

"Mind if I join you," said Rocker. "I do believe that chair belongs to me." He used an old George Strait line from the song of the same name, *The Chair*.

"If it fits, feel free to wear it," she responded with an extremely flirtatious smile.

He countered with his pearly white smile. From there, the volley began but it was really no contest. Each playing their version of the little game, it would most likely end in a tie.

For now, she decided to play it dumb and pretended she didn't recognize him. She could tell that this ploy bruised his massive ego but controlling the game was vital and right now she had the advantage. Soon she would take the news anchor where he had never gone before. She hadn't decided if and when she would admit she knew his identity.

At first it bothered Lance that she did not recognize him but what the hell, he had reeled her in so easily. The end game was what counted and he planned to rock her world. He sensed no drugs would be required for this conquest but he had them just in case.

She was a little older than what he preferred but she oozed intrigue and mystery and had a killer body. If what was underneath those clothes rated anywhere close to what he was looking at now, it would be worth the gamble.

"Buy you a drink?"

"Well, that's certainly a great start."

"And the ending?"

"I visualize something hot and sweaty," she said with the most sensual smile. "You do like creating fantasies as we go don't you?"

"You cut to the chase don't you?"

"We can play any game you'd like if that's what turns you on, sugar, but I think we both want the same thing. Getting there is just part of it." She twirled her drink with her fingers then inserted three in his mouth.

"You're not a hooker are you? I don't do hookers," he mumbled as he suckled her middle finger.

"I can be anything you want me to be but no, this won't cost you anything but time. You see, I'm a slow burn and require both care and patience but I promise I won't disappoint."

"Are you a nympho or some sort of sex addict?"

"You sure do ask a lot of questions and worry even more. You haven't even asked me my name or told me yours so that tells me you won't be making an honest woman out of me will you sweetie?"

"You're a real piece of work aren't you? I'm not sure I've ever met anyone quite like you."

"That, I can certainly guarantee. Do you want to sit here and play questions and answers or should we go somewhere and ravage one another? It's your call. I vote we head someplace private and pound our brains into oblivion." She pushed the envelope even further pouring on the slut.

"I'm not really interested in your brain but I'd sure like to take a peek at the rest of the package," said Rocker as he ran his finger over her lips then inserted it in her widening mouth.

"So let's go, lover boy. You staying in a hotel or are you a local?" She continued to pretend she didn't know the news anchor.

"Local and my place is about 45 minutes from here. I'll drive," he said as he left a generous wad of cash on the table for the waitress.

"Thanks but I'll drive my own car and I'll follow you. That'll make it easier for both of us later."

"You've done this before haven't you?"

"First time...with you...and I don't sense you're exactly a rookie either."

Janice had finally hit the gold mine she had been hoping to find. She had never landed a celebrity like Sir Lancelot before and would cash in on this prize, her ticket to a better life!

In the parking lot, purely by chance they were parked side by side, her in a burgundy Honda Accord and him in the Z28, his man toy.

"Nice car...sorry I won't be riding with you. I just love the feel of the wind blowing through everything."

Oh, you'll be getting the ride of your life so don't look so disappointed. "Stay close and we'll be there in no time."

She kissed him deeply before she sat down behind the wheel. "Let's go."

I've been waiting for you to come back outside bitch! You had some friggin nerve earlier when you turned that little Jap-trap in front of me like you did! I don't think you had the damn right of way did you? But that didn't seem to bother you. I see you had a rendezvous, how convenient!

Talking just above a whisper, "Lance Rocker, Mister Alive and Reporting, the Super Sleuth, it's time I ended this little connection of ours once and for all. And you inconsiderate and reckless driving bitch, you will help me with this little finale! I tried so hard to stay off these God forsaken highways and enjoy a weekend of solitude and fishing but your kind are just determined to ruin my life. Stop trying so hard. You ruined it already. Bradshaw was just a tumor but the cancer continues to spread."

Possible Burglary, Mega Bucks Bingo,
544 and Big Block Road
10:19 PM

Deputy Trudy Wagner examined the broken front plate glass window shattered by a large brick found inside. She and the bingo parlor owner had just walked the premises and nothing had been discovered missing but two gumball machines and the donation box for the animal shelter containing very little cash.

Trudy laughed. There could be some possible prints on an unbroken window pane. An obvious face smudge and a full set of right and left hand prints were clearly visible. The perpetrator had apparently tried to take a peek inside before breaking and entering...priceless and perfect for a segment of dumb crook news.

She had investigated a couple of fender benders earlier but otherwise the night had been very boring and way too long. It gave her too much time to think about her mom, her situation with Brady and the killer running rampant on the Grand Strand. Unfortunately she had not solved any of these looming dilemmas.

She and Brady had talked a couple of times but had firmed up no definite plans for spending any time together in the very near future. Checking at home, her mom had been doing okay or at least had done nothing Lulabelle couldn't handle. There was nothing new on the case. The coroner's reports were still pending on Sonny Boggs and Rachel Winslow.

Sheriff Singleton had made it perfectly clear, stay away from Tim Ford. As for Lance Rocker, simple, he had been warned to drop all communication. Hank stated he would have the badge and ass of anyone discussing the homicides with any news media, television or newspapers. She didn't intend on being the first to cash in on that.

She had a long night ahead and found herself missing the company of Woody Anderson. She had gotten spoiled having him as a partner. She would never admit that to him of course. How could her life have possibly gotten so screwed up in such a short time?

She wound up the preliminary investigation of the break-in and decided to take a break. She had seen the *Hot* sign on at Krispy Krème, the kiss of death for police stereotyping. The uniform had nothing to do with her weakness. In her present mood, a dozen ought to do it.

Rocker-world
1:10 AM

The still burning lamp lay on its side on the bedroom floor, the only light in the bedroom, its shade crumpled. Ice cubes were scattered, forming water stains on the Berber carpet. The ice bucket lay upside down near the bedside. Soiled bed covers were waded on the floor and several pillows were stacked, still positioned strategically from the acrobatic activities.

The condo resembled a crime scene from the entrance door to the bathroom. Steam seeped from the shower like an incoming fog bank. In the massive oversized shower, Lance and Janice, naked as the day they arrived in this world, lay lifeless on the tiled floor. The pulsating hot spray pelted their bodies from multiple directions.

"Are you alright there, champ?"

"I was just about to ask you the same thing," replied an equally exhausted Lance Rocker. "What the hell just happened?"

"Well, I think that last little acrobatic move you attempted to pull caused us to slam hard on this shower floor. Thanks for breaking my fall but I'm afraid it knocked the wind out of your sails though."

"Damn, that was good! We're good together," he exclaimed in a most un-Rocker manner.

"Four or five tries already tells me we must like what we're doing," she laughed, a cute nasally snicker.

"Who's counting? You're one hell of a woman, Jenny." Rocker spoke in a much winded condition, unfamiliar ground for him.

"You're not so bad yourself Rocky old boy."

Neither had disclosed their true identities yet even though she knew his. He just didn't know hers. She played it close to the vest for now to determine how the night may end. So far it was going rather perfectly.

She still had maybe three more hours before she'd have to return, grab the litter and be home before Woody. That left plenty of time for more play if Rocky could hang in there with her.

Lance Rocker for the first time in his life had been smitten. This Jenny, or whoever she really was, had taken him to task and had been damn good at it. He was on the verge of allowing a repeat visit to Rocker-World, something he rarely ever granted. Hell he may issue her season's tickets. He never did this and it almost unnerved him thinking it.

Janice had managed to do a quick scope of his condo while he took a phone call in the kitchen before their marathon began. She had discovered the walk-in closet with the posted photos, dates, names and an assortment of under garments. She heard the cash register ka-chinging in her head. She envisioned getaway cash and an answer to her prayers. She had enjoyed his virility but blackmail sounded like a better option. She certainly wasn't in love.

Making their way back to the master bedroom, Jenny commented, "Looks like a hurricane stuck your place, at least a category one. I hope we didn't mess it up too badly."

"We may qualify for federal aide and we could probably use Red Cross assistance," Lance replied with a chuckle.

"We must be in the eye of the storm right now. You know they say the back side packs more punch!" She slipped her right hand onto his shaft.

"Yep, I think it will be coming real soon. You do possess a magic touch."

They moved it to the second bedroom then the couch and eventually a funky rocker recliner. Janice glanced at her watch and it was almost 4 AM. She needed to leave shortly.

"Rocky, do you think we have a chance at the perfect storm?"

"Definitely," he surprised himself with quick confirmation. "Here's my card. You can reach me on my cell. I do have a confession to make."

She read the card out loud and mustered up a little pretend squeal. "Lance Rocker, Channel 12 News, I thought I recognized you. I don't watch very much television so I apologize."

"I should have been more truthful Jenny." He again surprised himself. He actually felt sincere, another new feeling. What the hell had come over him?

"Don't sweat the small stuff, Rocky. I will call you and arrange a repeat performance. Here, keep my favorite monogrammed panties as a voucher. I saw the ones in your closet."

"J.A., what's the initial A stitched on them stand for, Jenny?"

"We'll solve that little mystery next time but now I must go." She kissed him passionately. "Rest up but don't get dressed yet. I would like to remember you just like this until I return. You don't have to see me to my car. You're one hell of a wild ride you know," she said as she pretended to snap a photograph.

"You better call me, Jenny! Tomorrow wouldn't be too soon! And for the record, you're one hell of a ride too. I think I'm in love." He couldn't believe what was spewing from his mouth. He sounded like a little school boy who had just gotten snatch for the first time. Hell, he did feel that way and it felt wonderful.

She lifted her skirt and shook her naked ass at him as she opened the door. Turning she did her best *Betty Boop* impression winking and blowing him a kiss. She'd have to kick it into high gear to make it home before Woodrow but that didn't really worry her this time. She had found an open door to freedom. *Love...in your dreams...*

Southern Shores Dune's Resort
Myrtle Beach
8:10 AM

Trudy on her way home overheard the call on the radio and informed the dispatcher she was less than ten minutes from the resort and would swing by there. She phoned Lullabelle to let her know that she would be running late.

Minutes later she pulled into the parking lot. Several people surrounded an automobile just ahead. She pulled up, stepped out of her cruiser and the crowd parted.

"Hi, I'm Deputy Wagner. Who called this in?"

"I did," said a lady in a hot pink silk bathrobe, oversized dark sunglasses and a head full of curlers. She held a petite reddish blonde Pomeranian in her arms. "I'm Abigail Fuller. I saw her slumped over the steering wheel when I was walking Misty for her morning poop. I tapped on the window but she paid me no attention. I think she's real bad sick or something, bless her heart."

Trudy tapped on the tinted window but the lady behind the wheel didn't move for her either. "Can you open your door? I'm Deputy Wagner. I'm here to help. Does any one know her?"

"No but I saw her when she arrived last night," responded Abigail, Misty squirming in her arms.

To Trudy, Abigail Fuller resembled Gladys Gravis, the nosey neighbor from the *Bewitched* sitcom. Every neighborhood seemed to have one. They saw all, told all. One just like her had saved Edward Bradshaw the first time.

"So you saw her and what time would that have been?" Trudy saw the Little River Rescue Unit pulling into the parking lot.

"It was shortly after 10. I was taking Misty out for her last pooh-pooh run. We always do that at 10 PM sharp."

"And was she alone?" Trudy watched as one of the rescue unit personnel attempted to gain entry to the automobile.

"Nobody else was in her car if that's what you mean, but I'm glad they went up to his unit when they first arrived last night. I thought they were going to do it right here in the parking lot. They couldn't keep their hands off one another. It was such disgusting behavior out here in the open."

"You saw someone with her." Trudy heard the driver's side door being opened and momentarily diverted her attention.

"Why yes, he keeps a regular revolving door going and the sounds I hear coming from his place. Let me tell you. It sometimes sounds like he's killing those poor women. I've never heard such screaming and moaning in all my days."

"Do you eavesdrop at this person's door or something," Trudy blurted out.

"Deputy, she has no pulse."

"I'm appalled by your insinuation officer! I live next door to him and last night there was all this screaming and wild animal sounds and stuff breaking! It was so awful. I didn't think it would ever stop. I heard things that just didn't sound natural! I don't know what he was doing to that poor girl but I almost called 911."

And that's exactly what should have been done. "I think I get the picture," interrupted Trudy as soon as she had an opening. She wasn't sure this woman ever took a breath. "What is this gentleman's name?"

"He's an animal I tell you and to be famous like that. You read about these celebrities and their dark sides in the tabloids. He sure has one let me tell you. I lock my doors so he can't break in my place."

Trudy thought, that's what you wish would happen now isn't it. "Name, please..." Trudy glanced at the paramedics behind her.

"Why he's Lance Rocker, that Channel 12 News personality. He's so handsome you know," she now swooned. "But he's a sex maniac I tell you! Oh, I could tell you some stories if I were the gossipy type. He has a different woman every time. Some are under age I'm sure."

"Lance Rocker," Trudy spoke out loud, her brain going into vapor lock. "How's it coming with our young lady in the Honda?"

"She's dead, I'm afraid," replied the paramedic. "And you better take a look at this deputy. There's some sort of cord wrapped around her neck with something heavy dangling at the other end between her legs."

"Step back please and don't touch anything else," commanded Trudy, kicking into CSI mode.

The female's dress was pulled up above her waist and she wore no panties, the cord parted her vaginal lips apparently positioned there intentionally. She still couldn't make out what was attached to the other end of the cord because it disappeared on the floor under her seat.

"My, do you think that nice young TV man could have murdered her? Oh he must have and right next door to me. He dumped her body like those killers always do on TV! Oh he raped her then killed her. I've been living next door to Ted Bundy and didn't know it! All those other poor women are probably dead and buried somewhere too! I should have called 911!"

"Calm down. Will everyone please stand over there so we can secure the area," ordered Trudy. "We'll wish to get statements from all of you."

Trudy radioed for back-up as she stepped behind the Honda Accord to run the plate. "Oh shit," she exclaimed seeing no license plate.

Stepping around to the passenger side door, she saw a purse on the front seat. She slipped on latex gloves and retrieved the purse. As she feared, the dear lady's wallet contained no driver's license. She had stumbled right back into the middle of it again. Like it or not, destined to be her case to solve, she had no doubts now but would Hank see it the same way.

She turned to the nosey neighbor one more time, "Do you see Lance Rocker's automobile in the parking lot?"

"You're leaning against it honey. It's that sporty convertible right there."

Turning, she now recognized his Z28. *So he's still here then.*

Have we been so blind all along? Could Rocker be our killer in the other homicides too? It could explain how he has beaten us to almost every crime scene. This was bad on so many levels.

She waited for more officers to arrive then asked them to conduct an exterior search of both cars, take any prints, but asked them not to compromise the insides yet. She asked two other officers to accompany her to Rocker's condo once Abigail Fuller confirmed the unit number.

Rapping on the door, "Police, open up," ordered the younger of the two officers.

The door opened. Lance stood in the doorway shirtless and barefooted, wearing black silk pajama bottoms and sporting a very un-Lance like bed head. Trudy had never seen him any way but picture perfect. He looked all too human and frazzled.

"What can I do for you officers," he asked before spotting Wagner standing behind the second and rather robust policeman. "Well, well, well, Deputy Wagner, to what do I owe the honor?"

"May we enter?"

"Why certainly, Deputy, but I must warn you, the place is a mess. I had a few friends over for a wild sexual orgy last night and I must report it turned out very successful and rewarding for all! You should have gotten here sooner. I'm sure we could have worked you in somewhere."

"Damn," exclaimed the young officer, "You put on one hell of party don't you? You celebrities really know how to live."

Trudy gave the officer *the look* warning him to stifle the comments.

"I do my best, officer. Now deputy, why are you here?"

"Would you care to share your guest list with us?"

"I really don't think my guests would appreciate that. I must respect their privacy. In my profession, we can't have unnecessary tabloid coverage."

"Just because I like you so much I'm going to get right to it," she said putting her index finger on his smooth shirtless and hairless chest. We have a dead woman in the parking lot in a burgundy Honda Accord and have witnesses stating she spent the night here with you. How's that for an exclusive and wake up call Mister Orgy King?"

Rocker, speechless, wavered then sat back on the cushion-less couch, the three cushions strewn all over the floor. "I need to call my lawyer."

His heart ached with pain like he had never experienced before thinking of sweet Jenny, dead. He could not bear this being the end of their beginning. "How did she die?"

"We were hoping you would be able to tell us."

He dropped his head and said nothing else. Rocker, speechless, very unnatural indeed Trudy thought. She doubted that even he would be so stupid as to murder her in his own parking lot but this case had been strange from the beginning. Maybe he was just ready to be caught if he was the road rage murderer. Her gut told her he wasn't, but instinct didn't hold up in a court of law.

Horry County Police Department
Sheriff Hank Singleton's Office
2:00 PM

Trudy should have been exhausted but instead she felt invigorated. Lulabelle remained with Amy; her day, too, had been extended. The crime scene had been tidied up, both autos confiscated. Lance was still being held for questioning but not yet booked.

"Sheriff, here's what we have. One female *Jane-doe* and you've read her description, found dead by one of the resort's residents while walking her dog this morning. We have a 1991 burgundy Honda Accord with no plates and we're tracing the serial number. We have witnesses placing the victim in the parking lot and in the condo with Lance Rocker last night and through the wee hours this morning."

"Stop right there, Wagner. I may know who this woman is. God I hope I'm wrong but her description and that of the automobile just can't be mere coincidence," sighed the sheriff as he leaned back in his chair rubbing his huge fingers in his eyes.

"Who do you suspect she is, sir?"

"Janice, God help me, Janice Anderson. She drives a burgundy Honda and that description fits her like a glove."

"You're saying Woody's wife? I haven't met her yet but you really think...?"

"God I hope I'm wrong but, like I said, the description matches her and the car she drives. What the hell was she thinking, doing this with Rocker of all people?" Hank slammed his fist on his desk.

"You don't sound surprised that she might have been unfaithful to Woody?"

"Rumors have been flying for years. I hate to admit, that she's been running around on Woodrow. I didn't have the heart to tell him and they were, after all, just rumors. He loves that woman. I truly believe he thought she hung the moon. They have been sweethearts since grammar school. I'll confirm her identity before I dare contact Woodrow. He called about mid morning saying she and the kids weren't home when he got off work. I didn't expect this. What else?"

"Think about it, sir. Rocker was at the Bradshaw murder scene."

"But he called 911."

"He was first at the three homicides at the Admiral's Quarters. He claimed he had evidence that Tim Ford was behind this after breaking in his house. He's been on top of the story, fueling the fire and fanning the flames the entire time. Could he possibly have been our murderer all along just to further his career?"

"He's one smartass cookie but I just can't peg him as a cold blooded murderer," replied Hank, rubbing the perspiration from his slick bald head with his handkerchief.

"I'm glad you said that. I can't either but there's more. A News 12 microphone and cord was possibly the murder weapon. She had been strangled with it. Her monogrammed bikini briefs were found in his condo. And there's still more. He has a perverted dark side."

"I'm still sitting. Continue deputy," he said popping a couple of Rolaids and choking back a burp from his growing case of indigestion.

"Our Rocker has an entire wall of female photographs and underwear displayed in a walk-in closet. We're in the process of trying to ID them to make sure none of the others are dead or missing."

"That sick bastard...did you find any driver's licenses or plates in his place?"

"We've found neither so far. That's why I say he's not our man. Sure, it appears he took trophies from what I assume must have been his many sexual conquests but I still can't see him as our killer."

The phone rings and Hank answers. He listens mostly asking twice is the caller sure. "Damn, we may have to recant our little collaboration," he said as he stood to his feet. "Janice's tag and driver's license have been found."

"Let me guess, in Rocker's possession?"

"I'm afraid so. Forensics found them underneath the carpet in the trunk of his car. We now have no choice but to arrest him on suspicion of her murder. They're checking for prints on both." The door burst open. "Woodrow!" shouted Hank.

"Where is the son of a bitch? Detective Benny Robinson called me and told me what had happened. I want to see him now! He killed my Janice! That bastard is going to pay for this shit. Where the hell do you have him, Hank?"

"Woody, I don't think he killed her," Trudy tried to say but too late as Woody had already headed back out the door screaming back at her. "He fucked my Janice! Then he murdered her!" He repeated it several more times at the top of his lungs running down the corridor toward the interrogation rooms.

Hank grabbed the phone. "Deputy Anderson is on his way there. Do not allow him access to Lance Rocker. I repeat, do not let him get his hands on Rocker! Tackle his ass if you have to and hold him until I get there."

Hank turned to Wagner. "Oh this is bad. This is so very bad! I've never seen Woodrow this pissed before."

"Well, I suspect he's never faced anything like this before either, sir. I still say it's not Rocker but I'm not sure we can convince Woody," replied Trudy heading toward the doorway.

"I hope we're both right about Rocker but the evidence is going to make it hard to dismiss. Let's face it. We both know he's a slime ball but a murderer. For poor Woody I don't think it really matters whether he's the murderer or not. He can't get beyond the fact that the two of them had an affair. I just hope we can prevent him from doing something stupid like killing our newsman!"

"I'll go try to talk to him," she told Hank now feeling the full extent of her fatigue.

"If you're waiting on me you're backing up," he said stepping around his desk. "Let's go."

She so wished this was a done deal; case closed, but she knew in her heart that the killer was still out there. She only hoped he had grown tired of killing now that he had pinned it on Rocker but she doubted it. They were sitting on a powder keg and the fuse had been lit.

Amy Wagner Home
5:00 PM

Trudy had been unable to talk any sense into Woody but she and Hank had convinced him to go home and spend time with his children. Hank had insisted he go on an extended leave. He had plenty of vacation time and comp time available and Hank would not take no for an answer.

Lulabelle, seeing Trudy's obvious exhausted state, encouraged her to go to bed and she would stay the night and care for Amy. Hank had ordered Trudy to skip tonight's shift and take tomorrow off. She agreed to skip her shift but planned to be at the jail talking to Rocker come morning.

Brady had left several messages on Trudy's cell but she hadn't returned any of them. She couldn't deal with the emotional baggage of a lover right now. The case had now become number one in the pecking order followed by her mom then Brady sitting dead last.

Right now she couldn't deal with anything, too exhausted to focus. She required sleep but she couldn't will it to happen. She grabbed a chilled bottle of Chardonnay from the refrigerator and after finishing off the last glass, she finally drifted off to sleep still gripping the glass in her right hand.

She didn't sleep very peacefully. Her dreams were a jumbled mess of Lance Rocker on a killing spree, taking Amy and Brady as his next victims while she watched helplessly on a Channel 12 television monitor. Dreams can be so crazy she heard herself saying in the dream. So much blood and gore eventually took its toll on her not so restful slumber.

Trudy sat straight up in bed shivering but wringing wet with perspiration. She glanced over at the digital clock radio on the nightstand and at first thought it indicated 10 PM but after shaking the cobwebs she realized the room was too well lit with natural light to still be night. She cringed. She had slept for over fourteen hours. She had never done that before.

She pulled a marathon, opting to empty her bladder in the shower then dressed in record time. Lulabelle waved her off and said she'd be staying for awhile. She had sent for her niece to bring her a suitcase full of clothes and specific personal belongings. She advised Trudy that she would be moving in until Trudy gained control of her life and Amy's. Trudy didn't argue with her.

She paused long enough to kiss her mom on the cheek but Amy never acknowledged the gesture. She had a case to solve and urgently needed to talk to Lance Rocker. Trudy felt worse than hell and not rested at all. For a fleeting moment she felt guilty for neglecting her mom but that passed quickly. She had a job to do and it was time to do what she did best. Taking care of her mom and being seduced by Brady didn't enter the equation right now.

She should be concerned by the impression she was probably leaving on both of them but it just didn't seem important to her right now. She had had a life before either of them intruded and she intended to recapture it, come hell or high water as the saying goes.

This was for her and her sanity. They would have to wait their turn and she hoped in the long run they'd understand. She hoped she could live with her decision. This stunk to high heavens but had to be done. If any pieces were left of her personal life, she'd pick them up afterwards. This is so badly screwed up she thought.

Horry County Police Station
Interrogation Room #2
11:23 AM

Trudy sat at the table waiting for Lance Rocker to arrive still having flashes of her weird dream. She had already inhaled her third cup of coffee and held her forth sipping it while gazing at the mirrored glass. Her reflection looked like crap. No, she looked worse than that she decided.

The door opened and the officer escorted in a shackled Lance Rocker. He engaged the camera mounted on the tripod to record the questioning. Trudy dismissed the officer telling him she'd be fine alone with Rocker. He reluctantly departed and joined Hank Singleton on the other side of the mirror in the viewing room.

"Orange isn't your color," remarked Trudy attempting to end the silence. "How are you holding up?"

"Would you please turn off the camera and switch the sound off to this room?"

"Sir Lancelot, you're all of a sudden camera shy. What's up with that?"

"Please, just humor me, deputy."

This wasn't the Lance Rocker she had grown to despise. She knew Hank would probably go ape on the other side of that mirror but her gut told her to do as Rocker had asked. She flipped off the switch to the camera and muted the interrogation room. She glanced at the mirror and shrugged and mouthed *sorry*.

"Your dime, Rocker, what's eating you?"

"How did Jenny die? Was she mutilated, raped? I've got to know. She was a remarkable woman."

"I can't discuss Janice Anderson with you, you know that."

"I didn't know Jenny was Anderson's wife."

"Would it have really mattered?"

He shrugged. He just sat there speechless for about a minute. He ached for Jenny, Woody's Janice. He could not believe she was dead. For the first time in his life he gave no thought to his career or personal appearance. It didn't matter that he faced murder charges. He thought only of her.

Trudy watched him intently. This was not the arrogant, all for Lance Rocker, scoop monger at all cost slime she had first met. He had miraculously transformed into something different, an actual human being possibly. She almost felt sorry for him.

"I didn't kill her you know," he said very soft spoken and in a matter of fact tone. "I didn't kill any of them if that's what you're thinking."

"I'd like to believe that."

"I didn't drug her or anything. She took my place by storm and humbled me with her escapades. I've never been humbled when it comes to sex but this wasn't really sex, not like what I'm accustomed to," he tried to explain, providing Trudy with way more information than she had expected.

"Well if it wasn't wild crazy animalistic sex, you two sure had a strange way of dismantling your condo."

"Oh the journey was highly sexual but it wasn't just sex. I felt like we were actually making love. I'd never made love to anyone before Jenny...Janice. I could have spent the rest of my life with a woman like that and thought maybe I had a shot at it."

"You really shouldn't be telling me this. She was married, Rocker, with five kids." She attempted to bring him back down to earth. It didn't faze him.

"I don't think Deputy Anderson really made her happy. He couldn't have or she would not have been out in search of happiness. She didn't deserve this fate."

And all this from one night thought Trudy.

Rocker had no clue that Janice had planned to blackmail him and take him for everything he had. No one did or would ever know that little scenario. The dead tell no tales except through forensics and DNA. Neither would expose this secret.

"Did you hear me? They had five kids together?" She tried shock therapy again.

"Even with those children, she was unblemished and still flawless. I'm an expert on this subject. She was perfect."

Janice Anderson must have been one hell of a woman to have smitten Lance Rocker like this. He's a broken man.

"You've got to capture the asshole that did it, Deputy Wagner." He raised his voice for the first time. "Now turn on the camera if you'd like to interrogate me. I've got nothing to hide and I don't need my lawyer present."

"That won't be necessary, Rocker. You've told me enough. She motioned to the officer supposedly standing in the viewing room on the other side of the mirror. "You'll be going up in front of a judge shortly and I suspect you'll be able to make bail. Stay out of Woody's way, please."

"I've already told my lawyer I would wave, refuse any bail. I'm perfectly content here."

"You'd rather stay in here? What are you doing, preparing a piece for what it's like inside the slammer?"

"What better way to prove my innocence," he said with a half Rocker smile. "Rage will kill again and when he does, I'll be set free, innocent of all charges."

"Damn good strategy you have there Rocker. I hope it works for you."

"I may be damaged goods but I'm still marketable. The world hasn't heard the last of Lance Rocker by a long shot. I'm down but not out."

She actually thought she saw a glint of the old Rocker in those troubled eyes. She had to admit. She liked the new reformed Rocker much better. She believed everything he had just told her. The tin man really did have a heart. Welcome to Kansas!

As predicted, Hank ambushed her outside the interrogation room. She fabricated a convincing response not revealing the conversation she had just completed with the new and improved Lance Rocker. He fell for it. She was getting just too damn good with this lying.

Now she had to somehow convince Woody not to go on a murdering rampage, if you called snuffing out Rocker an actual rampage. Bars couldn't protect him from Woody forever. She had to protect her partner from himself.

Meanwhile the news media showed no mercy. Lance Rocker, the alleged murderer of Deputy Woodrow Anderson's wife topped all of the local channels and newspaper front pages. It had even made the major networks; however, his little perverted closet secrets had not been divulged yet because of the pending investigation. When released, it would certainly deliver the final nail and probably bring an end to his career.

Lance had not been linked to the nine homicides nor had the terms serial killer or road rage been mentioned. Sheriff Hank Singleton made it perfectly clear with all law enforcement that this would be played close to the vest unless evidence linked Rocker to the other murders. Neither his finger prints nor anyone else's had been found on Janice Anderson's tag or license.

Lance couldn't help but think if Lance Rocker would have been investigating his crime, he would have already blown the top off of it. He wasn't. Those fellow newsmen who despised him, which accounted for most everyone, stirred the pot and maintained a circus atmosphere. Lance Rocker had a knack, even when not trying, to keep his face in front of the camera.

Lance sat in his jail cell, heart aching, spirit broken. His only prayer, catch the killer before the lynching commenced and keep Woody Anderson from doing him harm.

Amy Wagner Home
Two days later
2:15 PM

Trudy had gotten a three hour nap and now sat in the den with her mom relieving Lulabelle to run a few errands. Her mom had been rambling about people and situations that just didn't interest her. She nodded or said 'is that so' occasionally. This didn't seem to impact her mom one way or the other.

Her cell phone rang. She answered and immediately recognized Hank's gruff voice. "Were you asleep, Deputy Wagner?"

"No sir, just sitting her enjoying some quality time chatting with mom."

"I thought you may want to hear this. I think we have links to the Sonny Boggs and Rachel Winslow cases. It would make them homicides seven and eight of a possible nine," he said waiting for her reaction but Trudy didn't give him the wow factor he had expected.

Hank told her that during the autopsies, a BMW hood ornament from Winslow's BMW had been removed from her vagina. It had been a similar situation for Sonny Boggs except in his case it had been the missing metal John Deere logo from the side of his tractor and it was found in his anal cavity.

"So," she finally responded, "Winslow's tag and license were missing. Our killer has upped his creativity. It does clearly link them to Road Rage. As I originally suspected, Sonny didn't have a tag or require a license to operate the tractor so our killer had to prove his point. His John Deere was his prize possession."

"You got it. We're dealing with one sick mother here. I suspect we haven't heard the last of him yet either. Say hello to your mama and get some more shut eye before your shift starts."

"What about Woody?"

"Lying low so far but I don't expect it to last."

Hank had no sooner hung up when her phone rang again. Trudy almost experienced heart failure. Her mom didn't flinch and continued her conversation babbling crazy talk.

"Trudy, its Brady. How are you holding up?"

"Hanging," she responded. "Selling any of those funny pants, circus boy?"

"Well, they're not jumping off the shelves but sales are keeping me off unemployment. Do you think maybe I could take you to breakfast after your shift ends in the morning?"

"Too hectic I'm afraid. Between the case load and mom's condition, my social life will have to take a hiatus."

"Sorry to hear. I was really hoping to see you."

"Don't sweat it, I'm doing okay."

"I wasn't feeling sorry for you. I was thinking about me." He shocked her with his response. "I know you thrive on your work but I miss you something terribly."

"If we're meant to be, we'll survive the temporary madness." She tried to be stern in her response.

"And if we don't?"

"I've got to go, Brady. Mom has wondered off into the kitchen and I don't need her trying to burn the house down again."

He sighed. "You know where to find me when you do need me. Please be careful."

She halted the call and just sat there staring at her mom still jabbering on the couch. She should have never lied to Brady about her heading to the kitchen but she had panicked. She thought, I can't lose Brady but I can't work him into the equation right now. "I am so pathetic; so much for multi-tasking." She spoke out loud and her mom just turned to her and smiled.

Fast forward. Two and a half months had flown by and no more related homicides had occurred, at least not in Horry or the surrounding counties. Sure, there had been four homicides but none had the earmark of the Road Rage killer.

Trudy pondered the possibilities. Had he grown tired of murdering? Had he died? Had he moved to another state? Had he been picked up on some unrelated charges?

Tim Ford had coincidently been out of town visiting family and friends for the past three weeks. Did that make him the killer? He leaves and the killings stop. It made perfectly good sense.

Rocker remained behind bars refusing bail. Hank had actually agreed to a supervised visit between Woody and Lance only after Lance granted permission.

Woody confided in her their conversation. Lance had lied to Woody. He had painted a scenario where he drugged and seduced Janice, saying she would never have been unfaithful to him on her own. He was to blame, not her.

He never mentioned the monogrammed panties, their sexual marathon or his genuine love for *Jenny-Janice*. He restored her reputation for Woody and especially for Janice. It didn't minimize Woody's hatred for Rocker. Lance took it in stride and maintained his guilt for ruining a good woman.

Woody did walk away believing Lance wasn't the serial killer nor Janice's murderer but he still threatened to kill him the first opportunity he got. Who was this man in Rocker's skin she wondered, and would Woody go through with his promise? Boy how the world had turned upside down she thought.

Amy Wagner remained in her home but now confined to a hospital bed, unable to do for herself at all. Her bodily functions were now maintained by Lulabelle and a home healthcare nurse came three times a week. Trudy avoided these responsibilities as much as possible. She always allowed her work to provide excuses. She wasn't cut out to be a caregiver. Allison was even worse and had not visited their mom.

She struggled with admitting her mom to an assisted living home. She had heard good things about a place down in Litchfield, less than an hour away but was it the right thing to do? It wasn't that she didn't want to admit her to one of these places. She just didn't assert much effort thinking seriously about it.

She continued to talk to Brady weekly by phone but had managed to conjure up excuses for not meeting him for breakfast, lunch or dinner. She had to keep her distance because in her heart she knew it would just be too complicated. She simply couldn't stoke that fire right now due to her fragile emotional state.

Researching Road Rage theory, incidences and causes had become her obsession. Somehow she knew the killer wasn't finished. Her job, catch or kill him. Monitoring cases nationwide, she searched for answers. She had to climb inside the murderer's head. She had not found any incidences in South Carolina or any other southeastern states to utilize.

Evil must be nourished. Road Rage knows no boundaries. For now, the palmetto state had been granted a reprieve but true to belief, they always return to the scene of the crime. This would prove to be no different but the carnage left in its wake would be unmatched in modern day history, all incited by a mere roadway reckless maneuvers and a troubled soul unable to overcome the tragedy.

The following are a series of reports possibly related to the South Carolina case.

LOS ANGELES — the driver of a silver Bentley was shot early Friday in an apparent car-to-car freeway shooting in the southbound lanes of Highway 101 in downtown Los Angeles.

California Highway Patrol and police officers responding to a 3:25 a.m. shots-fired call discovered the bullet-riddled Bentley stopped on the freeway near the eastbound Interstate 10 connector.

Police Lt. Paul Vernon says the Bentley driver, who has several bullet wounds, was found slumped over the steering wheel. The lieutenant says he's hospitalized with serious injuries.

Vernon says no witnesses have come forward to the apparent car-to-car shooting. Investigators don't know if the shooting is gang or narcotics related or the result of road rage.

The Bentley, which is peppered with bullet holes, does not have license plates.

CHP Officer David Porter says the southbound lanes of Highway 101 are shut down from the downtown Four Level interchange.

Motorists are being diverted onto the southbound Harbor 110 Freeway and traffic is stacked up for miles.

Vernon says the police investigation will continue through mid-morning and the freeway will remain closed for hours.

Another report from California

The crash that killed at least 14 Russian visitors on a tour bus in southern California on Tuesday was caused by road rage, according to local authorities. The mini-bus plunged down a ravine and burst into flames after being forced off the highway.

Reporters at the crash site talked to witnesses saying they saw the bus driver arguing with an unidentified man prior to the accident.

"The drivers were bullying each other," said one witness. "There are infrastructure problems on that part of the road." 'This accident was the result of the drivers' thuggery. The two argued over who would be first to cross the mountain pass after the bus cut off the pick-up truck earlier."

Phoenix, Arizona — The scene of a bloody murder. Witnesses remember seeing the driver of white Ford Bronco exchanging obscene gestures with a dark colored late model Chevy pick-up Tuesday afternoon before both drivers pulled into a post office parking lot.

Police Commander Mike Sierra later investigated the homicide of the driver of that same white Ford Bronco not more than a mile from the post office. The driver had been shot once in the back of the head. His identification remained unknown because his plates and driver's license were missing. Police were searching for a black or dark blue Chevy truck. Road rage was suspected as the cause leading up to the homicide.

Houston, Texas — Investigators were still puzzled by the apparent homicide of a yet to be identified female driver of a beige 2000 Ford F-150 pick-up found on the shoulder of Interstate 45.

Police are puzzled by the peculiar circumstances. No identification was found in the lady's purse. A Yorkshire terrier in the backseat had not been harmed. The truck may have been stolen because it had no tag. Police are treating it as a murder. Information on the cause of death has not been released.

Bastards, you're all the same, in every state, every city! You think you own these damn highways! It's all about you! Guess what, I think it's all about me!

"*LADY*, get out of the friggin truck! Are you deaf or just damn stupid? I said get your ass out of that damn truck...now!"

Rolling up the window and locking your doors, bitch, when I told you to get the hell out of the truck! Oh now that does it!

"Hang up that phone! I said *HANG UP THE DAMN PHONE, NOW!*"

Crap, now I have to break the friggin window! You're determined to make me injure my hand aren't you?

"Okay, we'll do it your way! Damn that hurt like hell! I got you now bitch! Where did you get your driver's license, Wall-Mart?"

Shit... sirens!

"You just had to call 911 didn't you?"

Guess we'll just have to make this quick won't we? Cry all you want. You caused this. Now pay the piper.

"Done, I'm outta-here!"

Conway Medical Center
Emergency Room
10:23 PM

"Miss Wagner, your mother is breathing on her own but she had an extremely close call," explained the young physician on duty.

"What happened?"

"Aspiration is not uncommon for a person in your mother's condition. Have you considered an assisted living facility? It must be difficult caring for her at home. Miss Wagner, next time she may not be so lucky."

"I've thought about it but I knew she would be happier at home."

"Frankly, in her accelerated state, I'm not sure she knows home from the emergency room if you understand what I'm saying."

"What do you know about the Litchfield facility?"

"Excellent facility, professional, good people, you nor your mother would be disappointed," he responded with a nod and a smile. "She needs it and I can tell by looking at you that you probably need it even more. Being a caregiver can be quite stressful."

"Is it that obvious?"

"I've seen it too many times in my young career. People don't realize how the caregiver is impacted. Unfortunately, we have the market cornered on the elderly here on the Grand Strand I'm afraid to say. It's almost like they've instinctively migrated to the beach, their version of the elephant grave yard. Their arrival signals the need for caregivers."

"That's a hell of a thing to come out of a doctor's mouth. You watch too many of those old Tarzan movies but I can't deny I agree. I'll do it for her and for me. Thanks for the push."

"I apologize for being so blunt. I'll refer her there if you'd like. It might go faster. For the record, Johnny Weissmuller was the best Tarzan ever."

"If you say so, doctor. Thanks for helping."

She held her mom's hand and kissed her on the cheek. Amy never opened her eyes. She knew this was the right thing to do. She had known for months.

The doctor admitted her to the hospital saying he'd keep her for observation long enough for Amy to be transported directly from the hospital to Litchfield. She'd start the ball rolling tomorrow. She had the day off.

The Anderson Residence
9:30 AM

Woody remained on FLMA and struggled to hold onto his life with his five children, without Janice. He wasn't cut out for this Mister Mom daily grind. He'd never mistreat or neglect his responsibilities but even he knew his children were suffering under his rein.

He would have never guessed that a simple knock on the door would spell trouble. Someone had apparently reported him to social services after the three year old had almost been struck by a motorist yesterday. Little Bobby had wandered into the street when Woody had been preoccupied with a skirmish between two of the other children in the back yard.

Social Services took all five into temporary foster care because of the one accidental incident, how embarrassing. Being a deputy carried no weight and they simply whisked them away. He stood in the kitchen, alone and cried. He never cried. He needed to go back to work and get his life on track and then he'd get his kids back.

Rocker, all of this is Rocker's fault! Janice, now the kids gone, damn you Rocker! All for what, so you could screw my wife and get her killed just like that. Your ass belongs to me if they ever let you out!

Oh now that would just seal it wouldn't it Woody old boy? Kill him, and ruin my career and my kids' lives! What the hell is wrong with me? I used to be a damn good cop and not a bad person. I follow the rules or used to. I'm acting as crazy as that maniac running free out there! Poof, just like that and look at me.

Look Woody did, in the bathroom mirror and he didn't like what stared back at him. He showered, dressed in his uniform and headed to the station. Job, life, then my kids, he kept repeating as he drove.

Horry County Police Department
Two Days Later
6:00 AM

After a debriefing meeting, Trudy prepared to start her shift. She stopped to grab a cup of coffee when she saw a welcome familiar face.

"Deputy Woody Anderson, you look like warmed over dog crap."

"And you, the sheer vision of doggy-doo yourself!"

"Is this your first day back?"

"Second...so how's your mama?"

"Put her in an assisted living home," she replied, expecting a sarcastic comment. "And what about your kids?"

"Just got snatched up into foster care," he said as he avoided eye contact. "Guess I won't be in the running for Daddy of the year."

"I removed my name from the ballot for daughter of the year too. It just didn't seem fair to the other candidates."

"So, where do we go from here?"

"We go out and catch the bad guys, kick ass and take names."

"Rocker still a prime suspect?"

She shrugged. "Like magic, no similar homicides have been reported in the immediate area since his incarceration. Maybe our real killer is dead or moved on to greener pastures in another state."

"Or maybe we really have him behind bars after all!"

"Rocker...I still say he's not our killer but you're right, this isn't playing in his favor."

"For the record, I don't peg him for a killer either but I still hate the son of a bitch. What about our Mister Ford?"

"He's left the area. I heard he was visiting friends or family but the trail is cold. He doesn't have any immediate family that we can finger."

"So you don't know where he is?"

"We do not. So that definitely keeps him on our little list of two."

"Any hunches?"

"None that I'm ready to share...I've been researching Road Rage on the net, interesting subject to say the least. I've also jotted down my own little list of what pisses me off about irate driving."

"Let's hear it. Maybe I can add to it."

She pulled the sheet from her jacket pocket. Here, you read it while I pour us both a cup of coffee."

He began reading her hand written list.

The driver turning in front of you then drives very
slowly only to make another turn within a block
The lane changer using no signals
Being cut off
Driver rides your bumper
The Red Light runners
Pulling into the parking place you were waiting on
Flipping you the finger or shooting you a moon
The dreaded school bus stopping every block
Racers blowing past whipping in and out of traffic
Using no signals when changing lanes
Hitting the brake lights for no apparent reason
The dump truck driver that cracks your windshield
The horn honker
The moped rider backing up traffic
The cell phone user
The truck scattering debris ahead of you
The car with no tag and driving erratically
The rude 18 wheel drivers
Golf carts and tractors on the roadways

"Wagner, you're one angry driver aren't you? Hell, you could be our killer from what I just read!"

"Don't be ridiculous. Give me that list! I should have never shown it to you!"

"My, you are touchy on this subject aren't you?"

"It's time to start our shift. Be careful out there and I hope everything works out with your kids."

"Same goes for your mama." He digested what he had just read, seriously wondering if his partner could be capable of violent road rage. He laughed it off.

"By the way, read this," she said, handing Woody a printout. "See you tomorrow."

Woody slipped behind the wheel of his cruiser and unfolded the sheet of paper. His partner was onto something apparently.

Road Rage Statistics

Road rage consists of a wide variety of drivers in aggressive acts taken out on other drivers. Some include speeding, tailgating, flashing headlights, yelling at other drivers, running stop signs or traffic lights, passing on the right, and weaving in and out of traffic. However, according to a study published by the American Automobile Association (AAA) in 1997, 37% of road rage drivers used firearms against another driver, 28% used other weapons, and 35% used their car as a weapon against another driver. And the numbers continue to increase.

Studies point not only to traffic congestion, but also to longer commutes to and from work, and an overall increase in the daily stresses and intricacies of living in today's world as reasons for the increase.

Amy Wagner Home
9:00 PM

Trudy sat in front of her laptop sipping on a glass of wine and querying the bureau's national files for road rage cases. She paused and picked up her cell and toggled to Brady's number, stared at it for a couple of seconds then she placed it back on the kitchen table where she'd set up her one person task force office.

Her query revealed over 1500 suspected cases nationwide where road rage could have been blamed. She fine tuned her search to just include those cases where deaths occurred. Boom, this drastically reduced the number to less than 200. Most road rage cases only went so far as a verbal confrontation between drivers, some leading to blows but not often ending in death.

She made several attempts to screen this number by adding ticklers such as missing license plates, missing driver's license, and types of weapons used if any. While the query ran, she again picked up her cell, rested it under her chin as she tapped her fingers on the kitchen table pondering should she call him. She had not checked on her mom today either.

She pressed the call button and the phone began ringing, no turning back now because he'd see her ID as a missed called if she halted it. It rang a third time, no answer, so she started to hang up when she heard his voice. She almost melted.

"Hi, is there anything wrong?"

She launched into a tirade of psycho babble before finally asking, "Can I come over?"

"Only if you promise me one thing."

This didn't sound good. Why had she called him? She waited for the other shoe to drop.

"Grab what you need for overnight and leave now!"

"I'll be there before you hang up the phone." She was overtaken by a case of diarrhea of the mouth and said, "Warm up the bed sheets but don't start without me."

She rushed around and grabbed what she needed forgetting about the query. Lights off and doors locked, she'd be in his arms in less than thirty minutes. She'd call Litchfield on the way to ease some of the guilt about her mom. Amy had moved to number three on the list only inched out of second by Brady. The road rage case still remained number one but tonight she'd let it go.

Hopping in her cruiser she briefly considered using her lights and siren to shave some time off the drive. She luckily talked herself out of that little stunt. She should be there before ten. That will give them almost eight hours before she would have to leave for work tomorrow morning. They could do a lot in eight hours.

It always amused her how the traffic slowed and how everyone obeyed the law when seeing a police car. Who did they really think they were fooling? She knew they cursed her for all she was worth for just being here. One car did cut her off before she made eye contact with the driver in their rearview mirror. That would have normally enraged her but it didn't this time.

Johnny's Bar and Grill
11:00 PM

Woody sat on the bar stool drinking his fifth Miller Light. He had never liked beer and really wasn't much of a drinker. His taste had apparently changed and he was getting quite good at this guzzling thing. Loneliness brought out the stupid in people.

The five beers had not diminished all of his brain cells yet. He still dreamed of Janice, missed his kids and worried about Wagner's obsession with road rage. He envisioned her going on a rampage and killing those nine people. Sometimes people just snap and she had been under a lot of strain with her mom, her new start here and old Payne Stewart.

Could that drive someone like her to kill? Could it drive an officer like Wagner over the edge? Some people yes, but not Wagner. She loved police work too much. He decided to make it an even six pack before going home. He hated to break up a matching set.

He had enough ugly baggage in his life right now. He thought, hell I could be the killer and could be suffering from some sort of mental block. If I am he thought, I hope Rocker is my next victim.

He dismissed the crazed thoughts, finished the last Miller Light and headed home to the empty house that waited for him. He wasn't in uniform and had opted to drive the Honda, Janice's Accord. It had been released after having been gone over with a fine tooth comb. It was no longer needed as evidence. Forensics had discovered nothing to assist in the case. He opened the car door. The interior still smelled like her.

He eased into the driver's seat then cried. He never used to cry but boy the tears flowed freely now. He had been doing this a lot, too much. His hand trembled as he tried to put the key in the ignition and it had nothing to do with the six-pack he had just consumed. He needed closure. Without it, this would only get worse.

Brady Pierce Beach Home
1:15 AM

"I needed that," she moaned. "I've been needing that for sooooo long."

"What am I, your little sex toy?"

"There's nothing little about you, circus boy."

"It's just good old southern marketing strategy. I thought you had given up on us."

"You missed me, huh?"

"Felt like you missed me more," he smiled as he pulled her close. "How's your mother?"

"I placed her in an assisted living facility."

"When?"

"A few days ago. She thinks she's in a fancy hotel resort."

"You've never allowed me to meet your mother. You think I could visit her?"

"No, I don't think that will be possible," she said in a stern tone.

"Why not, what are you so ashamed of. This is not an uncommon disease."

"No one can visit her for at least thirty days. It takes that long for them to become accustomed to their environment. And I'm not ashamed. I just wish you could have known her when she was my mom. I don't want your only memory to be of her as she is now."

Brady dropped the subject and simply held her in his arms. For almost an hour neither spoke. Finally he asked, "How's your investigation going?"

"It's not. The murders have stopped and don't pull a Woody on me. It has nothing to do with Rocker being jailed."

"Speaking of pulling a woody on you," he smiled placing her hand on his growing erection.

She took the hint and they forgot about killers and illnesses for another forty minutes. She awoke to the smell of breakfast. She sat up in bed. Brady handed her a cup of coffee. "Sorry officer, I have no donuts. You better shower and dress, its 5:30 and I don't want you blaming me for being late for work. Breakfast is almost ready."

"Circus boy, I really came here because I missed your cooking."

"Then enjoy. I did.

Road Rage never sleeps.

"Son of a bitch, there's a double yellow line here fellow, not to mention we're on a blind curve! Are you trying to get us both killed with this stupid passing of yours?"

Tailgating me earlier wasn't good enough! And don't think I'm letting that previous horn honking slide! Speed limit said 45 and I was doing exactly 45! I was minding my own business but you had to make yours mine!

"Now haul ass since you've passed me. What you say I introduce you to high speed bumper cars?"

Let's just see how you like being tailgated and passed! Mighty curvy road ahead, this should be fun for me, deadly for you!

Butt ugly double curves ahead, who's slowing to 45 now? Bye-bye. This is where we part company road hog! And I mean that in only the most affectionate way!

Amy Wagner Home
Shift's End
8:05 PM

Trudy sat on the edge of the tub running a hot bath, glass of wine already in hand, recapping her mundane day. She had investigated three robberies, one domestic squabble with a stabbing, two vehicular fender benders on 501 and an amber alert that turned out false. Just another day in the neighborhood she surmised.

Sliding into the tub and feeling the hot water reach her nether parts she contemplated heading south to Brady's again. They'd made no definite plans for tonight but she didn't think he'd turn her away. She took another sip, set the glass on the edge of the tub, eased back and closed her eyes to milk it all in.

Thirty five minutes later she awoke with a shiver. The bath water had almost gone cold. She dried herself and slipped into jogging pants and an old faded Ohio State Buckeye tee shirt. She didn't especially like the Buckeyes but the shirt had been on the 70% off rack with an additional 40% off the lowest ticketed price at J.C. Penny's back in Columbus and she hated passing up a bargain.

She poured a second glass of wine and flopped down in front of her computer. Entering her login and password, the screen fired up revealing the results of the query she had started before heading to Brady's last night.

She began clicking keys and sorting through the results not expecting to see anything of notable interest. It slammed her like a runaway freight train. She sat straight up in the chair and sponged in the information with reckless abandon. "Oh shit!"

She pulled out her road Atlas and began fingering locations. She leaped up and rambled through numerous drawers until she located a half full box of push pins and began marking the map, penciling in dates.

After just over an hour of marking up the map, she squeezed the last drop out of the wine bottle and sat back in shock. She tried to take a sip of wine but her hand trembled so badly she had to set the glass back down. She didn't really need the wine right now.

She took the necessary time to validate the police reports and verify the locations and dates a second time. Nothing changed on her map. Trudy glanced at the wall clock, 10:49 PM. She contemplated calling the sheriff and opted to call Woody instead but first she should give Brady a quick call to let him know she would not be coming there tonight.

She phoned him. After numerous rings his voice mail kicked and she left him a message instead. Where was he this hour of the night? *Not my concern* she convinced herself. She then called Woody and he picked up on the second ring.

"We need to talk," she said emphasizing the urgency.

"So talk."

"Not on the phone. Can you come to my place?"

"Do you realize the time? We're still on day shift you know and that's a hell of a drive. Can't you just tell me over the phone?"

"I tell you what, let me print out some information and I'll meet you in thirty minutes at that Waffle House you took me to before. It should be about half way."

"This better be good, Wagner."

"Trust me! You won't be sleeping much tonight anyway after you see what I have to show you," she boldly predicted.

"Okay, I'm on the way." *This better be worth it.*

She printed her supporting data, snatched up her Atlas and was out of the house in less than ten minutes.

The Waffle House
11:41 PM

Trudy utilized their table to methodically illustrate her findings. She explained the markings and dates on the Atlas referring back to the file data and closely watched how Woody reacted to her theory.

"Damn, so you're telling me that each pin and date on the map represents a road rage incident."

"Not just any road rage incident," she clarified. "Suspicious incidences, a missing tag, a missing driver's license, a similar weapon or method of homicide to our cases here."

"Connecting the dots provides a time line."

"Yep, the sequence and path jumps out at you, doesn't it?" The first occurred in Atlanta three weeks ago and each pin on the map shows the next a little further west finally ending in Los Angeles."

"Then the track doubles back," he commented, as he traced the route with his index finger.

"The bastard is coming back to roost. He's heading home, back here," she finished for him.

"And killing whoever is in his path," responded a shocked Woody Anderson.

"And look at the details in these two reports," she said as she pointed to the highlighted sections on the print out. "We have witnesses and a possible vehicle. He's either gotten sloppy or..."

Woody finished the sentence, "Or he doesn't think anyone will make the connection because he's moving from city to city, state to state, unlike the killing spree here."

"Do you recall what type of vehicle Tim Ford drives? Is it a dark, late model, Chevy pick-up by any chance?"

"It doesn't really matter."

"It certainly does!"

"Not really, I saw Tim Ford yesterday in the Piggly Wiggly grocery store."

"Are you sure?"

"Spoke to him, asked him discretely where he'd been the last few weeks and he told me to shove it up my ass. Nice guy, that Tim Ford. I wish he were the killer. Besides, look at your Atlanta date. It was a week before Ford allegedly left town."

"Damn," she sighed. "So Tim is innocent. I guess we can take Rocker off that list too. He's still in jail. Guess his plan worked after all. Once the killer killed again he would be exonerated."

"For the murders maybe," snapped Woody. "But he doesn't get off that easy. He still screwed my wife and ruined my life!"

Trudy didn't comment one way or the other to Woody's remark and obvious distaste for Lance Rocker. She still worried about the outcome when Rocker was released and he would most likely be released once she pled her case with the sheriff. He'd have to be blind not to make this connection with the Grand Strand killings.

"Wagner, we're looking at quite an impressive body count here!"

"Throw ours on the pile with these and it's very staggering."

"And he's still got a half dozen or more states to cross before he arrives back here if here is his final destination."

"Oh our killer is coming here. I'd bet the bank on it. He's returning to the scene of the crime. They always do."

"Do we even know the murders started here?"

"Positive. There are no other matches that show the pattern here and the ones plotted on the map," she said with the utmost confidence.

"We just don't know the name or face of the killer."

"Let's start with the vehicle; dark, late model, Chevy truck. You take that one and run with it if you don't mind." She toned it down so it didn't sound like she was giving orders.

"I'll run this through DMV," he replied, feeling his juices flowing once again.

"We have somewhat of a description if we take this one homicide that happened in New Mexico at face value. Male, Caucasian, huge, possibly six and half feet tall, dark hair, no facial hair; the witness said he resembled a biker in stature, but he wasn't sporting a bike."

"That's more than we've had since this thing started."

Woody glanced at his watch, almost 2 AM. "Yeah, you were right, I'm not sure I'm going to get any shut eye now but its best we head home and try partner. We might just have a big day ahead if we can sell this to Hank."

"That's my job," she answered with a southern belle accent, smile and a wink. "I'll use marketing strategy."

"Ya'll sho know how to charm the boys that is for shore," he added, with the Woody exaggerated version of southern slang.

Horry County Police Department
Sheriff Hank Singleton's Office
8 AM

"Amazing," gasped Hank. "Ten states! This maniac has been killing folks in ten states!"

"Eleven," corrected Woody. "Don't leave out the Palmetto state."

Hank took a deep nasally breath and then asked, "How many?"

"If we account for the ones I've marked on that map, 29 on the trip out to California and back to Texas," Trudy tallied. "And that doesn't count the 11 we associate here."

"And he's got seven more states to cross if he follows his current course," Woody added in his two cents.

"We've got to call in the FBI," remarked Hank as he stood from his desk, turned away and placed both hands on the wall behind him. "They're better equipped to handle these matters than us. Across state lines...its their case now."

"I disagree if you'll excuse my boldness, sir. I really don't think that's a smart thing for us to do right now," advised Trudy.

"This better be good Deputy Wagner," demanded Hank, turning to face her, his face reddening.

"Well, sir, we know he's heading here. He doesn't know we know. He thinks he's outsmarted us still. At least I believe he does. If we bring in the Feds and they tip him off then we may miss our only chance."

"Our chance to nab him here you mean," finished Hank. "And if we don't, the Feds will have our asses. He's crossed state lines. This isn't just a local matter."

"Sir, it started here," she stated boldly. "Let's end it here."

"You're asking a lot, Deputy Wagner. I'm not so sure I'm ready to put my pension on the line." He pounded his fist on his desk. "When do you estimate his arrival?"

"I can't really say. He's not a vacationer returning home. He reacts when drivers piss him off."

"We know Ford's not responsible for these murders and I guess we owe him an apology," stated Hank, sitting down in his chair,

"And Rocker's off the hook too," added Trudy.

"Don't even think about it," warned Woody. "That asshole won't get a *sorry* from me!"

"Alright, I'll give you your chance Deputy Wagner, I'll give you until Monday morning to break this thing open and if you can't show me substantial progress, I call the Feds. Don't make me regret this."

"Thank you Sheriff, we'll do our best."

"Best doesn't cut it. You apprehend our culprit. Pick your own team, work your own hours and tell me what else you require to assist your investigation but I'm in the loop every step of the way."

"Yes sir, thank you. Woody is on this with me. I'll need a psychologist with experience in profiling serial killers. Do you have a computer geek on staff, someone that can research and process data quickly?"

"I've got a couple of folks in mind. Let me make some calls. Anything else you need?"

"More time would be just wonderful," added Woody.

Hank rolled his eyes. "Wagner, like I said, keep me in the loop at all times. Don't go out on a limb because we're all sitting on it with you. You fail, we all do! You got that!" Hank stood up adjusting his trousers and looked as if he had aged a few years during Wagner's revelation.

"Yes sir, I understand perfectly."

"If you're waiting on me, you're backing up. Get out of here. And be careful out there."

They had no more than exited the office when Woody expressed his discontent. "What in the hell are you thinking? Five days, we have just five days to catch this psycho. We don't even know if he'll be back in the state in five days! Hell, we're not even 100% sure he's even headed here!"

"You want off this case?"

"Hell no, let's do it. This bastard has killed possibly forty or more people, including my Janice. I owe him!"

"He's ours to catch. I feel it!"

"Or ours to lose."

Task Force Meeting
Wednesday
10:05 AM

Joining Deputies Woody Anderson and Trudy Wagner were Detective Timothy Burroughs with a degree in computer science. Burroughs wore thick, black rim glasses and resembled a young, slightly thinner version of comedian *John Candy*.

Science Professor, Victor Swanson, MBBS/M.D./PH.D/Psy.D, sported a thick grayish mustache, waxed and curled up on the ends and matching bushy, wiry gray hair. His red bowtie, white long sleeve shirt and matching red suspenders were out of place for beach attire.

Rounding out the hand picked team, Detective Shannon Chestnut, forensic science. Chestnut was clean cut with jet black hair cropped in a crew cut. He resembled a marine recruit sergeant and carried himself like one.

The team had been formed and now they had their work cut out for them. Each, a specialist in their field, had been untested in such a high profile case.

"Alright, we have the introductions out of the way. I'd like to personally thank each of you for accepting or volunteering for this assignment," Trudy extended a hardy welcome to her new team. "And with that said, I'll be the liaison for all activity. This includes correspondence to the sheriff, other departments and the news media, no exceptions."

She continued, "We have five days to crack this case or to at least present enough evidence for Sheriff Singleton to extend our life. You've each had an opportunity to review your folders and what we know about these murders."

"Am I reading this right?" asked Detective Chestnut. "Potentially 40 homicides connected to one killer."

"Yes, your eyes are not deceiving you detective, eight in Horry County, one in Georgetown and the others spanning westward over ten states."

"Then where's the FBI?" he asked.

"For now we are it. Come Monday if we don't break this case, the FBI will be contacted and will head the investigation."

"Isn't that against policy and the law?" asked Chestnut.

"Only if the Federal Bureau of Investigation is privy to this information and right now they are not. Let's keep it that way. Got it?"

"Yes ma'am, I got it," he answered with a mock salute.

"So you have every reason to believe this killer is returning to Myrtle Beach?" asked Detective Burroughs.

"We do and that's where you come in. You'll be monitoring the web to track his progress if additional killings do occur."

"I don't get it," he said. "Sounds like to me we're hoping this person kills more people just so we'll know where he is. Shouldn't we put out an alert to warn other law enforcement to be on the lookout?"

"We have," spoke up Woody. "We have put out a Nationwide all points bulletin for a suspected vehicle with a description of a person of interest so technically we are following the book."

Trudy added, "We just didn't specifically mention the homicides outside South Carolina and fudged a little on the actual body count. My discretion, with the Sheriff's blessing of course. Think about it. How could they stop a killer who doesn't pick a specific type of victim?"

Trudy read the concern on their faces. "I admit we're coloring a little outside the lines on this one. Okay, we are coloring a lot outside the lines. I understand and respect your concern. If you're uncomfortable in this assignment feel free to walk away now but, if you do, I ask you to keep a lid on it until after Monday. For all intents and purposes, you were never in on it."

Woody spoke up. "Guys, you all know me. I wouldn't ask any of you to stick your necks on the line without mine being there too. We have an opportunity to bring to justice the worse serial killer to ever wreak havoc in our great state and community. Do we want to let the Feds botch this up for us? It started here in Horry. I say it ends here by our hands! My Janice was killed by the son of a bitch and I need this. Please work with us the next five days. After that, do what you will."

"I'm in," said Burroughs.

Me too Woody," said Chestnut. "Let's nail him!"

"Professor Swanson, I haven't heard you mutter a word," commented Trudy.

"I was merely waiting for you fine people to work through your BS so we could then begin."

"Alright then, let's talk assignments. Detective Burroughs, as mentioned already, you will be our watch dog and point man for computer research. You will alert us if you detect any criminal activity that resembles Mister Road Rage's work. You'll assist us in researching and compiling data."

"I'm on it, Deputy Wagner."

"Detective Chestnut, use your forensic expertise to go back over the nine cases we have and assess what you can from those others. Be very discreet when requesting out of state assistance."

"Sly as a fox," he replied.

"Professor, please build us a profile on the killer. My instinct tells me you'll be inventing a new chapter on serial killers. I don't believe Road Rage fits the stereotype."

"I'm intrigued already and concur with your preliminary assumptions."

"Woody, work with DMV and try to track down our vehicle. Expand that search to include motorcycles. One witness said Road Rage resembled a biker."

"I'm all over it, partner."

"I'm going to visit all of our known crime scenes, conduct some door knocking and see if I can flush out any new witnesses. Keep me posted on everything and I mean everything! And I repeat, mums to the media. It is 11:25. Let's meet back here at 16:00. And guys thank you for your help."

Horry County Jail
Wednesday
11:30 AM

Lance Rocker signed for his personal belongings. He ventured outside for the first time in months to no reporters, no fan fare and fortunately no Woody Anderson ready to ambush him. His thoughts retuned to *Jenny-Janice* but even he knew he had no choice but to put her behind him and move on.

He wondered if he'd still have his job. He doubted it. His contract was up for negotiations at Channel 12 and he felt confident Sir Lancelot would be no more. His reputation had taken a significant beating and the incident had tarnished his and the stations integrity. It was time for him to pull a Rocky Balboa maneuver and regain his title but not necessarily with channel 12.

Lance thought about a little freelancing and investigative espionage to get his creative juices flowing again. He owed this to *Jenny-Janice* to identify her killer and, if he could, he would break this case wide open. If he accomplished that he would be back on top. He'd call in all his favors and unleash his crude and unorthodox journalistic techniques.

He closed the door on his Z28. It felt wonderful to touch the leather and grip the steering wheel. He was in control again. "What a glorious day! It's great to be alive and vindicated! Beware Grand Strand. Lance Rocker is back! And I will leave no stone unturned and take no prisoners! I have a damn killer to identify."

Business 17, Hamburger Joe's
Surfside
Wednesday
1 PM

Trudy hadn't eaten today and had a ravenous craving for a cheeseburger. She knew she could get her fix at Joe's. She sat at the table cramming down the burger while jotting down *to-dos*. Fifth and six on her list, call Litchfield to check on her mom and then call Brady.

Sitting there so deep in thought she hadn't noticed the arrival of Tim Ford. He spotted her and swaggered over to her table. He stood directly behind her for a few seconds before she even looked up.

"Trying to catch the real killer," he asked, having taken time to peruse the open folder and her notes.

She gathered up the contents and quickly closed the folder. "Mister Ford, how have you been?"

"Pretty damned good since you and your bunch of keystone cops stopped harassing me."

"We do apologize for our actions. We had to follow our leads."

"You never did tell me what you were looking for back at my place."

"And I won't be sharing that information with you now."

"Do you have a suspect for Bradshaw's death?"

"Ditto, I cannot and will not discuss this case with you.

"If you find the guy that did it, I'd like to buy him a drink. I owe him."

"What makes you think it was a guy? It could have been a pissed off lover."

"If you thought it was a pissed off lover you wouldn't have been so determined to pin it on me."

"Unless you were the pissed off lover..."

"You're a funny lady. By the way I couldn't help but notice you've got quite a list of dead people there in that folder, Bradshaw being one of them. So mister TV personality was right, you do have yourself a serial killer in our fine tourist community."

"Would be best you forget what you thought you saw in this folder Mister Ford."

"Or what...it could disgrace your fine well oiled police machine, ruin the beach tourism, not to mention play hell with your investigation. Now, wouldn't that be a crying shame coming from someone who knows a thing or two about receiving bad PR. Deputy you really ought to finish that burger before it gets cold." He walked over to the bar and retrieved his take-out.

She watched him stroll out the door and drive off. Something still disturbed her about Ford. She couldn't quite put her finger on it but she always got bad vibes when he was around. He was one creepy individual. All of a sudden she had lost her burger craving. She had two more crime scenes to revisit before heading back to the station. She had forgotten about her to-do list. Her mom and Brady would have to wait their turn.

I-40
Little Rock, Arkansas
Wednesday

"You cut me off asshole! You really do have a death wish don't you?"

"Yeah that was me tapping your fender. Where are you going?" The driver of the Dodge floored it.

"I'm in. Let's see what that Dodge of yours has under the hood, *Bama boy!*"

The driver of the Dodge van could not believe the actions of the pickup truck driver. Unnerved he sped up again.

Road Rage followed suit and pulled along side him and looked over and smiled. "Roll down your window and repeat what you just said. I said roll it down and I won't have to keep trying to read your lips!"

Fine, have it your way, both barrels! Kiss your black ass good bye!

Horry County Police Department
The Crime Team
4 PM

Trudy reconvened the team. "Woody, vehicles, what do you have?"

"Too many...and without more to go on, we have potentially hundreds of trucks meeting the vague description from the witnesses and that's just in Horry County. Hell, it'll take the next five days just to make a dent."

"I was afraid of that and Burroughs, anything new?"

"Call me Tim. We might have another suspicious incident in Little Rock. Witnesses saw a truck possibly fitting our suspect's description driving wildly on I-40. Preliminary reports from the Little Rock highway patrol stated that the two vehicles were driving at high speeds, weaving and cutting one another off."

"Is that it?"

"The driver of the Dodge Ram Truck was killed by duel shotgun blast through the driver's side window resulting in a fiery crash."

"So what ties this to our Mister Road Rage?"

"The Dodge Truck's plate was missing. Initially the state trooper who first arrived on the scene thought it had been dislodged by the accident until the screws were found on the ground behind the overturned scorched truck. He reported it as an oddity in his report."

"Did any of the witnesses see the driver of the other truck?"

"No, it happened before daylight this morning and those who saw the behavior of the drivers kept their distance. The driver was an Alabama resident."

"Time?"

"Four forty nine AM which means Road Rage could be somewhere in Mississippi or Alabama by now if he's indeed heading here."

Trudy marked the new accident on the map and connected the last incident with a marker. "I believe this has to be our boy. Is there anything new on forensics, Chestnut?"

"Since we're one happy family here, I'm Shannon. "I'm still digging but I must admit I am impressed. Road Rage somehow keeps it pretty damn clean, no finger prints, no fibers, hairs, odd DNA, nothing. I'm re-examining the weapons, the baseball bat, the cell phone, the drill, the hammer, the microphone."

"Keep me posted."

"One more thing...I saw the coroner's reports on that realty lady and that farmer. We definitely have a connection between those two now."

"Don't leave us hanging," butted in Woody.

"The Coroner located Rachel Winslow's BMW hood ornament shoved deeply up her ass during the autopsy."

"Let me guess. You found that missing metal John Deere logo didn't you?"

"Yep, the same way, buried up Sonny Boggs' butt," finished Shannon.

"Good work but we already knew that. The Sheriff called and filled me in."

"Well it ties right into what our boy did with the cell phone in the Costello murder," stated Woody. "But you knew that too, right?"

"How do you see this Professor Swanson?"

"Well Deputy Wagner, the brutality illustrates that our subject is deeply troubled by a life altering event leading him to commit these heinous murders, his exclamation point. Something extremely traumatic has obviously triggered his hatred for undisciplined drivers."

"You've got the spotlight, Professor, please continue."

"Please refer to me as Doc," he smiled. "It's so nostalgic don't you think, like out of one of those Mickey Spillane crime novels. Did you ever read Spillane's novel, *The Erection Set*? It was quite the classic. His wife, Sherri Malinou, posed nude for the 1972 cover. Sadly they are divorced."

"Interesting but what about our case?"

"A very troubled soul, our Mister Road Rage as you refer to him; much like the characters in Spillane's novels. Most do not realize that Mickey lives here in Murrell's Inlet. He and I have shared exquisite seafood at Oliver's Lodge and swapped many fabulous stories. Did you know he received an Edgar Allan Poe Grand Master Award in 1995?"

"Professor, I mean Doc," she interrupted, "We appreciate the little journey down memory lane but we have less than five days to catch a killer."

"*My work may be garbage but its good garbage*. That's one of Mickey's best quotes. It rivals his saying - *I have no fans. You know what I got? Customers...and customers are your friends*. The man's a genius. We should bring him in as a consultant."

"Maybe next time," she sighed. "Let's take a break. I need a coffee." She really needed something much stronger than java.

She whispered to Woody, "Who did Hank send us, the Nutty Professor? Is he going to send us the Shaggy Dog and Mary Poppins next?"

"A bit eccentric for our little merry band, that's for sure. Did you turn up anything?"

"Cold I must confess, not a warm trail to be found. I don't like our odds in solving this before we have to bring in the Feds."

"Told you fives days was pushing it!"

"We're not out of the gate too quickly I will admit and Hank's not going to be very tolerant if the body count continues to rise."

"Maybe we should let the Bureau take this over." It would take the potential heat off of us. You do realize we're going to get crucified once the media gets wind of this, don't you."

"That reminds me, I ran into Tim Ford at lunch. He peeked over my shoulder before I realized he was there. He took note of my crime folder. He's sort of on to us and it wouldn't surprise me if he tipped off the news media just to get even with us. That's his style."

"That's all we need, another whistle blower like that damn Rocker. We don't have a chance in hell do we, partner?"

"We're on the side of justice, we will prevail."

"Even I recognize a crock of shit when I hear it.

"You can't blame a girl for trying."

"Deputy Wagner, Sheriff Singleton on Line two," paged the dispatcher.

"This can't be good," commented Woody.

Trudy picked up the line. "Yes sir. No sir. We will do our best, sir. I understand, sir. I don't blame you, sir. Goodbye, sir."

"Short and sweet so what's up?"

"Sheriff received an anonymous phone call threatening to expose our investigation to the news media if he didn't resign from his post by noon Friday but not before firing both you and me. He asked if I had any idea who would be threatening us and I sort of lied, told him no. He said if we didn't break this thing open by tomorrow afternoon he would request FBI assistance and tell them what we had discovered."

"Damn," said Woody kicking the metal waste basket.

"He said it would be the only way he could save our butts and steal the caller's thunder," added Trudy. "We now have less than 48 hours."

"Ford, you think?"

"It would be my guess or possibly Lance Rocker. We certainly busted his balls too if you think about it. It really doesn't matter who the culprit is I suppose. We're backed in a corner and we can't blame Hank. He gave us our chance."

"Yeah, we're down by two points, no time outs left, out of field goal range with one second remaining on the game clock and we need a miracle to win the game," barked Woody.

"Thank you, John Madden," responded Trudy. "You don't happen to have a trick play up your sleeve do you?"

"And I don't have a horse shoe up my ass either. I reckon we can go back in there and consult Spillane's biggest fan, *Son of Flubber*, and see if he can offer up insight into our killers' mind."

"We're screwed aren't we?"

"Pretty much, partner."

Wednesday
6 PM

Lance Rocker, emerging from the dark abyss, attempts to resurrect his life. He begins by calling in all favors with connections to the sheriff's department or any other law enforcement agencies that can offer leads to the rash of killings.

On a mission now, he hasn't felt this sort of vigor in a very long time. Being in jail probably had something to do with it. Jenny-Janice has not been forgotten though and remained a driving force in bringing this maniac down. The aspect of fame and fortune ran a close second.

As suspected, he had received his walking papers from Channel 12. The station did not renew his contract and had released him. From here on out, the burden of his expenditures would tug at his personal savings.

Rolling the dice, this would now be an all or nothing shot. If he succeeded he could most certainly cut any deal he wanted but if he didn't he faced an almost certain death in any entertainment or journalistic arena. The stakes had never been higher.

Lance, working at a disadvantage, had no clue the clock ticked against him too. If the story broke and he wasn't the one to break it, the game would be over.

While his sources dug up the dirt, Lance began leisurely researching the phenomena called road rage. To understand the killer he needed to climb inside his head.

Most common offences leading to road rage:

Aggressive behavior 22.1%
Dangerous driving 18.8%
Dangerous overtaking 11.6%
Other 11.1%
Cutting me off 8.8%
Speeding 6.7%
Driving too close 5.8%
Using phone while driving 5.2%
Erratic lane changing 3.9%
Ignoring traffic signals 3.1%
Driving too slow 2.9%

"Interesting stats," remarked Lance out loud. "I guess Mrs. Missouri, using your cell phone ensured you made the hit list."

Bad drivers:

76% male

13% female

"You must have worked much harder to qualify based on the male-female ratio. Can you hear me now?"

Reasons Violent Traffic Disputes Occur

"It was an argument over a parking space..."

"He cut me off"

"She wouldn't let me pass"

A driver was shot to death *"because he hit my car"*

"Nobody gives me the finger..."

A shooting occurred *"because one motorist was playing the radio too loud."*

"The bastard kept honking and honking his horn..."

"He/she was driving too slowly"

"He wouldn't turn off his high beams"

"They kept tailgating me..."

"She kept crossing lanes without signaling -- maybe I overreacted but it taught her a lesson."

"Every time the light turned green he just sat there -- I sat through three different green lights."

Lance thought how often he shared these same sentiments. Reading on...

Weapons Used by Aggressive Drivers

In approximately 4,400 of the 10,037 known aggressive driving incidents, the perpetrator used a firearm, knife, club, fist, feet or other standard weapon for the attack. In approximately 2,300 cases the aggressive driver used an even more powerful weapon -- his or her own vehicle. And in approximately 1,250 cases the aggressive driver used his or her own vehicle *and* a standard weapon like a gun, knife, or club. No information was available for 1,087 of the cases reviewed.

Without question the most popular weapons used by aggressive drivers are firearms and motor vehicles. In 37 percent of the cases a firearm was used; in 35 percent the weapon was the vehicle itself.

Other weapons used by aggressive drivers have included the following, in order of their frequency:

Fists and feet: In hundreds of cases hostile drivers have used their fists and feet to express their displeasure with other motorists.

Tire irons and jack handles are frequently used as weapons, probably because they are readily accessible in most vehicles.

Baseball bats: Mizell and Company recorded over 160 cases in which baseball bats were used to settle traffic disputes. There are, of course, thousands of cases in which baseball bats have been used as weapons in other situations, such as gang fights or street robberies.

Knives used include bayonets, ice picks, razor blades, and swords. A knife is used criminally and violently almost every day by an angry motorist.

Hurled projectiles: In at least 313 cases in the sample angry motorists hurled beer and liquor bottles, the most popular of hurled missiles, rocks, coins, soda cans, and garbage. Aggressive drivers have also thrown a wide range of partially eaten foods, including burritos and hamburgers.

Other clubs: Angry and impatient motorists have used a wide range of weapons to bludgeon one another. These "other clubs" include crowbars, lead pipes, batons, 4x4 timbers, canes (a favorite with the elderly and the disabled), tree limbs, wrenches, hatchets, and, in six cases, golf clubs.

He had gained access to the coroner's information from the related cases. It had cost him a wad but his source had come through for him. Lance began to jot down notes.

Baseball bat - Bradshaw

Golf Club - three Admiral's Quarters murders

Drill - Farmer

Microphone cord - Jenny-Janice

Drowning - the Q-tip driving the golf cart and maybe the realtor lady

Hammer - the Mexican

Tire iron/fist - the Ohio guy

"We have mister versatility here don't we and eleven bodies and why is Ford no longer a suspect? That's the question."

Lance poured a Brandy while he tried to process the road rage statistics and what he now knew about the murders. "Damn, we really do have the Grand Strand *Jack the Ripper* and it will be my case to break, my guaranteed ticket out of here! I've got to zero in on this homicidal maniac before they do."

Amy Wagner Home
Friday
11:14 PM

Trudy had finally conceded, giving up for the night. She had to get some rest. The team had been spinning their wheels. They would regroup at five AM sharp, hopefully with more success after a little down time. Road Rage didn't sleep. He stayed on track in route homeward. She could feel it.

Trudy was sure she'd not be able to rest either but soon as her head hit the pillow she was gone. She woke to her cell phone ringing. Glancing at the digital clock on the night stand, 2:13 AM, she sat on the edge of the bed before picking up her cell trying to clear the cobwebs.

"Hello, what...when...is she...I see...I'm on my way...thank you," she said as she ended the call. *Not now mom, I don't need this right now*! She regretted thinking it the instant the thought filled her head. "I'm on my way."

Amy had suffered congestive heart failure. She had been transferred to the Litchfield Medical Center. From Little River she had a forty minute drive. She decided to use her lights and siren. That would allow her to shave a few precious minutes.

She arrived at two fifty-nine AM, record time. Her mom was on life support, unconscious and in critical condition in the emergency room. She consulted the on duty physician and he didn't offer much hope for recovery saying she could remain in a comatose state for an extended period while on life support. Trudy loved her mom but struggled to prioritize her obligations.

After completing the necessary paperwork, they transferred Amy Wagner to ICU. Trudy sat in a very uncomfortable chair beside her hospital bed holding the lifeless hand of her mother but staring at the hands on the mounted wall clock thinking about the case slipping away, as was her mother.

It finally dawned on her that she should call her sister, Allison in Atlanta. She dreaded doing this any time but especially at 4:07 in the morning but it had to be done. In fifty three minutes she was supposed to meet the team at the police station. They had less than thirty remaining hours to catch a break before she assumed Tim Ford would screw up their chances or Hank would pull the plug.

Tim Ford, that asshole, it had to be him seeking revenge or could it really be Rocker? Three more minutes had passed and she still had not called her sister. The team would be arriving shortly. Should she call Woody first? She stared at her mom and sighed. She had lost control once again and resented the feeling.

Four fifteen AM she sat beside her mom in a daze. She couldn't help her and apparently she couldn't help herself either. She really needed to make those phone calls. The demons were sucking the life out of her and were stealing her soul one slurp at a time. She wanted to scream but she wasn't a screamer. She should call Brady but her body felt like it weighed a ton right now and she simply couldn't muster the energy to move.

She could have cried but she knew no tears would come. She couldn't comprehend why she was acting this way. She didn't normally act like this. She was a control freak. Right now she was simply out of control instead.

A nurse walking into the room snapped her out of the funk she had succumbed to and she grabbed her cell and stepped into the hallway to allow the nurse to do her thing. She called her sister first.

"No, there's nothing you can do here. No, she doesn't know me. She's on life support. The doctor says that's the only thing keeping her alive. I understand. Come when you think you can. No, I'm fine."

Her sister was worse at this sort of thing than she. She didn't hold it against her sister. She hated being here too. She didn't want to watch her Mom die either. Her sister was pretty worthless so the burden fell on the shoulders of the self proclaimed only child, the orphan, the adopted one, the anointed caregiver. Boy, this wasn't a real step up was it, she thought.

At four forty-five AM she made her second call, this one to Woody. He had already arrived at the station. She explained the situation saying she'd be there as soon as possible.

Five-o-five AM she called Brady. She never wanted him to see Amy in this condition. He was on his way. She returned just as the doctor arrived. After a brief examination he said there were no changes in her condition. She remained critical. I need to be with my team thought Trudy.

Road Rage had killed another erratic driver, this one in Columbia County. He was back in South Carolina and less than three hours from home but Trudy didn't have that information yet. The team soon would.

Lance Rocker's Condo
Thursday
5:30 AM

Lance had been unable to sleep and had finally gotten up at three AM. Still he was no closer to becoming the hero. His mind raced as he reviewed the confidential information supplied by his mole. Nothing jumped out at him. Had Sir Lancelot lost his touch?

He tried a new path. Thinking out loud because that's how he did his best thinking, "Let's recap. Tim Ford had been the prime suspect, why?" He clicked the keys on his laptop.

"Ford lost his wife and daughter in the original accident caused by Bradshaw. He had the perfect motive to kill Bradshaw and did attack him once before our Mister Bradshaw ended up dead. So, if Ford didn't kill Bradshaw and the others after snapping, who could have had a similar reason for killing him and the others?"

He thought surely the cops had already played up this angle so he was probably wasting his time. "Humor me Rocker, let's probe this and see where it takes us." He mumbled as his fingers typed vigorously on the computer keys.

At precisely six forty-nine AM, he almost choked on his coffee. "Oh shit, it was there all along! Talking about not seeing the forest for the trees, timber! Okay Lance, take a deep breath. I've got to prove this before I dare go public. I can't afford another show stopper. Time to call in one last favor and I better make this one count because it's for all the marbles! It's time to rock their world!"

Litchfield Medical Center
Thursday
7:35 AM

Brady sat with Trudy in the ICU waiting room. Trudy stared expressionless at the wall on the opposite side of the room. Brady held her hand and watched her with loving and passionate eyes. Trudy never noticed.

"I know you're worried about your mother."

"I should be but strangely I'm not." She blurted it out without thinking about the consequences of her statement. "I mean I'm worried about her but I'm concerned about the case. That almost makes me a worse monster than the murderer we're chasing. Mom could not have picked a worse time to do this. I know it wasn't her choice. How could she have given life to someone like me? I don't deserve to be her daughter."

Brady was so taken by that response he could say nothing. He thought it did seem like a heartless thing to say but he knew how seriously Trudy treated her work. He had certainly played second fiddle too many times in their short relationship. He knew deep down she must love her mother.

Then he said something he didn't even believe he had said, "Go, and find that killer. I'll stay here and keep you posted if anything changes."

This next shock rattled his cage even more when she said, "Okay," kissing him on the cheek and waltzing out the door without a second of hesitation.

Where had Trudy Wagner, the Trudy Wagner, he had grown to love, still loved, gone? She looked like that same wonderful woman but certainly didn't act like her.

Brady walked into the ICU and met Amy Wagner for the very first time. Amy didn't know he was there. He couldn't help but notice how she so resembled an older and much more fragile version of Trudy. He wished he had known her before her illness. He hoped she would hang in there until Trudy returned or her sister arrived. It wasn't in his hands he admitted. He then bowed his head and prayed; something he hadn't done in a very long time.

Horry County Police Department
Crime Team
Thursday
8:40 AM

Trudy glanced at her watch just before she entered the investigation room. Woody, Shannon and Doc sat at the conference table. Tim sat in front of a laptop breaking the silence clicking the keyboard loudly.

"Woody, bring me up to speed." She took charge.

"How's your mama, partner?"

"No change," she answered in almost a mechanical tone. "Brady is with her. Do have anything new?"

"We've had another one, West of Columbia, near Lexington, a young woman."

"It's our boy," spoke up Tim Burroughs. "No witnesses this time but preliminary report from the investigating officer stated they have not identified the victim yet."

"No driver's license or tag," added Shannon Chestnut.

"When?"

Woody clinched his fists. "Enough time for him to be back in Horry County already."

"Any leads on our perpetrator?"

"Doc has put together a profile but nothing really jumps out at us from it," Woody answered as he handed her the folder containing the profile.

"Intriguing individual and you were certainly correct with your original assumptions," spoke up Professor Victor Swanson, aka Doc.

"And that would be?"

"It differs from any serial killer profiles on record," smiled Doc, proud of his role in the investigation. "We certainly have a new brand of murderer challenging our ensemble of worthy investigators."

Her cell phone rang and she almost jumped out of her skin, dropping her coffee cup to the floor. All eyes turned to her, perplexed at her antics. She had her cell phone set on vibrate. "Sorry, I have a call," she explained, expecting it to be Brady breaking news about her mom's death.

"What in the hell do you want?" she shouted then stepped into the hallway.

"Deputy Wagner, I have missed that sexy and charming voice of yours too."

"What do you want Rocker, more apologies? I can put Deputy Anderson on the phone. I'm sure he'd accommodate you."

"I'm sorry about that situation and I've told you, and I have told Anderson, it was entirely my fault but I think I have a break in your serial killer case if you're interested."

"Don't start this crap again," she warned him. "Haven't you learned your lesson about playing junior detective? I certainly have had my fill."

"Give me fifteen minutes and I'll explain. You can be the judge but I don't think you can blow this off. I'm within walking distance of The Trestle. I'll spring for the coffee."

"Rocker, why can't you just butt out of this and let it go?"

"I want to see her killer fry for what he did to her. This is personal, not professional, this time." He told a half truth.

"Fifteen minutes, I decide and you accept my decision."

"That's all I ask..."

"And let me finish that for you," she said. "You want the exclusive if it pans out."

"Only if you insist," he said, as he set the hook and began to reel in his catch.

She peeped back in the room full of sleuths. "I've got to leave, should be back in less than thirty. Any luck on that truck, Woody?"

"I hope that wasn't about your mama."

"No, it was my sister."

"We're narrowing down the truck list. Hopefully we'll have something we can wrap our arms around by mid morning."

She nodded then headed for her appointment with the infamous Sir Lancelot. As she walked the two blocks she contemplated calling Brady but covered the short distance too quickly so she didn't. She didn't really want to call him any way.

Rocker sat at a table in the back. She wanted to trust the supposedly reformed and repentant Lance Rocker but she didn't totally believe the transformation.

"Okay, I'm here." She sat down across the table from him. "The meter is running."

"You are a sight for sore eyes and ravishing as always." He opened with a Rocker-like flirt. "You're not in uniform?"

"Why am I here? Get to it."

"You were onto something with Ford. That was definitely the correct angle to play, but I believe we both agree, Ford cannot be the serial killer. He wouldn't have planted that evidence at his own house."

"I'll give you that one. So what do you have?"

"That original accident, Bradshaw's little screw up I am convinced started the dominos falling so I re-examined the accident."

"Continue...I'm listening. You have eleven minutes."

"Ford lost his wife and kid. There were three other fatalities and two more survivors."

"Clock is ticking."

"Joanna Preston lost her life and her husband Carl survived with no life threatening injuries. They had recently retired and moved here to our fine beach community."

"You're not trying to tell me that you think this retiree is doing the killing." She stood up; had heard enough.

"Sit down, please."

"I think I'll stand."

"You're drawing attention, please sit."

She did.

"He's dead too. He committed suicide shortly after Bradshaw's exoneration. Guess he couldn't take losing his wife then seeing the killer walk."

"Eight minutes."

"Victims four and five were Ace Robertson and Sugar Willis, bikers." He was drawing her back in again.

"Last survivor but in critical condition, Junior "Tank" Patterson had an extended stay in the hospital. He was released shortly before the Bradshaw trial."

"Four and a half minutes..."

"Sugar was his little biker babe and Ace was his cousin. This Tank has quite a rap sheet and is one big son of a bitch, about six foot five and tipping the scales at nearly three hundred pounds."

"Two minutes," she said pointing to her watch. "So what has convinced you this is our man?"

"Let's see. I believe you're looking for a dark colored, late model truck. I'd suggest you run his plates. By the way, he lives in Socastee. I'll make it easy for you. Try Folly Road."

Trudy's mouth became unhinged. "Where'd you get that information?"

"A newsman always has his sources, darling. You should know that. Witnesses said they saw a biker looking dude, right? I'd say the shoe fits our boy Tank."

"Hold on Rocker."

"And seems we have a serial killer that's taken his show nationwide. I'm sure the FBI would be shocked to hear this! Were you planning on telling them anytime soon?"

"You bastard, you wouldn't?"

"Freelancing and surviving, sugar britches," he said, placing his hand on top of hers. "Don't be pissed off at me for making the case easy for you and your team of crime fighters. You should be thanking me," he added, puckering his lips for a kiss.

Trudy dropped her head and rubbed her eyes and face with both hands. This was totally unbelievable.

"And I know about the little theme here. The licenses I have seen but the missing tags, nice touch. He really hates drivers doesn't he?"

"What do you want?" she choked on the words.

"What I always want," he opened the negotiations. "I want to be there when you make the arrest and you've already offered me the exclusive. I think we're good here."

"I want the name of the worthless piece of crap on the force that has leaked this information to you!"

"You know I can't divulge my sources." He smiled now stroking her arm.

Oblivious to his fondling, her mind raced. Which one of her newly formed teammates had betrayed her?

"I also know about the threat. This should get you off the hook for Tim Ford's Friday morning deadline. It wouldn't be the same law enforcement agency without you, Woodrow and the big chief on staff."

She had no grounds to argue. He knew every thing. Rocker should have been a team member instead of that wacky professor. He certainly got better results. She had a killer to apprehend. "Alright, come with me. I'm not letting you out of my sight until we close the deal." Actually her only motive, watch her cohorts' expressions when Rocker walked into the room. If lucky, she'd expose the snitch.

"Perfectly fine with me Sweet Cheeks," he said, giving her a little love pat on her fanny.

She ignored the pat staying focused on the pending next steps. Verify his findings. Verify the truck registration. Verify the accident specifics as described. Confirm this Tank's home address and plan to have him picked up for questioning. Flush out the mole on her team with Rocker's assistance of course.

Horry County Police Station
CSI Team
Thursday
9:30 AM

She and Rocker waltzed into the room. She watched for obvious reactions. No line, no waiting, no suspense, she flushed out snitch immediately.

"Well, hello again Sir Lancelot," greeted the Professor. "We're so privileged to have you as an honorary team member. That is why he is here isn't it my dear deputy? He is quite the Mickey Spillane expert, knows him personally, as do I."

"Professor," she began but was interrupted.

"Doc, my dear," he said. "You're supposed to refer to me as Doc."

"You spilled your guts to Rocker didn't you?"

"Spilling my guts, such a harsh term don't you agree? He had some wonderful assumptions and we merely compared notes. I promised not to divulge our conversation until he contacted you first to expose our killer's identity. After all it was he who cracked the case as Spillane would say if he were here."

Woody clearly befuddled asked, "What's he babbling about?"

"Run the plates for a Junior Patterson, aka Tank. Confirm the vehicle make and his last known address, please. Don't look at me like that, just do it. "Tim, check him for priors.

"And you two gentleman must be detectives Burroughs and Chestnut. Professor Swanson speaks highly of you both," Rocker said, extending his hand. He received no shakers. "Has your maniac scored any more kills since the Arkansas one?"

Neither spoke a word but if looks could kill, the Professor would already be in the ground and buried beside Rocker. Trudy poured a cup of coffee then just stood on the far end of the room assessing the situation. Rocker chatted with the Professor looking like long lost, best friends.

Woody returned with a sheepish look on his face. "The truck closely resembles the description of the one reported by the witness. One Junior 'Tank' Patterson resides over on Folly Road in Socastee. I recognize this name from somewhere."

"Indeed you should," she replied. "Besides Ford, he's the only other survivor from the Bradshaw accident. He lost his girl friend and cousin in that accident. They were all Harley riders."

"Damn! Bite me! It was under our noses the whole time," Woody grumbled.

"Our Tank Patterson has one hell of a rap sheet to boot," added Tim Burroughs. "Assault (three counts), drug possession (two counts), suspected but not convicted of distribution, robbery (one count), suspected racketeering but not convicted, tax evasion (six counts), jumping parole four times, spousal abuse and 43 unpaid parking tickets and this is only his accomplishments in North and South Carolina. He served a total of seventeen years behind bars in five states. We have a real poster boy here. He's a monster by this mug shot and tops the scales at two hundred eighty seven pounds, and a good head higher than anyone in this room."

"Woody, have him brought in for questioning."

"On what grounds?"

"Forty three unpaid parking fines for will work for starters."

"I'll request an arrest warrant. Burroughs, Chestnut, your heard her...bring our Mister Tank in for a round of discussions once you have it."

"I'll brief the sheriff," added Trudy.

"You don't mind if I tag along with the two officers do you? I will be shooting my own footage."

She nodded. "You stay inside the cruiser until the arrest is made! I mean it! Doc, you're officially off the case. Woody, please get him out of my sight."

"Yes sir, I mean ma'am," he said, clicking his heels together and giving her a hile Hitler!

"Burroughs, make sure he stays put even if you have to cuff him to the patrol car."

"Tim and I'll take care of him."

Litchfield Medical Center
10:00 AM

Brady felt a squeeze to his hand and looked up to see Amy Wagner staring him straight in the eyes. She had a little twinkle in her eyes and he sighed, believing she would be just fine. She squeezed his hand a second time, smiled then closed her eyes. A series of alarms erupted. He noticed the monitors to her left had flat lined. Her grip had gone limp.

A doctor and nurse rushed into the room asking him to step into the hallway. Only a few short minutes later they had pronounced her dead. Her heart had just given out.

Brady couldn't help thinking how she had died with a complete stranger by her side but at last she seemed at peace. She would suffer no more. Now he had to make the most dreaded phone call of all. No, this was something he needed to do in person.

Folly Road, Socastee Community
Thursday
12:00 PM

Burroughs and Chestnut, accompanied by Rocker, pulled up in front of the residence of Tank Patterson. The dark blue 1989 Chevy pick-up was parked in the drive along the left side of the small, white, wood framed house.

Two vintage Harleys were parked out front. Tank apparently had visitors. The officers hadn't counted on this development. They paused and discussed should they wait until they leave or proceed as planned. They decided to serve the warrant and bring him in for questioning.

Two uniformed policemen were parked on the opposite side of the street just in case. Burroughs and Chestnut, in plain clothes, crossed the overgrown lawn, grass reaching well above their shins. The front door was solid with a peep hole and a screen long ripped from its hinges. With chipped and peeled paint it matched the rest of the house's exterior, long overdue for a makeover.

Officer Shannon Chestnut, standing directly in front of the entranceway, knocked on the front door. Officer Tim Burroughs stood next to him scanning the perimeter. Chestnut knocked a second time but before he could make an announcement the wooden door exploded into splinters, Chestnut launched ten feet off the porch and onto the front lawn. Failing to follow procedure of standing adjacent to the door had cost him his life. Rocker had caught it all on tape from the backseat of their cruiser not believing what he had just witnessed.

The shotgun blast had launched Detective Shannon Chestnut through the air where he landed lifeless on the front lawn. Tim Burroughs had already spun to the side, leaped off the porch and dropped to the ground. One policeman rushed toward the scene while the second called for backup. Rocker continued to film the melee, trapped in the backseat of the detective's cruiser, unable to breach the locked doors from the inside. He kept his camera rolling thinking prime time.

A yell came from inside, "You're not pinning that shit on me assholes!"

Rocker assumed the voice belonged to Tank Patterson. Windows on both sides of the front door shattered with additional gun fire. The approaching policeman was hit and dropped to the ground. Tank was not alone in the house and his visitors were armed and dangerous. All hell had broken loose.

Rocker whispered from the safety of the backseat, "He's damn serious about not paying those parking fines!"

Horry County Police Department
12:35 PM

Hank Singleton walked into the investigation room, sweating like a mule, perspiration dripping off the tip of his nose and staining the front of his shirt. The big man's hands were trembling. Woody had never seen the sheriff appear to be so shaken and out of sorts.

Hank's gruff voice crackled as he spoke, "We have officers down."

The room became deadly silent, hanging on Sheriff Hank Singleton's next words.

"Socastee, gunfire has erupted while delivering the warrant at the Junior Patterson residence. We have back-up on the way and are blocking off six square blocks. This thing has gone to hell in a hand basket. We underestimated the situation. I think we have our man cornered but he's not alone."

No one asked who the injured might be and hoped it wasn't the worse case scenario. "Woody, let's go," barked Trudy, rushing pass Hank and in route to the scene.

Trudy slammed into Brady as she stormed through the front door of the station. Eye contact told her everything she needed to know. She gave him a quick hug, said nothing and continued on her way.

Brady Pierce just stood there perplexed not knowing what to do next. Unclear now what he had signed up for with Trudy Wagner? It got weirder by the moment. Her Mom was dead and she didn't seem to care. The entire police station appeared in turmoil. An elderly gentleman wearing red suspenders approached.

"Excuse me sir, do you have any idea what's going on?"

"Quite a stir I must say," answered Professor Swanson. "Mickey would paint an exquisite and vivid scene of a shoot out on the pages of his novel."

"Mouse?" asked Brady.

"Spillane, you silly man..."

"So are you telling me there's some sort of police gun battle ongoing right now?"

"Please, call me Doc my good fellow. Yes, I do believe we have the rat trapped in his hole and guns are blazing. I just love that sort of dialogue don't you?"

"Who, where?" asked Brady scrambling for answers.

"The serial killer of course, have you just awakened from your forty year slumber? We're teetering on a historical event here in our grand community. This ranks up there with Dillinger or Bonnie and Clyde. It's fascinating don't you think?"

"Do you know where this historical event is taking place?"

"I do believe the good sheriff said in Socastee. I assisted in breaking the case you know. I am a crime investigator."

Brady heard all he needed to hear and hoofed it to his automobile as more police sirens wailed away. The eccentric professor cocked his head sideways watching the stranger sprint away. "Strange fellow...he certainly seems to be in a hurry. I must call Mickey. This is great material for a novel. Possibly he and I can co-write the next best seller."

Folly Road, Socastee Community
Thursday
1:15 PM

Over thirty county and city law enforcement agents had the area cordoned off and the residential area completely surrounded. Gunfire continued to erupt from at least three separate locations within the house. With two of their own down, police returned fire with vengeance.

Burroughs had managed to flee to safety. Chestnut's bloodied body remained in plain sight on the lawn. The wounded officer had been dragged to safety and now received medical assistance. His wounds while serious were not life threatening. One medic had been winged during the rescue but the bullet had passed cleanly through her forearm. Rocker now filmed from across the street and out of gun shot range, savoring every moment.

Woody and Trudy arrived unprepared for the spectacle unfolding before them. All the local television and radio affiliates were present. The circus had come to town. Another deputy waved them over.

"Woody, I just received a call from the station. They've had to rush Hank to the emergency room. They think he's suffered a heart attack," reported the balding rather big boned deputy named Jameson.

"That explains all that sweating and pale appearance," answered Woody. "Keep us posted on his condition, Officer Jameson."

Spurts of gunfire continued from both sides. The wood on the house resembled Swiss cheese.

"Catch us up to speed Mack," said Woody, addressing Sergeant Mack White, twenty three years on the force.

"We have at least three shooters inside. We're running the plates of those two bikes parked out front."

Trudy, rubbing her hands through her hair, asked, "How did this get started?"

"I can answer that," said Tim Burroughs.

Trudy asked Tim was he was okay, noticing blood splattered on his clothing.

"I'm good. It's Shannon Chestnut. He's dead. That's his body on the front lawn over there."

"What happened?"

"We approached the house following routine procedure except for one critical error. Shannon should not have been standing directly in front of that door. He knocked and they opened fire though the door, took him out clean with the first shot. I think they knew we were coming. Someone tipped them off. They were ready. We weren't."

"Rocker," exclaimed Woody. "He'll do anything for theatrics!"

"Couldn't have been Rocker," explained Burroughs. "He was locked up snug as a bug in the back of our cruiser and didn't make any phone calls on the drive here. I had confiscated his cell phone to keep him on the up and up."

"Have you tried to contact those inside?"

"They won't stop shooting long enough for us to try. It reminds me of one of those scenes where the cops won't take them alive."

"Are there any hostages?"

"Not that we can tell."

Mack interrupted. "We have identified the owners of those two Harleys, real bad asses. They make Patterson look like an Eagle Scout."

"Call a cease fire," commanded Trudy. "I don't care how much they shoot, don't return any more fire. Let's try to negotiate removing Chestnut's body."

Mack hoisted his pants and asked, "Who put you in charge?"

"Just do it, Mack," added Woody. "Sheriff assigned us to a special task force and this is related to our case."

Mack gave the command then stated, "You know we don't have a chance in hell of talking them out now don't you? They've killed a police officer."

And possibly forty other innocent people thought Trudy. "Who said anyone really wants to see them walk away from this?" This took her by surprise realizing what she had just said. Luckily only Burroughs and Woody had heard her little slip.

She scrambled to explain. "Someone wanted them or at least Tank dead. That's why they were warned ahead of time. I don't yet understand why but I do believe in the premise." That was a half truth. She really wanted them dead too. She wanted this nightmare to be over.

Brady stood four blocks away with hundreds of rubber-neckers, each trying to catch a glimpse of the gun battle. He finally sat down on the curbing, thoughts returning to Amy. He had no marketing strategy for this mess, for Trudy, or for their questionable future. Numb, he just existed in this new world he had stumbled into and thought about how his life had once been so simple.

Tank Patterson Residence
2:50 PM

Fox and CNN, through local affiliates, now stayed deadlocked on the unfolding saga. Like it or not, this had become national news. Shots of Chestnut's lifeless body on the front lawn played over and over. The department had only released snippets mentioning this had been a routine arrest for traffic violations gone badly. No newsperson but Rocker knew the serial killer ramifications.

Horry County's finest had been unsuccessful in their attempts to talk with the wild bunch still holding up in the four room house. The shooters inside had not allowed anyone near Chestnut's body. With Hank out of the picture, Woody and Trudy had co-chaired the command. The officers trusted Woody but they didn't really know her.

"You know we're going to have to take them out don't you?" stated Trudy.

"Yeah, I know it, partner. The rest of these officers know it too. They can smell it."

"Let's pull everyone back but law enforcement. We don't need any cameras or media close enough to see what we're about to do. That includes those circling copters."

"What about Rocker?"

"He has enough footage. Get him out of there."

"We'll hit them with everything we've got. And what's left of them, we'll read their rights, book them and then send them to the morgue," stated Woody sarcastically.

Another burst of fire suddenly erupted from inside the house followed by one single shot. All went silent. Woody and Trudy made eye contact, both confident of the meaning of that last volley.

"Clear the media and tear gas it then we go in," said Trudy. "And you can let Rocker stay. We need this documented now."

"CAOA," answered Woody. "Cover All Our Asses."

"Is there any news on the sheriff?"

"He's in ICU but stable."

"How about your mama..."

"Deceased..."

"Sorry...this has to be tough."

"Don't be. I'm not. She's better off. What she had wasn't a life."

"And Payne Stewart..."

"He's MIA for good maybe, and it's entirely my fault. He was with her when she died. I can't seem to do anything right lately. Let's do this!"

"For Chestnut, time to remove the garbage," nodded Woody.

Horry County Police Department
Thursday
9:11 PM

Trudy sat at Sheriff Singleton's desk behind closed doors, alone, replaying the day's events and trying to make the puzzle pieces fit. She wasn't having much luck. She had never liked working puzzles.

The three shooters were dead, as was her mom. The preliminary investigation pointed to Tank killing his two accomplices with an automatic weapon then turning a pistol on himself, one shot under his chin. Best she could figure the other two weren't going to give up. Tank Patterson had possibly had enough and ended it on his terms.

They had found enough weapons inside the house to have instigated a small war. Officers had discovered over a hundred thousand dollars in cash, several pounds of marijuana, a substantial amount of cocaine and a fully functional methamphetamine lab in one bedroom.

Woody, Burroughs and she had searched the premises thoroughly but had found no evidence that linked Tank Patterson to any of the road rage homicides, no vehicle license plates or drivers' licenses, nothing. Could Rocker have been wrong again? It was his MO.

Sheriff Hank Singleton remained in serious but stable condition. She had not talked to Brady yet nor viewed her mom's body. She had talked to both the medical and the assisted care facilities.

Lance Rocker sat outside with Burroughs waiting patiently to talk to her. She still wasn't sure if Tim Ford planned to keep his promise in the morning and blow the lid off this mess, if indeed Ford was the blackmailer.

She needed a stiff drink. She needed Brady. Refocusing, she began playing the *what if* game.

What if Tank and his henchmen were not involved in the road rage string of killings? If they found no evidence to link them that would mean the killer or killers were still out there and most likely back in town. What if Ford made good on his promise? This case would become a political nightmare and career buster.

What if Ford didn't report it? The Sheriff was in serious shape so maybe that would go a ways in satisfying the revenge factor. But then he wanted Woody and me off the force too.

What if Brady doesn't want anything else to do with me? After all, I deserted him leaving him with mom, a perfect stranger, and she died on his watch, not mine. I'm such a worthless and selfish bitch she thought. What is my sister going to think or will she even care? She'll probably be glad it's over too. I guess we're both orphans now.

We have a mountain of dead bodies and plenty of concerned family and friends deserving an answer. I have nothing to offer. I certainly miss Columbus right now. This is either going to launch my career or end it. There's no middle ground. Someone knocked on the door and she turned to face the music.

"It's Burroughs. Rocker wants to talk to you. He's getting quite impatient."

Leaning back in the sheriff's cushy leather chair she told Burroughs to send Rocker in. She figured she might as well get this over with and see what the bastard wanted now.

"Deputy Wagner, you look like you've been rode hard and put up wet, and I can't claim responsibility. That alone saddens me."

"You never lose your edge do you? Well, maybe that one time when Janice Anderson was found dead outside your condo. I'm sorry. That was very inappropriate. I shouldn't have said that. I apologize."

"Accepted, so does this close your serial killer extravaganza?"

"I'm surprised. You typically know before us. Losing your touch?"

"It's tough to tap my sources when you have me under lock and key. What was the other two thug's tie to Tank Patterson?"

"Oh, so now you're part of the investigating team and we're supposed to chat openly about the evidence. I think not," she said, leaning on the desk with her elbows and rolling her eyes.

"Deal, remember, I get the exclusive on this."

"You've got plenty but before you cash in your check, I'm going to ask you to hold off a little longer. Things have become complicated."

"Explain complicated."

"We haven't completed searching through the evidence yet and I don't intend having this case scrutinized until we have it open and shut."

"So deputy you're asking me to sit on this powder keg until someone else puts two and two together and scoops me? I don't think so!"

"I figured you would say that," she said pressing the button on the intercom. "Burroughs, front and center, please."

Burroughs entered immediately and eyed Rocker suspiciously.

"Deputy Burroughs, I'm placing Mister Rocker in protective custody until further notice. Please make him comfortable."

"You're protecting me from whom?"

"From me for starters..."

"That's bullshit. You're hiding something!"

"And tag, you're it...your turn to seek. And deputy, temporarily relieve him of his camera equipment, cell phone or any other communication devices including that little pocket recorder of his. You may give him a note pad and pen. He'll have plenty of time to write his memoirs."

"You know you won't get away with this."

"I just did. Take very special care of our guest and get him out of my sight."

"This isn't over, sweet cheeks; not over by a long shot."

"I'm sure it isn't. Enjoy your stay."

Her cell rang. Brady's name appeared on the caller ID. It rang a third time before she answered. "Guess I sort of deserted you didn't I?"

"Are you alright?"

"I'm just hunky dory. Mom is dead. One of my officers is dead. Three suspects are dead and Sheriff Singleton is fighting for his life with a bad ticker. Lance Rocker is in lock-up and not guilty of anything but being a thorn in my side. It couldn't be any better. Oh yeah, and a serial killer is probably still out there stalking his next victim. Life is a beach."

"Have you been to the medical center yet?"

"I haven't worked that in to my agenda yet."

"I guess I'm on your short list again too."

Now that stung Trudy even though she knew it had been a fair and truthful statement.

"Are you at home?"

"I'm still at the station tidying up this mess."

"What say I come by and pick you up? We'll go by the medical center so you can do the needful. Afterwards I'll prepare you dinner, draw you a bath and put you to bed."

"So I guess we're still dating?"

"Only if that's what you want."

"Guess you're on your way then."

"Be there in ten minutes..."

"I'll be waiting."

Her phone rang again while she still held it. She almost wet her pants taken by surprise. "Hello, this is Trudy."

"It's me, Woody. We just did another sweep of the Patterson house."

"And..."

"And nothing...I'm beginning to think he's not our man."

"I agree. I've been thinking."

"I hate it when you do that."

"Hear me out. Hank's out of commission for now and besides you, Burroughs and me, no one knows about the cross country romp, except for Rocker and I have him in lock-up."

"Lock up?"

"Long story but it was necessary, trust me."

"Don't forget about our nutty professor."

"Okay, so we may still have a minor problem. Follow me. Let's say Ford, or whoever our caller is, doesn't blow the whistle in the morning."

"We've bought some time."

"Scary, you're sounding more like me, partner."

"Partners begin having that affect on one another. Okay, so we stay mum for how long?"

"Until we apprehend Road Rage..."

"Guess that's our best hope."

"It's our only hope."

"You do realize Hank is going to crap a brick when he finds out."

"Yeah, it stinks I know."

"Okay, I'm heading home. I'll meet you bright and early, Wagner."

"See you in the morning Deputy Anderson and God help us if we don't find that murdering bastard real soon."

"And again, I'm sorry about your mama."

She mustered up a nod and a smile. *I'm sorry too.*

Intersection of Carolina Forest and
Highway 501, Conway
Thursday
10:00 PM

The black 1991 1500 Chevy Silverado with dark tinted glass slowed at the intersection from the west. The driver watched traffic approaching the light just ahead.

The driver almost began crying, reflecting. *My world ended right here. I hate this damn place; both of them dead and for what, careless driving. What the hell am I supposed to do now? It doesn't matter where I go; you maniacs just won't leave me the hell alone! You made me what I am! You made me do it! I didn't want to but you made me just the same!*

Anger quickly replaced remorse. "Damn it! There you go! Ran right through that red light and you never looked. You never even slowed down. You just don't get it do you? I'm here to make it right!

Speeding up, Road Rage pursued the traffic violator for no other reason than to protect people involved in the near miss. The meth and pain pills worked their magic once again, righting the wrong, clouding everything else.

Brady Pierce Beach Front Home
Friday
1:03 AM

"She died peacefully," Brady said as he poured her a second glass of Bourbon on the rocks.

"And with a total stranger thanks to me..."

"You look just like her you know," he said, trying to comfort her. "You have your mom's eyes."

"I should have been there," she said, turning up her glass almost killing the contents in one gulp. "I screwed up."

"It couldn't be helped," he tried to reassure her.

"Oh, it could have been helped. I just did what I always do, prioritize and justify, putting me and my needs first. I should have been there with her, Brady. I miss her. Before the sickness, she was my mom. The woman who died was almost a stranger."

"So what now?"

"I make love to you then I bury my mom. I'll not make the same mistake with you. I've neglected you long enough."

"We'll lay your mother to rest."

She nodded. "Then I catch a serial killer but not before I check on the Sheriff. You first then I'll work on the pecking order of the others."

"You prioritize well in my book...another drink?"

"More you," she answered. "And fill her up!"

"Yes ma'am."

Horry County Police Department
Friday
6:15 AM

Trudy sipped her third cup of coffee while she flipped through the folder on the desk. Obviously they had missed something and she intended to find the missing puzzle piece. She really did hate puzzles but she so enjoyed solving crimes. Go figure.

Detective Tim Burroughs walked into the room with a cup of StarBucks in one hand and a powdered Krispy Kreme Donut in the other. A ring of white coated his mouth. He greeted her then wiped his mouth with his sleeve. Computer Geek was such a slob.

"Good morning detective. I need you to access that computer of yours and Google me up some information about the Bradshaw accident."

"The Edward Bradshaw murder?"

"No, the original Bradshaw accident."

"Anything in particular?"

"Survivors."

"We only have one and that would be Tim Ford. Everyone else connected to that accident is now dead."

"No, I'm looking for family members, survivors of those killed or injured."

"I'm not following you."

"Just humor me, please. I still believe the key to this lies in the Bradshaw accident. We're missing something. I just can't put my finger on it."

"I guess Woody told you we didn't find any..."

"License plates or driver's licenses in Tank Patterson's residence...yeah, he did but today is a new beginning. My gut tells me this might just be our lucky day." Her gut really felt sour and knotted from too much whisky and Brady and no sleep.

"Do me one more favor. Look in on Lance Rocker. And Burroughs, wipe your mouth and not on your sleeve this time."

She braced for the next shoe to drop, that dreaded phone call from Tim Ford instigating a media feeding frenzy. While she waited, she called the hospital to get the latest update on Hank's condition, stable but not out of the woods. He had undergone a triple bypass.

She thought how she had totally botched this investigation by allowing her emotions and personal challenges to interfere. She vowed to not make that mistake again. She had regained control of her life and that was vital for a control freak.

She still had arrangements to complete for her mom's funeral. Allison would be in town later today so she could hand that off to her. She'd try to ease Brady off the burner until this case was solved. That would be a tough one because she needed him more than she cared to admit.

Refocusing, this was her case to solve. She had to take full advantage of Hank being incapacitated. His condition could change at any time which meant he would surely bring in the Bureau. She had a temporary reprieve. There was no way in hell she'd allow someone else to break this crime of the century, not on her watch.

What did she know about the Bradshaw collision? Tim Ford's wife and daughter had been killed and he underwent tough rehab. He had tried to kill Bradshaw once. Did he try and succeed killing him that second time. Was he Road Rage? Conflicting incident dates threw a monkey wrench in that theory.

Tank Patterson had lost his girl friend, Sugar Willis and cousin, Ace Robertson. Badass that he was, evidence, or lack thereof, indicates he didn't go off the deep end and commit these homicides. That theory was probably history. He was now dead by his own hands so he might still be the one if they could just find those mementos from the killings and prove it.

That left Joanna Preston, dead at the scene and her husband Carl who survived but sadly he had recently committed suicide. Road Rage had killed after Carl's death so he couldn't be our suspect she surmised.

So who do we have left? Tim Ford just won't go away. He had been the prime suspect from the beginning, low hanging fruit, too obvious. That just didn't seem possible. Maybe that's what he was counting on. She was running herself in circles.

Woody says none of them owns a pickup matching the type reported by witnesses. So, what do I take away from this? Am I so damn sure the key is the Bradshaw case? I am. It all just feels right she thought but I don't know why.

Burroughs returned. He still had that white powdered crap in one corner of his mouth. She motioned him over and wiped it off with her thumb. "Do you have anything for me?"

"Well, Lance Rocker is madder than a fire ant mound under attack by a lawn mower. He wants to know when you plan to release him and he's threatening law suit."

"Well, I'd be foolish to release a person threatening to sue us wouldn't I?"

"You can't keep him there forever you know?"

"Forever is such an unfair assessment. I don't think solving this case will take quite that long. Anything else?"

"I finished my preliminary research on the victims' next of kin."

"That quickly, I'm impressed!"

"Hey, that's why I'm the computer guy, right?"

"Let's hear it."

"I started with Tank Patterson. Mother is deceased, seventeen years, and there is no record of a father. He had one brother, killed in Vietnam. He has an ex-wife from three years ago, last known address in Tennessee, no children and no other immediate relatives."

"Tim Ford, one older sister living in Florida, married once, widow with three teenage children. Her husband died of cancer three years ago. Ford's parents are still alive and reside in Charlotte, North Carolina. His father is a prominent executive with Bank of America and his mom is a fifth grade school teacher. There's an abundance of cousins scattered up and down the eastern seaboard. Ford's wife's parents are deceased and she too has one younger sister, unmarried and living in Asheville, North Carolina."

"What else?"

"Carl and Joanna Preston were both retired from cushy government jobs, relocated here from New Jersey to enjoy their retirement. That didn't go so well as we all know. They have only one child, a son, one Joseph Randle Preston, formerly a resident of San Diego, California, never married and moved here to live with his parents after they retired. Apparently he's a seasoned construction worker. Good place for him to move with all the building activity." He finished, handing her the entire printout.

She reviewed the report jotting down notes. Burroughs watched her intently trying to make out her chicken scratch. After a couple of minutes of frowning and scribbling she looked up from the printout and asked, "Where is this Joe Preston now?"

"Like I said, his last known address was his parent's home in Pawley's Island. That's as far as I've gotten."

"Burroughs, locate him. Find out where he works and what he's been up to since his parent's deaths and find out what he drives. If he's still in the area, I'd like to question him."

"Will do but I thought that we agreed you'd call me, Tim."

"Hindsight, too personal ...let's keep it professional. I've decided that I don't do personal well." She thought about Shannon Chestnut...no more first names.

"Shannon," he said, verifying he understood.

"Detective Chestnut, he will be missed." She glanced at her watch, almost eight AM. Would Ford make good on his promise if Ford was indeed the culprit?

Burroughs nodded and departed to begin his newly assigned task. He wished he processed data more like a full fledged detective and not like a computer geek. Maybe working with Anderson and Wagner would transform him into a real cop to be reckoned with. He could only hope.

Trudy's cell phone rang. Caller ID indicated Woody Anderson.

"Yeah, Woody, what you got?"

"Are you sitting?" he asked then paused before saying, "We have another one."

"Where?"

"Here."

Platinum Gentleman's Club
Seaboard Street, Myrtle Beach
Friday
8:30 AM

"Bartender from the club noticed her car still in the lot this morning and found her body in the backseat," recapped Woody.

"She was a dancer?"

"She was stripper. There is a difference."

"I see the license plate is missing on her late model Toyota Corolla."

"Seems our boy has kicked it up a notch, again," stated Woody, pointing to the young hard body's face.

"Is that what I think it is?"

"Best I can tell, but we'll know for sure once the coroner removes it. It's definitely a driver's license and I suspect it belongs to her."

Wedged between the young blonde's lips and gums was what appeared to be a driver's license. It reminded Trudy of how she and her friends would take a section of orange peel and wedge it in their mouths. It resembled a clown smile. "Any witnesses?"

"Nope and something tells me they won't line up to admit they were here and saw anything. This is a titty-bar, so don't hold your breath."

"Humor me and call it a strip club. How old was she?"

"Nineteen and she had two kids and a live in boyfriend who managed her career."

"A pimp you mean."

"Humor me, partner and call him an agent," smiled Woody. "Owner said she didn't report to work last night at eleven as scheduled so we have a good idea when it happened."

"Are you thinking what I'm thinking? She pulled some stupid driving stunt on the way to work and pissed off Road Rage."

"That would be my guess. Are you ready for the real kicker? She lives in a condo off 501 in the Carolina Forest community."

"Isn't that the same place as the Bradshaw accident? He's returned to the scene of the crime. I knew there was a tie to that Bradshaw accident!"

"Maybe he's ready to be caught."

"Could be...could be it's time for him to hang it up, dead or alive?"

"Well, we can certainly help him with that decision can't we."

"Call us the grand strand *make a wish foundation*," she said with devious smirk.

"Open for business, twenty four-seven " he added.

"Partner, let's go apprehend us a serial killer." She patted Woody on the back. "I'll meet you back at the station to regroup."

"I told the on scene officer in charge to keep us in the loop. By the way, did the crap hit the fan yet?"

"So far, so good. Ford, and I do believe that's where the call came from, has not acted on his threats yet. That alone is damn strange to me."

"Maybe it was all just a big tease. He's got a sick sense of humor and probably just wanted to mess with us."

She shrugged. She didn't believe it had been a bluff. Something impacted his decision and she planned to find out what. She hoped Burroughs had located one Joseph Randal Preston. She needed to investigate someone, having grown tired of chasing phantoms.

Waffle House
Ocean Highway, Pawley's Island
Friday
9:45 AM

"What can I get you?" asked Boo, the middle aged, pot bellied, spiked haired waitress with the tongue piercing and probably other piercings you didn't even want to know about.

"V8, large glass and no ice, please."

Boo returned with the glass of juice. "Where you been? I haven't seen you in here in a while."

"Lost my job and been doing a little traveling to clear my head to figure what I'll do next."

"Have you decided?"

"On what I plan to do?"

"No silly, on what you want to eat." She giggled and retrieved the pencil from her hair. "Don't have one of them cream milk shakes. I had two last night and let me tell you, they had me running to the John every few minutes, cleaned me out like a handful of Correctol."

"I'll have country ham, three eggs over easy, hash browns with onions and a toasted cheese sandwich."

"Well, your appetite is doing just fine...more juice?"

"Yeah, you can bring me a refill with my order."

"It sure was terrible them finding that young dancer dead this morning over on Seaboard. I hear she left two little ones behind. Probably one of them dope heads or homeless people killed her is what I figure. What you think?"

"What do I think? I guess I think we don't always know the circumstances behind this sort of thing. Shit just sometimes happens and who can say whose fault it might have been."

"But, she was murdered. It was the murderer's fault," she said, making a screwy face, surprised by his comments.

"Could be she brought it on herself and if there were no witnesses, who are we to pass judgment one way or the other? Circumstances determine the outcome."

"That's the strangest thing to say. Let me get that meal of yours turned in to Butch in the kitchen," she said, walking off mumbling to herself.

"**Justice served.**" *The bitch ran the red light. She almost took out those poor folks ahead of me. She orphaned her two little ones, plain and simple, circumstances instigated by her. The thoughtless pole humper did it to herself, end of friggin story. People just don't get it. I'm saving lives by ridding the roadways of those who have no business there. I'm an American hero. One day they'll understand. I'm Road Rage.*

Horry County Police Station
10:35 AM

"You know Wagner...we're not going to be able to keep this case to ourselves too much longer don't you?"

"Yeah, we do have an impressive pile of bodies. Selfishly, I wanted us to crack it but realistically I know we're not optimizing the resources that could possibly assist us with this investigation. That's not fair to the families of the victims."

"Hank gave us a chance and he put his ass on the line for us so I think it's time to call in the dogs and do what's right."

"You're probably right but damn, I think we're close," she exclaimed, pounding her fist on the table.

"We really need to make that call to the feds. I hate it as much as you do but who are we fooling? This is a national case, not just little old Horry County," Woody said, as he stood up cracking his knuckles.

"You know we're going to get crucified by the press, the Governor and the Bureau don't you? We'll be damned lucky to still keep our badges!"

"We knew that all along. You want me to make the call?"

"I got us into this. I'll contact them."

In burst Burroughs through the door skidding sideways on the slick tile floor making an entrance like Kramer from Seinfeld waving a printout at them. "You're going to just love this," he screamed, almost too girlie for Woody's taste.

"Catch your breath son," said Woody.

"The truck, I think I have our truck!"

"Where, Who?"

"Pawley's Island and it belongs to none other than Joseph Randal Preston. A black 1991 Chevy Silverado and I did some hacking and guess what?" Burroughs could hardly contain himself.

"On with it," barked Woody.

"Our buddy, Joe, uses his Capitol One card for every thing. He probably cashes in on those reward points. I have one and ..."

"And get on with it," Woody interrupted.

"He took a little trip to the west coast recently and I can place him in the proximity of most of the cross country homicides, simple as connecting those dots on your map! That happened after he was fired from his construction job, the same construction company that released Tim Ford the very same day. And, the Walter Ozolins' assault happened about an hour after they both got canned, according to their foreman."

"And there's more. Preston was pumping gas on 501 last night at 10:23 just west of the Carolina Forest. The station is located at the high school intersection just across from CVS, same CVS I use for my allergy meds. That places him in close proximity of the residence of Jennifer Wilson. She could have been in route to the strip club and crossed paths with him."

"Good work Tim," shouted Trudy, giving him a big old hug.

"I guess we're back on unprofessional terms, huh," he grinned.

"Yes we are Tim. The next Starbucks and donuts are on me."

Woody rolled his eyes. "I hate to break up your little foray of law enforcement bonding but do we know where our new suspect is right now?"

"No sir," answered Tim. "I figured you two needed to do some of the work."

Trudy asked, "How about a picture or description?"

"Not yet but I'm working on it."

Woody patted Burroughs on the back. "We ought to bring him in for questioning; don't you think and get a search warrant for his parent's house? And that means we venture into Georgetown County so we'll have to bring in the local boys there."

"Alright, let's take a breather," said Trudy. "We need to do this by the book but we will limit our information sharing with the Georgetown police. We certainly can't afford any more screw ups or leaks now."

"We certainly can't," said a voice at the doorway. "Count me in teammates and mums the word!"

Trudy couldn't believe her eyes. "Rocker, who in the hell let you out and how long have you been standing there?"

"I get that one phone call Sugar Hips and my lawyer did a wonderful job springing me don't you think? You really didn't have a leg to stand on but you knew that didn't you? I've heard enough to allow you to include me in on your merry band of crime fighters. As previously promised I'm part of this through your apprehension of the most notorious serial killer this county has ever seen. I have earned the exclusive."

Trudy sighed. She had to hand it to him. He was damn persistent.

"I can be persuaded to stifle my plans to sue if you cut me in on this, darling."

And just that quick, Woody landed a right cross sending Lance Rocker spinning to his knees. "You should have caught that on camera Wagner! Damn, it was a Kodak moment too!"

"Welcome back to the team smartass, but you play it by our rules or I'll feed you to the gators!"

"Are you sure about this?" asked Woody, as he pondered popping Rocker a second time.

"Yeah, I'm sure. We'll allow him, as originally planned, to document this historical event but, as before, Rocker, you break the story when we say you can."

"I would have it no other way, Princess. Do I get deputized this time?" he asked, still rubbing his red, splotched, swelling left eye and cheek.

"You know what? That might not be such a bad idea."

Both Woody and Tim did a double take on that comment. What the hell was she thinking?

She was thinking once deputized, he'd be in for the ride...good, bad or ugly. He'd reap the benefits of success or go down in flames with the rest of them. Trudy felt that would keep him in check.

She rounded up a badge and made short work of the swearing in process, and just for good measure, she had Woody film the event. She even presented Officer Rocker with a regulation issue revolver and holster, minus the bullets of course.

Trudy glanced at her three partners in crime and said "Okay F Troop, let's determine our next move and put an end to the bleeding."

The Preston Residence
Pawley's Island
Friday
1:05 PM

Joe Preston packed two large suitcases for another road trip. This time he would not be returning to South Carolina. The Palmetto State offered nothing but bad memories. Both parents now dead, the only child's world had transformed into a living hell. He wasn't completely sure he could outrun his demons but staying here served no purpose. Unfortunately running had not worked so well but what other choice did he really have?

His inheritance would last him for quite a few years if he didn't get reckless with it. His folks had left him well off, their lives cut short, unable to enjoy the fruits of their work all because of Edward Bradshaw. The roadways were filled with Bradshaw types.

Joe Preston knew he wasn't a crazy maniac. He certainly was no serial killer. He didn't venture out every day with an urgent lust to kill just to satisfy some insane need. He was simply a self appointed avenger ridding mankind of the sorry asses wreaking havoc on the roadways.

His mission, balance the checkbook and rewrite the statistics. For every death or close call as a result of inconsiderate *all about them* drivers, he intended to tip the scales back in favor of the innocent travelers.

Those driving responsibly would be in no danger, at least not from him. For those so arrogant as to abuse the privilege, vengeance would be his and had been countless times already. He should have regrets but he didn't.

Joe was not troubled by what he had done. He felt no blame for his actions. He had done what had to be done. He still mourned his parents' deaths. He feared that this would not go away easily. The drugs helped numb those feelings but offered no permanent relief in healing the pain he endured because of Edward Bradshaw and others like him.

He took no pleasure in revoking the offenders' driver's licenses and confiscating their vehicle tags. These were not trophies. He was simply doing what the DMV should be doing to people that had no business operating an automobile in the first place. Sadly, too many people still chose to drive without a license or a plate, so he had taken it a step further to ensure this didn't happen. He revoked their lives.

He drew comfort in the thought that the American population would one day recognize him with the likes of the Dark Knight or Superman, and he too would be a folklore hero. He even resurrected a hero persona and dialogue when on the job and ridding the world of evil. His alter ego neither talked nor acted in any way like him.

This was not crazy talk. This world revolved around true heroes. Hell, the world needed his kind. It would be a better place in the wake of his do good deeds. He wondered if he should recruit a sidekick. Most prominent heroes had a reliable side kick. He'd give it some thought on his road trip.

Joe did like the name that Channel 12 newsman, Sir Lancelot, had given him during one of his reports. Every good hero deserved a good hero's name. Road Rage, it did have that certain ring to it. It certainly beat the original name he had given himself, The Highwayman. Road Rage oozed respect and was self explanatory just like Mel Gibson's *Road Warrior* character.

Continuing his packing, he retrieved the L.C. Smith double barrel shot gun that had belonged to his daddy. His daddy had been an avid hunter so ammunition, if needed, would be no problem. An abundance of assorted birdshot, buckshot and slugs were boxed up in the gun cabinet.

He would take the 30-06 scoped deer rifle too. Unfortunately his daddy had no hand guns. He would have probably been better at using one of those. He really hated using the fire arms but sometimes there really wasn't any other way. It didn't make any sense leaving them behind for strangers to confiscate. They did after all belong to him now.

Both guns were loaded and ready for use, just the way his daddy liked to keep them. He had never fired either except when he had to reconcile a driving offense. Hunting had never really appealed to him. He didn't even own a gun and how he used them really shouldn't be considered hunting.

He really missed his mother. He was a self proclaimed mama's boy. He never denied that. She had let him get away with murder all his life. He chuckled to himself when he realized what he had just thought.

She had been the buffer between him and his daddy. She stood up for him when he bucked his daddy about going hunting. He had no such protector now because of Bradshaw and his kind.

The bags now packed, he stood on the back deck overlooking the marsh and drank one of the three Milwaukee's Best beers he had found in the refrigerator. He made a toast to his parents and walked back through the house, pausing to take a long look at the avenger's reflection in the floor to ceiling mirror.

Standing six foot, six and almost three hundred pounds, he could strike fear in most any would be adversary. Truth be known, he was really just a big old pussy cat or had been until Road Rage had arrived in his life.

Thirty three years old, he had never been married, had never even been close. He stared at his face. He wasn't particularly handsome but he wasn't a toad either. If not for his girth, he would have easily blended in any crowd unnoticed. He had never tried to be a standout.

Since being let go from his job, he had allowed his brown hair to reach shoulder length and his beard was full and untrimmed, almost too gnarly. It made him appear more vicious than he really was. He suited his Road Rage persona.

Both forearms were tattooed, a result of a wild hair he had when he owned a Harley some ten years back, just a phase he had gone through. He regretted having done that but the tattoos did contribute, along with his size, to having that badass biker look. It had a tendency to attract the slutty biker babes and he often cashed in on that notoriety, but not since his parents had died. Sex no longer lured him. If it had, he would have done the little stripper last night. She was young and hot but stirred nothing in his loins.

He took one last look at his folks' retirement home then closed the door behind him. He would never set foot in it again, his choice. He probably should sell it and maybe some day he would but now wasn't that time.

His old Chevy had one of those lockable flat fiberglass covers on the bed so there was no fear of his belongings blowing out or getting wet. He pushed the duffle bag containing the driver's licenses and tags toward the cab before loading his suitcases and the guns.

A small six pack cooler containing the two remaining beers and a 20 ounce bottle of Diet Pepsi rested on the seat beside him in the cab. He had no real reason for drinking diet sodas. They certainly had no impact on him trying to lose weight. He just didn't like the sugary taste of regular sodas.

Joe Preston had no particular destination in mind. He'd just drive and see where it took him. His trip to California had purpose. He had retrieved some personal belongings in a rental self-storage unit.

He might consider driving northwest, maybe even up to Alaska. He had always wanted to go there. Traffic should be much better in the remote wilderness areas. He could become one of those real mountain men. He certainly had the looks for it. He turned the key and allowed the engine to warm.

Highway 17 South
Friday
3:40 PM

Converging on the Preston residence, Woody led the procession, followed by Trudy then Tim and Lance in the third cruiser. Trudy had contacted Georgetown law enforcement informing them that they wished to investigate Joseph Preston for his possible involvement in a hit and run. Stretching the truth had seemed like routine procedure in this case.

Georgetown deputies arrived at the scene ten minutes ahead of Horry County's crime scene investigators. The commanding officer radioed them stating they did not see the suspect's truck or any vehicles at the residence. Trudy asked them to stand down and wait until they arrived with the warrant.

"Damn it," exclaimed Trudy. "We really didn't need this."

Woody radioed back. "You want to hold off until we have the fish in the bowl?"

"Nah, let's search the house," she replied. "We might get lucky."

"I think we just did," broke in Tim. "Eleven o'clock, north bound, looks like our Chevy truck."

Lance had the video rolling and zoomed in but couldn't make the driver due to the tinted glass. He did make the tag after the truck passed and it matched.

"Pursue and apprehend?" asked Tim Burroughs.

Playing a hunch, Trudy radioed, "No, we'll just shadow and observe, but not all of us. That would be too obvious.

Woody, proceed to the residence and complete the search with the Georgetown boys."

"On top of it, partner, but you be careful."

She radioed the trailing cruiser, "Tim, make the turn at that crossover coming up and I'll take the next one. Discretely Tim...I do mean discretely, catch and pass our suspect, maintain a ten car length lead."

"Then what?" asked Tim, suddenly craving a donut and a cup of Starbuck's best.

"Just cruise ahead of him. He'll slow to stay behind you. That will buy me the time to catch up and maintain my own ten or so car lengths behind him. We do not want to spook him. Let's just see what he's up to, where he's going. Maybe we can catch him in the act if he is indeed our Mister Road Rage."

Preston continued north on 17, passing the famous hammock shops. Tim Burroughs trailed him now by five car lengths with two vehicles between them. Trudy was a quarter of a mile back and gaining.

Lance spoke play by play in his recorder. Tim warned him to keep the camera out of sight. So far, Lance complied with the request. Maybe the badge idea was working.

Tim pulled into the left lane and began his nonchalant calculated pass. He instructed Lance to pretend to be talking with him and not to look in the direction of Joseph Preston. Again, Lance Rocker followed instructions to the letter.

Trudy, now close enough, watched Tim Burroughs pull it off flawlessly. The computer geek made a passing grade on that one. He pulled away taking his assigned spot approximately ten car lengths ahead and back in the right lane. Four vehicles were between him and the suspect's truck.

Trudy closed to within twelve car lengths and maintained that distance with a box truck and an SUV separating them. She hoped they were doing the right thing, just following. Now approaching where HWY 17 split to bypass on the left and business on the right, Preston took the business route. They were back in Horry County.

Burroughs unfortunately had gambled and taken the bypass. He'd have to double back over at the next traffic light at the Inlet Square Mall. Trudy radioed telling him not to take it because it might look suspicious. He complied. She told him to travel ahead and cross over on 544. She'd radio him if the route changed.

Traffic had gotten heavier and she had lost a little ground. She dared not do anything foolish and tried to remain patient. The box truck still ahead and a transit bus paralleling it in the left lane almost completely obstructed her view. They now approached Garden City, having just passed the mall.

The bus finally pulled and eased over in the right lane ahead of the box truck. She made the left lane pass by them and her heart skipped a beat. She didn't see Preston's truck. He was no longer on HWY 17 business but where had he disappeared?

The traffic light was green at the intersection she now approached. Left would take her into a neighborhood and right would take her to the ocean and the Garden City Pier. She gambled and took the right turn.

Immediately she realized this had been the wrong choice. The straight stretch of road leading toward the ocean did not reveal his truck. She whipped the cruiser into *Johnny's Bar and Grill* on the left and radioed Burroughs telling him to hightail it over to 17 business and park, watch for the truck. She had lost him.

She eased through the parking lot making another left to head back to 17. Murphy's Law, another bar and grill was on her left in the same parking area and The Pink Pony Gentleman's Club was on her right. Preston's Chevy was in a parking spot splitting the difference between the two. She couldn't tell whether he was behind the wheel due to the tinted glass.

Passing behind the truck, the Pink Pony's flashing marquis lights in front of the truck helped her determine that no one was seated in the truck cab. She sighed, relieved she had located the truck but now wondered where he had gone, in the bar and grill or the strip joint.

She opted to do something very stupid and against police protocol. She didn't radio her location but instead she retrieved her overnight bag from the trunk of her cruiser. She still had a slinky little black dress and heels in it from a previous night out with Brady. She decided to go undercover.

Parked between two large SUV's, she changed quickly inside the cruiser. She had a matching purse just large enough for her keys, revolver, badge and cuffs after dumping the contents in the floor. It would be tough to remove any of them quickly due to the snug fit.

Consumed by her mission she made an even worse mistake. She failed to call in what she planned to do. Trudy usually didn't make mistakes but she had committed a biggie this time.

With no room for a cell phone or radio handset, she now could not call for backup if the situation warranted it. She was on her own but that thought never entered her mind, consumed by tailing Preston. The control freak had again lost control.

She had this primal urge to get close to the suspect, Joseph Preston. She had to know what made him tick but she had to find him first. She ran her fingers along the metallic surface of the truck as she passed almost expecting to receive some sort of vibes about the driver. She felt none. The engine still pinged as it cooled.

She opted to try the Pink Pony first. This would be her first experience venturing into a nudie bar. She didn't have a clue why she chose it first other than it seemed like a place for a deranged guy to visit. With daylight blazing the trail she awkwardly made her grand entrance.

A lady in possibly her forties greeted her in a small alcove just inside the door. "Well hello sugar, are you here applying for one of the open spots? Nick's not here right now but he should be back in about thirty. He does all the interviewing. He'll sure like you. With those heels you must top out at over six feet with legs from your feet to your sweet spot."

At first insulted by the assumption, she then thought, I must not look half bad if she thinks I'm here for a job. The heels did put her at about six three and the dress rode up over her thighs. She saw her reflection in the glass doorway and she had to admit, she did look like a stripper.

Seeing there was an eight dollar cover charge for patrons, she decided to play the part. "Yes ma'am, I'm here to try out." She wasn't sure how to audition for the position.

"No need to sweetie; call me Belle. Just go on in and have a seat. I'll tell him you're here when he gets back," instructed Belle, the door mistress. "And what name do you go by?"

Trudy thought she apparently didn't mean her real name but was asking about her stage name. "Veronica Goodhead," she quickly replied, almost blushing by what she had spat out of her mouth. That was the only name that came to mind. She remembered the Goodhead character from an old James Bond rerun she had recently seen on TBS.

"Original one honey," Belle smiled, apparently having never seen a James Bond flick. "The boys will be drawn like flies to that one!"

Getting into character the best she could, Trudy replied, "I usually have to swat them off." She tossed in a fake whorish laugh before entering the next door.

It took her a few seconds to adjust her eyes to the darkness and flashing strobes. Once she did, she realized her third mistake. She had no clue what this Joseph Preston looked like except she knew he was supposed to be a big old boy.

She saw three men scattered about, one sitting on a couch with a dancer on his lap, a second pressed up close to the stage watching a girl clinging to a pole and the third standing at the bar talking to a redheaded bartender with extremely large breast.

She recalled the witness saying the driver looked like a biker. The guy hunkering over the stage definitely didn't have the look of a biker. He looked more like a perverted, middle aged school teacher.

The man standing at the bar was dressed like a golfer, not like circus boy but instead in shorts and bright green shirt with some sort of golf logo. She couldn't make out the identity of the guy underneath the girl on the couch.

A waitress with a tight tee shirt and perky nipples came over and asked if she could get her something to drink. She ordered bottled water. "Slow in here, huh," Trudy made small talk.

"Don't worry," answered Nipples. "About nine you'll be beating them off with a cue stick. We don't have but four girls on duty until seven."

"Where is the forth?"

Nipples answered, "Oh, Angel is entertaining in the VIP room. You're new. Are you starting tonight?"

"Don't know. I have an interview with Nick." She poured on a little southern charm.

"Oh," Nipples smiled. "Nick is going to just love this little job interview for sure."

Trudy didn't like the emphasis or tone of her last comment. She finally got a glance at the couch potato and he looked like a seventy year old granddad, a very sleazy old codger. The flashing lights and loud booming music made it difficult for her to focus on her mission.

She asked Nipples how long the patron had been in the VIP room and she said about twenty minutes. Angel had negotiated an hour and ordered two bottles of Champagne. Angel would be busy for a while.

The golfer from the bar strolled over and sat in a chair next to her placing his hand on her exposed left thigh. "What deal you offering up tonight Blondie?"

"Fifty a dance..." she tossed out that price figuring that it would deter his advances. Mistake number four, he smiled and said he'd take two.

Rocker-Burroughs-Anderson

Tim Burroughs had totally lost it after being unable to raise Deputy Wagner on the radio for the past thirty minutes. He had already contacted Woody. Woody reported they had found no incriminating evidence at the Preston residence. He left once he heard Wagner had disappeared off the radar screen.

Woody had driven the entire route up business 17 and hooked up with Burroughs and Rocker in the Old Time Pottery parking lot. He had not seen either her cruiser or the pickup along the highway or any parking lots close to the roadway. Unfortunately, both were parked out of view.

"I don't think he's coming back to that house anytime real soon," said Woody. "We found one piece of empty luggage on a bed and it looked like the drawers and closet had been picked over."

"So what do we do now?" asked Lance. "This story is slipping through our hands."

Woody just gave him a *go to hell* look. "It gets worse. We found an open and empty gun cabinet."

"What do you think happened to Wagner?" asked Tim Burroughs. "The last thing she said was she had lost him."

"Did she say where?"

"No..."

"Think..."

Deputy Rocker took charge. "We had just split on the 17 bypass and she took business 17 behind Preston. That call came less than five minutes later so she should have been in Garden City by then."

Woody momentarily forgot how badly he hated Rocker, slapping him on the back to acknowledge good job. Rocker flinched then smiled.

"Shouldn't we call for backup now?" asked Burroughs.

"We should but we're not. We started this as a team and we'll finish it the same way."

"This is going to be one hell of a headliner!"

"I hope she's alright."

"Let's go find our missing partner!"

Pink Pony

Nipples had saved Trudy's ass, telling golfer dude that she was not a dancer. She winked at Trudy from the bar afterwards. Trudy had a bad feeling about that wink but made mistake number five by nodding back. She feared she had just sent the wrong signals. Nipples smiled to confirm her fears.

Glancing at her watch, six forty and it should be about time for number four to exit that VIP room. Like clockwork they exited the room together. "Crap," Trudy grunted.

Angel had been entertaining a female customer. Mistake number six, she had picked the wrong establishment. Now thinking back, Murphy's Law, how appropriate!

The door opened to her right and stepping inside, a five and half footer dressed in kaki pants and dark black v-neck with several gold chains hanging loosely from his neck, most fingers flashing huge rings. He walked over to her table. He ran his hands through black, greasy looking hair. In a Jersey accent he said, "Howyadoing? I'm Nick."

She stood up and looking down on him, said in her own version of a Jersey accent, "I'm Veronica Goodhead, and I'm outtahere."

Stepping back outside and again allowing her eyes to adjust to the light, she saw that Preston's truck was still there. She exhaled, counting her lucky stars. She wished she had taken a pee before she left. The sudden rush of cool air up her skirt alerted her bladder and it ached something fierce.

It suddenly dawned on her that she had done the unforgivable. She had failed to let her partners know her twenty. They were probably panic stricken. How stupid had she been? She would radio them first then head inside the bar and grill.

Before she reached her cruiser, a figure stopped along the driver's side of the pick-up and had the look of a biker, a mountain of man. He had to be Joe Preston.

She kicked into her stripper persona again and approached the hulking figure. "High honey, you're not coming inside? I'm Veronica Goodhead and I would just love to take you back to the VIP room. I have something special for you."

"Sorry, not interested," he abruptly answered.

She felt insulted. Belle thought she was hot. Nipples wanted in her pants. Even golfer boy had offered her two bills. Now, Road Rage wasn't interested; if indeed he was their man. This would ruin her reputation. She could be much more charming with about three glasses of wine under her belt. The bottled water just wasn't cutting it.

She grabbed him by the arm and said, "Come on sugar. Let me show you how I earned my name."

"Give it a break. I said not interested." He pulled her hand free and accidentally knocked her purse to the ground spilling its contents, her badge, cuffs and revolver.

"You're no stripper. You're a damn cop," he snarled, kicking the revolver underneath the car parked in the next space.

He then grabbed Trudy by the throat almost lifting her off the ground. Thank goodness she stood over six feet and with the heels she managed to keep her toes grounded. He pushed her against the car.

"What do you want, bitch?"

She couldn't answer. She could hardly breathe but she maintained eye contact.

"I know who you are. I've seen you on the news with Lance Rocker. You're that hotshot deputy that keeps sticking her feet in her mouth. Well, here I am. I'm the one you've been hunting, so what are you going to do now?"

She struggled to keep her toes on the asphalt and now felt close to blacking out. She had both hands on his massive tattooed arms.

"I said what you going to do about it? Hell, you should be on your knees thanking me. I've speeded up the judicial process. I'm a hero."

Well she certainly was getting what she had wished for, up close and personal with the killer. She just didn't want to be his next victim. She felt faint. She certainly felt no positive vibes.

"I guess the more obvious question is what am I going to do with you?" he asked, glancing around the parking lot to make sure no one saw them. Fading due to the lack of oxygen intake, she barely heard that last question.

When Deputy Trudy Wagner came to, she found herself handcuffed to the truck's passenger side armrest. The cuffs were looped through it with both hands pulled taut. She was leaning slumped against the door, arms crossed in front with minimum opportunity to move.

Turning her head to the left she saw Preston sitting behind the wheel and staring at her. Worse still, she glanced down and her sexy little black dress now rode above her hips fully exposing her panty-less bottom. She made eye contact with Preston and he glanced down at her little peep show and smiled.

"Very nice for a cop and if I were a rapist you would have already been raped by now, probably numerous times, but I'm not." He continued to smile then pulled her dress down to at least cover her neatly trimmed landing strip. "And you are a natural blonde I see...rare in these times."

Trudy tried to regain her composure.

"Oh, allow me to explain. I removed your little panties after you pissed yourself." You must have one monster bladder. I'm just glad you did it in the parking lot and not in my Chevy."

She started to reply but realized her mouth was covered with a strip of duck tape, mandatory accessory for a serial killer she supposed. They weren't moving and after peeping over the dashboard she recognized the flashing lights from The Pink Pony.

She leaned over to remove the tape and he said, "Please don't think of doing that. I'm not in a mood for your conversation right now." She did what he said.

He spoke again, "Look, regardless of what you think, I'm not a wild crazed murderer and I am certainly not a serial killer. I'm no Ted Bundy or Jeffrey Dahmer. I don't rape or eat people. If I did, you would be my entrée right now."

"Now Road Rage, I like that one. That one fits me perfectly."

She searched for a way out of this stupid predicament she had gotten herself into, thinking she had responded like a rookie and she now paid the consequences. Her very long and deadly legs were still free and she could easily contort and plant a heel up beside his head when she had the opportunity. She'd definitely keep that option on the table.

"Okay, here's the deal. I'm planning to put some distance between me and the beach. I'll be out of your hair and you can return to a normal beach cop life, dealing with these stupid tourists."

He continued, "I assure you I'm not sitting here itching to kill somebody so don't fret your little heart, but I will not tolerate maniac drivers. My folks would still be alive if not for them."

Trudy tried to sit up straighter in the seat but the way he had her cuffed limited her movement. She surveyed the cab for something, anything that may offer her an advantage and spotted her revolver tucked between his legs.

"I saw that," he said reaching down and grabbing his crotch and the revolver with his enormous hand. "I don't really care for guns but I figured you did so best I keep this close by and out of your reach, unless it wasn't the gun that caught your attention. Where's your sense of humor? It's just a joke. Don't panic."

"How do they put it in the movies...oh yeah, you're my insurance policy. As long as you ride shotgun over there and behave I should have safe passage, right?"

"Look, I'm not really a bad guy. I had never done anything like this until after that Bradshaw ruined my life. He killed my mother and drove my pop to take his own life. Run me through your files. You won't even find a speeding ticket on me I assure you."

This wasn't going the way she had envisioned but there were worse alternatives. Her job, avoid the other possible scenarios and remain alive. Paying for my past sins she thought. She vowed to do better if given the chance.

"Alright then...since you don't require a bathroom visit now, let's be on our way." He fired up the Chevy and eased out of his parking spot. "Please don't try anything stupid. You should realize by now that I don't deal with stupid people all that well. Work with me and I promise I will set you free. It's really simple and your choice but don't piss me off. Road Rage has a bad temper when pissed and I can't promise you that I could protect you from his rage. Okay...road trip!"

Business 17
7:15 PM

The two cruisers now backtracked down highway 17 from the 544 intersection toward Garden City. The deputies surveyed the parking lots and establishments on both sides of the road. Woody took the left and Tim and Lance kept watchful eyes on the right.

They had yet to make Preston's truck or Trudy's cruiser. Woody felt time was running out quickly and hoped his decision not to call for backup didn't prove to be deadly. Preston had allegedly killed nearly fifty people so he probably wouldn't hesitate in killing one more.

"Anything..." he radioed.

"Nothing," responded Tim, driving on the frontage road and now pulling through another series of parking areas.

"Not looking good for her is it," commented Lance.

Tim Burroughs didn't answer keeping a vigilant watch for any signs of hope for Deputy Wagner.

Woody made the left turn toward Garden City Beach at the traffic light just past Johnny's Bar and Grill. Tim Burroughs completing his past through the Walgreens' parking lot on the opposite side and now about to re-enter 17 yelled over the radio, "Got him!"

"I copy. What's his twenty?"

"His pickup is exiting that lot between Murphy's Law and the Pink Pony!"

Woody hung a hard left through Johnny's parking lot. "I've got Wagner's cruiser here in the parking lot! Stick with him and I'll check this out!"

"Roger," answered Tim, entering 17 behind Preston.

"Those damn dark tinted windows make it impossible to see whose inside," remarked Lance. "I thought South Carolina prohibited such dark tint."

"There are limitations but if it comes from the factory like that or is out of state, they get a pass. He was originally from California. It may have met the state's requirements there," explained Tim Burroughs.

Woody checked Trudy's cruiser, locked. He could see what looked like the contents of a purse dumped in the passenger side floorboard. A chill rippled down his spine. He walked to the rear of the cruiser and stared at the trunk. He hoped he was wrong.

He grabbed the tire iron from his own cruiser and jimmied Trudy's trunk open. He raised it slowly and expelled a sigh of relief when he found no body. Just as he was about to climb back in his cruiser he spotted something in an empty parking space.

Walking over he stooped down to examine a black purse. Inside he found Trudy's badge. He radioed Burroughs. "Are you still on him?"

"I just made my way back onto 17 but I can still see him."

"I think he may have Deputy Wagner. Proceed with extreme caution. Don't do anything foolish! Whatever you do, don't spook him. He probably has her revolver too."

"Damn...this is getting better by the minute. I do hope the blonde Amazon is alright."

Again, Burroughs said nothing, staying focused. He had just passed the Pink Pony when Woody pulled out onto 17 behind him. The sudden flurry of law enforcement vehicles all merging from the same area did not go unnoticed.

"It appears we have company Deputy Wagner," said Joe Preston, adjusting his rearview mirror. "Looks like I'll be exercising my insurance policy sooner instead of later."

Trudy stretched her neck like a tortoise from a shell and could just make out the two cruisers in the side mirror. She thought this could be good or it could be very bad. She'd remain positive but she couldn't help being concerned and somewhat terrified thinking about the potential outcome.

She really needed a chance to work her charm on her abductor but the duck tape stymied her ability to do so. He had previously warned her not to remove it. He hadn't appeared to have changed his tune.

The wheels were turning in that brain of hers. She thought I'm no mere whiny little hostage. I'm a seasoned police officer. Isn't it about time I act like one?

"I see they're being coy," stated Joe Preston, staring in his rearview mirror. "Probably means they have called for backup and we can expect road blocks ahead. Well, let's just take a little detour out to the beach." He engaged his turn signal and eased into a right turn.

"Do you think he's made us?" radioed Tim.

"It's hard to say," responded Woody. "He's certainly driving like a law abiding citizen but if he has Wagner, he knows he holds the winning hand right now."

"That is if she's alive," added Lance. "He's got us either way doesn't he?"

Burroughs glanced over at Rocker but said nothing. He radioed Woody, "What do we do now?"

Woody was glad he had informed Tim earlier to change radio frequencies. If he hadn't they would probably have company from other law enforcement officers. "You pass by and catch the next right." I'll follow after I give him some leeway."

After turning right off 17, Joe Preston immediately took a second right, the next block. Woody made the first right turn and panicked when he didn't see Preston's Chevy ahead.

"Crap," he radioed. "I've momentarily lost him. If he tuned left ahead he's coming your way Burroughs. I'll take the next right. He didn't have enough time to do any thing else."

"Circling the wagons," chuckled Joe Preston as he made another right back toward 17. Checking his mirror he saw no signs of either of the cop cars.

Trudy decided she had two options, actually three if she bided her time and did nothing. One, she could barrage him with a flurry of high heeled foot kicks, hoping to score a knock out. Two, she could possibly reach the accelerator and goose it, but she wasn't sure that would gain her an advantage. One was probably her best option if she succeeded. If not, she could be sealing her fate quickly.

She opted for number three right now and wimped out. Three ensured she would remain alive. A potential dead hero didn't rate that high on her priority list. Option four, roll the dice and remove the duck tape, chance talking to him. Four it was.

She snatched it off before he had an opportunity to warn her. "Look, we really don't have to do this," she spoke, almost causing him to veer off the street.

"For an officer of the law you certainly don't follow orders very well." He placed his hand on her thigh applying an extremely painful grip.

"And I never was very good at coloring inside the lines either," she replied, trying to jerk free resulting in her dress hiking up and exposing her bare bottom again.

"You must be really proud of that little trimmed monkey of yours. Luckily I'm not a sexual predator but I must say it is an enticing proposition." This time, just to rattle her cage he released his grip and brushed his hand across her nether regions. "Tasty! You may win me over yet Deputy."

She couldn't pull down her dress but did immediately cross her legs, very tightly. He laughed then checked his mirror as he now made a left turn back onto 17, heading south. Still no police vehicles were in sight.

Woody could not believe how easily this bastard had shaken him and had done it so nonchalantly. He crossed every intersection looking both ways but still had not caught sight of the truck. "Burroughs, have you got him?"

"I've got nothing," answered Tim in an almost panic stricken voice. "We've been zigzagging down these back streets and we have seen neither hide nor hair of him!"

Woody pounded the steering wheel. What was this guy, some sort of supernatural apparition? This was damned embarrassing losing him in a low speed chase.

"We need to ditch my Chevy don't we? How about we go back and grab your squad car?"

"How about you show me where I may have my keys concealed?"

"Oh," he said placing his hand on her knee. "Is that an invitation for me to conduct a cavity search?"

"Remember, you don't like sex!"

"I never said I didn't like sex," he smiled, slipping his hand back up her inner thigh, her legs still locked like a vice. "I just said I was no perverted sexual predator. I'm a full blooded man and do so enjoy a meaningful sexual encounter. I'm sure you and I could make it meaningful." He laughed watching the expression on her face.

She tried to pull away. Just as quickly he released her again. Reaching into his pants pocket he jingled a set of keys. "I took the liberty of taking these when I confiscated your cuffs and weapon. I've been doing your dirty work. I may as well have your vehicle to reward my accomplishments."

He pulled back into the parking lot and into an empty spot on the passenger side of her cruiser. Both passenger sides now faced one another.

"Mister Preston..."

"Joe, after all we're old buddies now, aren't we?" He patted her on the leg and gave her a wink.

"Joe," she attempted a second time. "Let's end this. Let me get you some help. This only tarnishes the reputations of your parents. I can tell you loved your parents dearly. I just lost my mom. I still have arrangements to complete for her funeral."

"It saddens me to hear of your loss," he said with all sincerity. "Losing one's mother can be overwhelming, I would know. I so loved mine."

Bingo, she thought. She had struck a nerve and she needed to milk this for all its worth. "Do you have any brothers or sisters," she asked, knowing he was an only child.

"I'm it."

"That must make it even tougher," she said, mustering up a fake smile.

He nodded.

"And to have lost your father too," she continued.

"Bradshaw, he drove him to take his own life! He was grief stricken without my mother. They should be enjoying their retirement now! Senseless, it's just friggin senseless!"

Oops she thought. She had pushed the wrong button. "Your mother, what do you miss most about her? I miss the one on one girl talks with mine."

"She was always there for me. She respected my decisions and life choices. She...wait a minute, you're good. Did you major in psychology?"

"No, really, I can relate to your pain," she tried to explain but he'd have none of it.

"Time to pull the old switch-a-roo," he said walking around to her side of the truck, pistol tucked in his belt, handcuff keys in one hand, her cruiser keys hanging from a finger.

Trudy thought this wasn't working so damn well. Joe Preston opened her door almost dragging her out in the process. He unlocked the one cuff to slide it through the armrest. Trudy figured now or never. She launched those slender legs into action, assaulting first his groin then belly and placed several kicks to his face.

He staggered backwards, dropping both sets of keys. He reached for the revolver. Trudy did a side leg sweep sending him stumbling onto the asphalt. She scooped up both sets and hauled ass toward the doorway of the Pink Pony.

Heels free wheeling on the slick tile floor inside the alcove, she ended on her butt with her legs spread wide open, cuffs dangling from her one wrist like an oversized bracelet. She had completed her grand entrance through the swinging doors of the showroom. She received a standing ovation to the claps and howls of more than twenty five men now inside, providing her audience with full frontal.

"Hired!" shouted Nick as a line of men with waving dollar bills formed behind him.

She rebounded quickly and twirled expecting to see Joe Preston standing in the doorway but he wasn't. Her new found fan base closed in and she opted to exit the joint and take her chances in the parking lot.

Peeping out the door first, she saw Joe Preston firing up the Chevy and peeling out of the parking lot. He must have had a second set of keys. She sprinted toward her cruiser, unlocking the cuffs on her little jaunt. Keeping an eye on which direction the truck traveled, she unlocked the door and made haste in her pursuit.

Preston headed south on 17 back towards Pawley's Island. She radioed Woody and Tim this time. "Guys, I've got him, he's southbound business 17 just leaving Garden City, Pink Pony parking lot!"

"Where in the hell have you been?" shouted Woody, relieved to hear her voice.

"Moonlighting...I can't depend on being a cop forever."

"I always knew she had balls," remarked Lance. "That will fill my fantasies for a while."

Tim Burroughs responded, "Damn right, she's one hell of a broad!" They both laughed and high fived, glad to know she was still alive and kicking.

Southbound HWY 17
Friday
8:49 PM

Three cruisers were now in pursuit of Joe Preston's Chevy pickup. Trudy thought it odd that Preston had not floored it. He maintained a speed of fifty, just five miles over the posted speed limit. She stayed two car lengths behind him and in the same lane. He did have her revolver after all.

Woody followed four car lengths behind her and in the left lane with Tim and Lance another three back. "What the hell is he doing," radioed Woody. "I feel like I'm in that O.J. Simpson white Bronco pursuit."

"I'll be damned," she replied. "He's really trying hard not to break any traffic laws."

"And what does that mean," radioed Woody. "He's a killer. I'd say that qualifies for breaking the law."

"I'll explain later."

"I agree with short stuff. I'm reliving the O.J. Simpson pursuit too," said Lance. "I thought hot pursuit equated to high speeds, near misses and an adrenalin rush."

"Just film it," answered Tim. "It's your exclusive remember."

Woody radioed. "We're back in Georgetown County, Wagner. We better radio the locals again and let them know what's going on because this could get very messy and extremely complicated."

"Speed limits now fifty five and this guy is maintaining it," stated Tim.

"And we have BrookGreen Gardens coming up on our right but looks like we won't be visiting it today," added Lance.

"Make the call to Georgetown," she replied. "Just keep it to a minimum. Tell them we're following a traffic violator into their county."

"He's obviously not heading home," radioed Woody. "We just passed the turnoff to his parent's home. Where is he taking us? We're approaching Willbrook Boulevard."

The traffic light changed to yellow just ahead but Preston, too focused on Deputy Wagner in his rearview mirror, never saw it. Now red, the Channel 12 News van, exiting Heritage Drive, clipped Preston's truck, hitting the rear passenger side's bumper sending it into a spin.

Crossing the grassy median the Chevy pickup stopped in the path of northbound traffic momentarily. A PT Cruiser with Ohio plates T-boned the truck's passenger side door panel sending it back into the median.

"Damn, did you see that?" yelled Lance Rocker. "There is a God and I got it all on film. Now that's taking *live on the scene* a bit too much even for Channel 12!"

Brady Pierce, trailing the news van, leapt from his vehicle and sprinted across the two southbound lanes and arrived first at Preston's demolished Chevy. Channel 12 had been covering a charity event sponsored by Brady at the Tradition Golf Course.

Trudy recognized him and began shouting, "No, stay away, Brady!"

Through the shattered passenger side window Brady spotted the driver of the truck slumped over the steering wheel. Running around the truck to the driver's side door, he yanked the door open. He touched the driver's shoulder and Preston flinched, sitting straight up.

Joe Preston, bleeding from his nose and mouth, deep gashes above his left eyebrow, turned to face Brady Pierce. "Are you alright?"

Joe nodded, wiping the blood from his mouth with his hand. He quickly glanced left then right. He spotted the first cruiser, Trudy Wagner inside, no more that forty yards away. Traffic had come to a stand still; north and south bound 17 in the melee.

Throwing up his hands in disgust Brady asked, "What the hell were you thinking, man? Didn't you see that red light or did it just not matter? You could have gotten yourself killed, not to mention other innocent people!" From the time Brady had arrived until now had taken only a couple of precious minutes.

Brady spotted Trudy exiting her vehicle and heading toward them. Why was she wearing that hot black dress from the other night he wondered? Were they supposed to meet some where this afternoon? Brady turned to be greeted by a revolver inches from his nose. "Uh, I didn't mean to piss you off, sir, but you really could have caused a pile up by running that light. Let me get you a doctor."

"Who are you?"

"Brady Pierce and I really think we need to get you some medical attention if you'll be so kind as to lower that gun."

"You think I caused this don't you?"

"You did run that traffic light but that happens a lot around here. I see three and four vehicles shooting through them all the time after they turn red." Brady chattered away trying to get this man with a gun pointed at this face to lighten up.

"I was distracted. I didn't see the light change. I caused this mess didn't I? Innocent people could have been killed...lives shattered...senseless...so very senseless."

Trudy stared in disbelief. Brady was about to be killed with her gun. She stood there weaponless. Some police officer, why had she left her shotgun in the cruiser? She saw Woody and Tim, guns drawn but they would never make it in time.

Brady still staring down the barrel of the cannon didn't understand why this guy was so enraged at him. He didn't realize that the stranger really wasn't angry at him. "You should really stop waving that gun around. It isn't helping."

"Did anyone get hurt?"

Brady glanced around at the other vehicle involved and everyone seemed to be standing outside and behind them, fearing what the gunman might do. "It looks to me like everybody is alright. You took the worst of it. Consider yourself lucky. I didn't get your name."

Shaking his head back and forth Preston said, "I'm the avenger. I am *Road Rage*. I rid the highways of the assholes who don't respect their right to drive. Wrong must be righted! There are no exceptions! Live by the sword, die by the sword. You're sure no one was hurt?"

"Not that I can tell. You're *The Road Rage*. You have been quite a busy man haven't you," blurted out Brady. "Do you suppose you could remove that gun from my face? It makes me quite nervous."

"You've heard of me, but how? I've not been on the news other than that one mention by Lance Rocker."

"Between you and me, she sort of filled me in," Brady said, nodding towards Trudy standing less that twenty yards away, hoping to stall for time; anything to get Road Rage to lower the pistol.

"The officer is your wife?"

"Not yet...maybe one day, but that depends on you," said Brady, trying a different marketing strategy.

"Brave woman and she's a natural blonde. You are a lucky man."

Brady didn't know what to make of that last comment but figured it best to keep Road Rage talking and not pulling that trigger. "So does Road Rage have a real name?"

Joe Preston stared at Brady with dark empty eyes, sighed then pulled the trigger. The shot sent all the onlookers scampering for hiding places. Brady stumbled backwards, landing on his back in the median. Trudy heard the shot and saw him fall, his body now concealed by the smashed Chevy truck.

Unarmed she covered the distance at lightening speed, throwing caution to the wind. She arrived to find Brady in blood splattered khaki knickers sitting on the ground and in shock. Joseph Preston had placed Trudy's gun under his own chin and pulled the trigger rectifying his sins. He had become one of the people he had hated the most. Road Rage had no choice but to eradicate the cancer.

"Circus boy, you're not shot?"

Brady smiled then passed out. Trudy stood to face a very dead Road Rage dangling from the driver's side door, still fastened in his seat belt. "Joseph Preston, you're under arrest."

Lance, Woody and Tim stood just behind her, startled by her comment. She just shrugged and smiled.

"And this closes the final chapter of the evil known as Road Rage but not the phenomena called Road Rage. Let us all learn a valuable lesson, but I dare say will we? Deputy Lance Rocker at the scene of a most incredible ending but to every ending, there is a beginning and I, Sir Lancelot, will share this incredible story with you so please stay tuned."

Lance, not one to pass up an opportunity in front of the live news feed, had gotten the last laugh on Channel 12. *This will pave my way to the top. I'll name my own price.*

"Well, partner...I guess we can tell Hank now."

"I guess we can, partner," she smiled placing her arms around Woody and Tim.

"You best see to lover boy," said Woody. "Something tells me it will take some tender loving care for him to get over this experience."

"I think I need it more but first we need to tidy things up for my mom. Would you take care of this?"

"Done, and Deputy Rocker, give me that damn badge and revolver. You're fired."

"With pleasure," responded Lance offering Woody a hand shake instead.

Woody balled his fist and muttered, "If only the cameras weren't rolling I would rock your world." He then turned and walked away to tend to the crime scene.

"I loved her too," Lance whispered, then he got back into character for his audience.

Conway Medical Center
Wednesday
8:25 AM

"How are you feeling Sheriff?" asked Woody.

"Can you believe it? They want me to lose might near a hundred pounds. What am I supposed to do, go on that Biggest Loser TV show? Sheriff Hank Singleton patted his hand over his heart in a fluttering motion.

"That or survivor," replied Woody. "They tend to drop a few pounds on those islands and you might take home the million."

"And how are you doing Deputy Wagner? Sorry I didn't make it to your mama's funeral. These men in white coats wouldn't issue me a kitchen pass."

"I'm fine sir. Thanks for asking. And those doctors were doing the right thing keeping you here."

"So they tell me everything was in the back of his truck."

"Yes sir, we have the evidence to basically link him to every murder, ours and the ones nationwide."

"You know I ought to bring you and that damn motley crew of yours up on charges. You went beyond bending the law. If those federal boys catch wind of it there will be hell to pay." He shifted in his hospital bed, and then smiled and said, "Fine police work."

"Thank you sir but we just pretended we were only trying to solve ours and didn't know about the others."

"I saw a promo on Fox that Rocker has a three part report coming up next month on prime time. Guess we at least get that boy out of my jurisdiction so reckon I ought not to complain. Hope he doesn't make us look like a bunch of country hicks."

"I think Deputy Rocker will report it correctly."

"Deputy?" asked Hank, now sitting up in bed.

"Trust me Sheriff, you don't even want to know," added Woody. "Let's just say the department comes out smelling like a rose on his special."

Leaning back in bed he acknowledged he probably didn't. "Hey what about that beau of yours, Pierce? How's he taking this?"

"He's doing the best that can be expected sir but seeing a man blow his head off just inches away will keep him in therapy for a while."

"It beats the bullet being in his head. Well you take care of him. He seems to be a decent enough feller."

"I plan to do just that, sir."

"I hear that young Burroughs did a good job for you."

"Tim was outstanding. He's going to be fine officer. Woody and I will let you get some rest. You'll be up and at it before you know it."

"We'll see."

"Take care Sheriff," added Woody. "We've got bad guys to catch."

"Keep my county crime free then."

Tim Ford Residence
10 AM Wednesday

"Thank you for agreeing to meet me Mister Ford," said Deputy Trudy Wagner. "We certainly have met under extraordinary circumstances in the past haven't we?"

"You were trying to do your job I suppose. I can't say I liked your approach."

"I do appreciate your understanding the awkward situation we found ourselves in. Your attack of Edward Bradshaw did complicate our investigation."

"Water under the bridge so let's just put it behind us. I understand you finally solved that little crime spree of yours so I guess it all worked out for the best. I also saw where Lance Rocker landed his own little special on Fox. It's crappy how the sleaze balls profit from the misfortunes of others."

"Rocker is a survivor and an opportunist and the Joseph Preston case has put us on the map for all the wrong reasons. Life isn't always fair."

"It appears all of you are very famous because of the crime of the century here in our humble county. You should write yourself one of those tell all books and take early retirement."

"You would definitely occupy a key chapter if I did."

"Then I guess I will deserve my cut when you strike it rich. Maybe I should write one."

"Do you still draw satisfaction that Bradshaw is dead? You were so adamant about his death when this began."

"No need lying about it. It tickled the crap out of me that he got what was coming just like I'm sure you're losing no sleep about getting your man."

"What makes you so confident that we apprehended Bradshaw's murderer?" She tossed out the first tad of bait and watched closely for Ford's reaction.

"What, I mean...I thought he was one of the first victims," answered Ford, obviously rattled by the statement.

"Oh, you're absolutely dead on. He was one of the first homicides alright but I'm still not so sure Joe Preston committed the murder. He had motive, don't get me wrong but I don't think he killed Bradshaw."

"Why would you say something idiotic like that, Deputy?" Tim Ford spoke in a higher pitched voice. "I thought the evidence matched the others. What kind of damn silly game are you playing?"

"I'm not sure I follow you. What evidence?"

"The driver's license, the license plates," he blurted out. "Wasn't Bradshaw's with the others?"

"Where'd you hear about that? We haven't released specific details to the news media yet." Rocker would break it on his little exclusive.

"I'm sure I heard it on the news or read in the local paper. What are you trying to pull here deputy?"

"You do seem to know too many of the specifics but I assure you it has not been released. It's just you and me here so we can be honest with one another can't we?"

"Like I said, where the hell are you going with this deputy? I don't know what you think you know."

"Let me recap for you what I do know and you feel free to fill in the blanks where you see fit," she said, now seeing him beginning to squirm on the hook.

"You almost killed Bradshaw the first time but the Calvary, Deputy Woodrow Anderson, arrived before you could finish what you started, correct?"

"I don't deny the bastard deserved to die and you know I kicked his ass, so what?"

"After you were released from jail, you returned to finish the job and took all the precautions to conceal any evidence that you committed the murder. You knew you would be the prime suspect but figured you could play the harassment card if we couldn't provide tangible evidence which as it turned out we couldn't. You did your homework and didn't leave us a thread of evidence. Smart move, you allowed Preston to take the fall and look at you. You are a free man."

Tim Ford began to perspire, wiping sweat from his brow now. She had hit a nerve.

"I suspect you were in the house when Joe Preston the killer showed up, intent on murdering Bradshaw too, but you beat him to the punch didn't you?. You had to hide and did so in that front living room."

He sighed but still said nothing.

"I don't believe you saw the killer's face but it didn't take you long to figure out why he was there. Preston was probably pissed that he missed making the kill so he took some mementos, Bradshaw's vehicle tag and his driver's license."

Tim Ford started pacing and wringing his hands hard enough to start a fire from the friction. Trudy had witnessed her mother do the very same thing when nervous and confused.

"Before you could make your hasty escape, our beloved Lance Rocker shows up so you had to remain in hiding, still trapped, the rat that you are. We, too, complicated your dilemma when we arrived. You never expected so much company in the middle of your murder did you? I opened up your escape route when I deserted my post at that front door."

He sat down now and just listened to her intently; sweat clearly soaking through his shirt. It wasn't particularly hot in the room so she definitely had him on the ropes but would he talk?

"We were all distracted by Rocker and a very dead Bradshaw in the other room. I did make it easy for you to escape. That was a stupid mistake on my part, leaving that entrance unattended."

Standing back up, she noticed he was now clinching his fists. Tim Ford was not a happy camper.

"You just sat back and watched it unfold didn't you? You played it smug for a while then at some point you launched this plan to allow the killer to take the fall for Bradshaw too. I haven't figured out how you knew about the other crimes but you knew didn't you?"

"Worked like a charm," he almost surprised himself when he heard the words leave his lips.

"The killer played the game well too, planting the evidence in your house for Rocker then removing it before we saw it. But of course you never knew about that did you? Preston figured out that you murdered Bradshaw and robbed him of the opportunity. He didn't take that too well. He really stirred the pot and kept us on our heels. He wanted to punish you and Rocker and make us all look incompetent. It certainly worked."

Tim Ford had dropped his guard. "Yep, you knew I wouldn't plant evidence in my own house so it kept the heat off me for the murder spree. I didn't know about the evidence when you questioned me here about it. I only learned about it recently." He smiled as he grew confident in their little parlay.

"So you tell me, we're here, just you and me. I just need closure for my own sanity."

"This is off the record right? My word against yours in a court of law..."

Trudy nodded.

"And you're not wearing a wire are you?"

"Search me if it makes you feel better."

"I'll take you at your word, Deputy Wagner. You don't seem to be the lying type."

She smiled.

"His missing tag and license did make the link with Bradshaw for sure. You're correct, I heard your serial killer enter the house just after I bashed in Bradshaw's brains and I had to hide." Now with new found confidence he began to lay it all out. "Preston raved and ranted about someone else killing Bradshaw. And you're correct. He was highly pissed about it. He talked out loud about taking those items and vowed he'd make Bradshaw's killer pay for denying him the pleasure of doing it. I heard him get in a few licks with the bat just for good measure. I never saw his face."

"So, you figured you were on his hit list?"

"I won't deny it. It scared the crap out of me. He must have read about my first attack and figured I murdered Bradshaw. That's why he kept messing with me."

"Messing with you how?"

"I kept getting these weird phone calls. The psycho told me about each of the other murders, play by play. I figured he was overloading me with information to eventually set me up for the fall. How could I ever pass a lie detector if I knew everything about the killings? That's why I put you onto Tank. I had to make sure you got him before he got me."

"And Tank wasn't even the killer."

"Look, his description matched who I thought you were looking for and he was involved in the original accident. He was a badass and I thought he was our man."

"Our man...so when did you know he wasn't *our man*, Road Rage?"

"Well, I didn't know it until the calls continued after Tank was dead. Then I had no idea who was making them but he would tell me my days were numbered. He enjoyed screwing with my head. He said he knew I killed Bradshaw."

"So you did nothing?"

"What could I do? My best chance was to ride it out and hope you caught him before he followed through on his threats."

"Let's fast forward a bit. How did you gain information about the nationwide killings and I am assuming you're the one that alerted Tank we were coming?"

"You're going to just love this," he snickered. "My wife, rest her soul, taught at CCU and was an associate of Professor Swanson at the university. He was very fond of her. When Sheriff Singleton asked for his help on the case, Professor contacted me telling me not to worry that I was no longer a suspect and that it had gone nationwide. He told me of your suspicions about Tank Patterson."

"That sorry professor was blabbing to everyone," she responded in a highly agitated tone.

"It gets better. I also knew Tank. Let's just say he helped me with my medical requirements."

"You were buying drugs from that crazy bastard, I'll be damned." She shook her head in disbelief. "You also threatened to blow the lid off our case didn't you?"

"I was playing all my options. I figured if I gave you the deadline on reporting it to the news media it would prompt you to immediately go after Tank."

"Well we sure played into your hands didn't we? And the good old nutty professor informed you we were going after him didn't he?"

"You've got to believe me. I really thought he was the serial killer. If you hadn't have gone after him, I intended to blow the lid off and make your lives a living hell. Either way, it would keep you off me and make sure he got captured or killed."

"Just what the hell did you tell Tank?"

"I told him you suspected him of being this hot shot drug dealer who was responsible for an ass load of murders and that you did not intend to take him alive. I told him the police didn't want him to go to trial and risk any plea bargaining."

"And he believed you?"

"Why wouldn't he? I was just some poor grieving husband and father on drugs, a dependable paying client. Why would I have reason to lie to him?"

"You do realize you were the cause of a good man being murdered don't you? Detective Shannon Chestnut lost his life serving a warrant."

"Prove it. I wasn't there nor did I pull the trigger. I certainly didn't know he'd have that wild bunch inside with him"

"So after Tank and his guys sucked on bullets you were home free and had no cause to play your *alert the media* card. You were home free until Preston continued to phone you."

"Yeah, but like I said, I didn't know he wasn't the killer at the time or I would have gone through on that threat to tell the media."

"And your buddy, the professor, no longer had connections to the case after I found out he was already snitching to Rocker and I kicked his ass off our team. You didn't know we were still searching for the real killer did you?"

"Like I said, I didn't know Tank wasn't the killer until the bastard called me and then I didn't know what to do. I'm curious. So what made you think I killed Bradshaw?"

"Not following through on your threat to go public raised the first flag because if you were truly out for vengeance, the Tank incident would have just added fuel to the fire. But I must admit I couldn't shake the feeling you were somehow involved from the start. You expressed too many times your hatred for Bradshaw. You were a man on a mission. Woody and I both had hunches but I kept mine more to myself."

"But still, you couldn't be sure I killed him?"

"Well, I must confess, everything I had was mere conjecture on my part. I had no real evidence, not until now."

"What a shame, this little moment of honesty doesn't give you any real evidence either now does it? It's my word against yours so, if it suits you, I say let your serial killer take the fall and life goes on for both of us. If I hadn't beaten him to it, he would have disposed of Bradshaw anyway. Dead is dead, right?"

"Who am I to judge you. I've certainly made my fair share of mistakes lately. Grief can certainly skew your thinking. I could just let you slide. After all, like you so eloquently put it, dead is dead. What harm would it really do I suppose to allow Preston to lay claim to one more?"

He smiled and nodded in agreement. "See that wasn't so hard. We can both walk away from this knowing justice has been served; no harm, no foul. My wife and daughter are dead because of his reckless driving. That Preston guy lost his parents because of him too."

"And let's not exclude Tank and his two cohorts."

"Everyone comes out alright on this and you'll probably receive all sorts of commendations and most likely a promotion. We can just put the whole ordeal behind us can't we?"

"Well, see I have a big problem gnawing at my gut. I have a dead detective on my hands and a hell of lot of grief for the department and me personally because of your self centered motivations. And I am an expert on being self centered." She smiled as she unbuttoned her blouse exposing the microphone clipped to her bra.

"You lying bitch! You can't submit that as evidence. You entered my house without a warrant and wire taping is illegal and I asked if you were wired and you said no."

"Well, actually, you invited me in your home. I don't remember storming in here and I certainly haven't conducted an unauthorized search. I never said I wasn't wearing a wire. I told you to feel free to search me and you chose not to. We were just two old friends discussing life's tragedies. Where's that confident smile?" She pointed out the huge living room window and Woody filming the incident from a van.

"This is bullshit! You told me this was off the record. Your little recording will prove it!"

"I don't think you'll hear me telling you that anywhere on the final footage." She smiled knowing she had stood with her back to the window when she nodded.

"This is illegal as hell!"

"Actually it's not. You see we do have legal permission from the District Attorney to tape and photograph this blessed event. The warrant is on that table over there. I placed it there when I entered. By the way, her deceased nephew just so happens to be Detective Shannon Chestnut so our magistrate will support our actions. She was surely fond of her nephew and is grief stricken. She wanted to make sure she brought his murderer to justice and I think she will be happy with these results."

"Wait a minute! It doesn't have to end like this. We can cut a deal."

"Deals, tell that to the Chestnut family. We now have you on the premeditated murder of Bradshaw and an accessory to Detective Shannon Chestnut's death, not to mention that Tank debacle. We have you on attempted blackmail, withholding evidence and probably drug possession just to mention a few other little infractions. The hits just keep coming and you really thought you were going to just walk away from this? You underestimate the Horry County Police Force."

"But you don't understand. He killed my wife and daughter! He destroyed my life! He destroyed a lot of folk's lives. Even that Preston guy was an innocent man until..."

"Hold it sport. You destroyed your life! This is some legacy you are leaving your wife and daughter because of an unfortunate vehicular accident that took their lives. Bradshaw was not a sweetheart, I agree, but he was no murderer either. Your killing him wasn't an accident and that makes you the real murderer here."

"You don't know how it feels to lose someone you love!"

"I believe I do. I recently lost my mother." She certainly missed the remorse train when her mom had died and she did regret how she had handled or mishandled her illness and death. "But what was I suppose to do, take out some vendetta on doctors for not coming up with a cure for Alzheimer's? Maybe I should have taken it out on all the caregivers. No, you made this bed, Tim Ford."

"You heartless bitch," he yelled, grabbing for her collar and the microphone.

A lightening right hook decked him on his ass. Trudy turned to the window talking into her bra and said, "Woody, I sure hope you got him resisting arrest on camera to add to the charges. By the way, I want a copy of that wicked punch I just landed. Damn it felt good!"

Woody gave her the thumbs up.

"Now, allow me to read you your rights Tim Ford. Unfortunately, you still have them and it is my job to obey the law." She really would have rather just kicked his ass into oblivion but that's not the way we do things in Horry County. Just ask Hank Singleton.

Trudy decided she would wrestle with her personal demons another time. Today she would just savor the victory and start a new priority list. She mentally penciled Brady Pierce in the number one slot and ended the list at that, today. Tomorrow she'd reevaluate it but for now Brady deserved to be number one.

Driving down 707, a moped pulled out directly in front of her, the driver oblivious or unconcerned, causing her to brake hard to avoid a rear end collision. She clutched the wheel with her left and almost gave him the finger with her right then laughed at her reaction. *Patience, Deputy, patience...Brady will be there when you arrive.*

Epilogue

A couple of months had passed since Amy Wagner had been laid to rest. Her death had worked a miracle of sorts. Trudy and her sister Allison had actually reconciled their differences. Trudy was no longer an only child. This summer they planned to visit Disney World as a family.

While Trudy still struggled with how she had reacted to her mother's illness, she now at least drew some comfort from attending sessions with other caregivers. She realized that her reactions and denial of the circumstances were common among those responsible for providing care.

Brady had endured his own struggles, having witnessed Joe Preston commit suicide just inches away from him. He suffered horrific nightmares of the anomaly known as Road Rage. Therapy had helped. His doctor said he had shown some progress and should be fine eventually.

He had proposed to Trudy. She had accepted. They hadn't yet worked out the details of their wedding but Allison had agreed to be her matron of honor. When the time came, Woodrow Anderson would proudly escort his partner down the aisle.

Woody had stopped drinking and had gotten his kids back and for the first time in his career he actually took vacations to spend more time with them. Lullabelle assisted while he pulled his shifts. Each day was a challenge for him to put Janice's death behind him. At least he didn't have Lance Rocker's face on the nightly news to remind him of their affair. Rocker had moved from the Grand Strand to greener pastures. Woody no longer wanted to kill Rocker but had not forgiven him for what he had done. He probably never would.

Lance Rocker had successfully completed his series in the Road Rage murders rating him his very own syndicated show. He had a book deal in the making. He was now rocking the tabloid television world. He, too, found it difficult to forget about Jenny-Janice but in true Rocker fashion had reconvened his whorish ways. A zebra never changes its stripes.

Sheriff Hank Singleton...well, he was Hank Singleton. Those hundred pounds he was supposed to lose weren't exactly peeling off of him. That would require actual dieting and exercising, something he had not yet embraced. His career and potential pension had dodged a serious bullet. The Feds had never gotten wind of how they had actually handled the Road Rage Case and they never would.

Tim Ford remained in custody awaiting trial. Shannon Chestnut's aunt, against her sworn oath, chomped at the bits to see justice served for her nephew's untimely death. Ford denied everything saying he had been framed but the footage didn't lie.

Hurricane Hugo had all but destroyed Mickey Spillane's Murrells Inlet home back in 1989. At the time, a television interview had shown him standing in front of the home in ruins. He had to rebuild the house almost from scratch. He had received an Edgar Allan Poe Grand Master Award in 1995. His novels went out of print but in 2001, the New American Library began reissuing them. Professor Swanson, aka Doc, watched the file footage wishing he had actually met the man he so admired. Doc owned a copy of every one of his novels.

Road Rage never dies. It exists in each and every one of us. How many times did you experience it today? What are *YOU* going to do about it? How many times did *YOU* cause it? You better check your rearview mirror. Is the face in the mirror one of rage?

Coming in 2012 from T. Allen Winn

Dark Thirty

Breaking in another batch of tormentors at a new school, not exactly how Dale Thomas Jackson had envisioned his sixteenth year. Much worse things exist to haunt his darkness and it would be waiting patiently at nightfall. Dale feared the bullies for obvious reasons. He feared the other for reasons unknown. Meeting and greeting the newest horde of bullies loomed just two weeks away. Dark Thirty dwelled on the fringes of twilight. Dale had no plan of resistance for either, only submission and more humiliation.

North of the Border
(Another Officer Trudy Wagner suspense thriller)

Jorge Cruz stops along the secluded road, spotting the stranded Mustang and the lady with her head buried in the steering wheel. He offers his assistance. He's no mechanic but does his best to mimic one, peering under the Mustang's hood. Unable to repair the broken vehicle, Jorge offers her a ride. She accepts. Without warning, the syringe penetrates his neck, feeling like a bee sting. How had he been so stupid? With his hand placed on hers, the Good Samaritan makes brief eye contact with the lady in distress, questioning her intentions, and then collapses on the ground. Trudy Wagner and Horry County's finest will again have their work cut out for them for a new terror has discovered the beach community.

Foot

Indian folklore becomes reality for trapper turned wagon master, mountain man B.N. Carlson, when he leads a handful of hopeful frontiersmen westward. Some aspiring to cash in on the gold rush while others leave their sorted past behind, all are in search of a new life. Their second mistake would be trespassing into the northern woods, their first, trusting in their fellow man. Myth and legend has a beginning. In the mid eighteen hundreds in the Washington State Mountains, the Spokane tribe called it *S'cwene'y'ti.*

The Perfect Spook House

Halloween 1968, too old to trick or treat, eleven high school students vent by exploring old deserted houses, something they've done countless times. The house on the Cedar Springs Road changes the game. Nineteen years later, they're still searching for answers. A historical town isn't interested in digging up old bones. History can be worthy of rewriting but often it is best left alone. Sometimes you don't have a choice but choices unfortunately come with consequences. Reminiscing is not for the weak hearted but the truth can set you free or can it? Ask Payne Lewis, one of those eleven now seeking the truth, wondering if he has made a wise choice and will live to see the consequences of his actions.